PENGUIN BOOKS

King Death

Toby Litt grew up in Ampthill, Bedfordshire. He is a
Granta Best of Young British Novelist and a regular on
Radio 3's *The Verb*. He was the winner of the 2009 Man-
chester Fiction Prize. He is currently working on the film
version of *King Death*. His website is at www.tobylitt.com.

King Death

TOBY LITT

PENGUIN BOOKS

PENGUIN BOOKS

Published by the Penguin Group
Penguin Books Ltd, 80 Strand, London WC2R ORL, England
Penguin Group (USA) Inc., 375 Hudson Street, New York, New York 10014, USA
Penguin Group (Canada), 90 Eglinton Avenue East, Suite 700, Toronto, Ontario, Canada
M4P 2Y3 (a division of Pearson Penguin Canada Inc.)
Penguin Ireland, 25 St Stephen's Green, Dublin 2, Ireland
(a division of Penguin Books Ltd)
Penguin Group (Australia), 250 Camberwell Road, Camberwell, Victoria 3124, Australia
(a division of Pearson Australia Group Pty Ltd)
Penguin Books India Pvt Ltd, 11 Community Centre, Panchsheel Park,
New Delhi – 110 017, India
Penguin Group (NZ), 67 Apollo Drive, Rosedale, North Shore 0632, New Zealand
(a division of Pearson New Zealand Ltd)
Penguin Books (South Africa) (Pty) Ltd, 24 Sturdee Avenue, Rosebank, Johannesburg 2196,
South Africa

Penguin Books Ltd, Registered Offices: 80 Strand, London WC2R ORL, England

www.penguin.com

First published 2010

1

ISBN: 978-0-141-03972-5

www.greenpenguin.co.uk

Mixed Sources
Product group from well-managed
forests and other controlled sources
www.fsc.org .Cert no. SA-COC-1592
© 1996 Forest Stewardship Council

Penguin Books is committed to a sustainable future
for our business, our readers and our planet.
The book in your hands is made from paper
certified by the Forest Stewardship Council.

'Land and sea, weakness and decline are great separators,
but death is the great divorcer for ever.'

–Keats, Letter, 30 September 1820

I.

I am writing in Japanese because it will be easier for me. My English is okay but not good enough to tell this complicated story. And this story happened in English, except what happened in my head. When I write my diary, that is in Japanese. Japanese is for being very clear and also private.

At first through the window we could see nothing but the lit-up windows of houses. Then, closer to sunrise, traces of the houses themselves began to appear – and the empty fields around them.

We were returning from a long weekend at Brighton with Skelton's parents. He couldn't sleep and I didn't want to talk.

It was already over between us, though neither he nor I had said anything. There had been no horrible argument. The weekend was perfectly pleasant and completely dead.

Skelton's father had driven us to the station in time to catch the early train. I think he felt when we said goodbye that he probably would not see me again. At that moment, I liked Skelton's father. He seemed a better man than his son.

Apart from ourselves, the carriage was empty. A year before, this would have made us joke about having sex. But we did not make jokes like that any longer.

I felt like a dead body, and was trying to move as little as possible to preserve this. Sometimes I looked at my reflection, to see how dead it was.

There were more houses and fewer fields, and then there were only houses and the fields were parks that we didn't see because they were hidden behind houses.

The train stopped at London Bridge station. It is important now that I am very precise. The time was 5.34 a.m. exactly, because the train was on time.

We heard footsteps along the platform and then the doors beeping before they all closed. There were still very few people around, though one or two got into our carriage.

Skelton was sitting with his back to the driver. I always prefer to travel forwards, so I can see things coming.

There were some routine shouts, and the train started to move. At first it went over something like a bridge. To the right was the cathedral of Southwark. In the summer it has stones that look golden but on a spring morning they are gentle gray like the rest of London. But I was looking out of the window on the left-hand side of the carriage. Skelton was looking that way, too.

The next thing the train reaches, after coming off the bridge, is the glass roof of Borough Market. Since the time I am writing about, this has been replaced by a modern imitation of itself. It is now something clean and easy to clean. But what I saw was Victorian, covered in lichen and with some of the long oblong panes cracked. I liked them very much. They were zigzag waves on a sea of green glass and the train was a ship ploughing through them.

The next thing I remember is the heart. I saw it sliding down the incline of the roof until it touched the lead guttering and was out of sight.

As soon as I lost sight of it, the rain began to fall. Welcome to London, I thought. The date was May first.

I expected the train to stop. To see a heart like that, naked, was such an extraordinary thing. The train didn't stop.

'It was human,' I said. I am not an expert on biology, but I knew for absolute certain. Not for one second did I doubt it.

'What?' Skelton asked.

'You saw it,' I said. 'Just outside the window.'

'It was probably just a piece of meat,' he said. 'Something from the market.'

'On the roof?'

'Some rats must have carried it up there.'

I didn't like to think about rats. Maybe they had, but it was still a human thing. We couldn't just leave it there for other rats to come along and eat.

'We need to go and see.'

'I can't,' Skelton said. 'You know I've got a session, and I have to go home and get changed first.'

A good example of why our relationship would soon have to end.

'You do that. Fine. I will go back by myself.'

The train was now waiting for permission to cross the bridge. I was impatient for the next stop.

'Do you think anyone else saw?' Skelton asked.

'That's not important,' I said. '*We* saw, so we must do something.'

'If it's what you think it was, we should just call the police.'

The train finally started to move again.

'It is our responsibility,' I said. 'And if you don't want it, it is my responsibility.'

We could see the waters of the Thames river, not brown and not green, but a colour.

3

'I saw,' said Skelton. 'I saw just like you did.'

The train began to slow. I picked up my weekend bag from the seat beside me. Skelton had an old-fashioned suitcase.

When the doors unlocked, I pressed the button and stepped onto the platform. Then I saw what I wanted: a train on a platform heading in the opposite direction, back to London Bridge.

With my bag clutched to my chest, I ran. Skelton was behind me, slower because of his suitcase and slower generally.

We ran down the stairs, across under the tracks and up onto the other platform. A few commuters were around but they didn't watch us – two people running for a train, big deal.

The doors began to beep, but I got there in time to climb in and hold them open with my shoulders.

Skelton arrived and tried to pull them apart. He wasn't strong enough. My shoulders were hurting a lot, so I stepped back into the carriage. The doors shut the whole way. Skelton was still on the platform.

Immediately, the train began to move. Skelton looked towards the driver, as if he might take pity and change his mind. Then Skelton's face passed out of sight.

I crossed to the other side of the compartment, so I could gaze out the window and see if I could see the heart. Skelton could either go to work or come and try to find me. It didn't matter which.

I felt very excited, almost as if I were going to try to save someone's life.

The train went too slowly. I had enough time to read every piece of graffiti between Blackfriars and London Bridge – or it seemed like I did.

I was disappointed when we went back over Borough Market. This train was on a different set of tracks – further away from the roofs. The gutter where the heart had fallen was out of sight.

There was a window, quite near by the place, painted English green. It issued from the top floor of an old brick house. If I could find the front entrance, perhaps this would be a way out onto the roofs – down the rail tracks.

I kept my eyes on the spot of the heart for as long as I could. Just before it went round the corner I saw a large crow come down and land exactly there.

Even before the carriage stopped I was already pressing and pressing the button to open the doors. And when they did open, I got out on the platform and began to walk very quickly towards the exit. I did not wait for Skelton on the next train. To see the crow had caused me painful anxiety about the safety of the heart.

At the end of the platform was a long passage sloping down past advertisements for crime novels and other happy things. When I got to the bottom I turned left and approached the ticket barriers.

A minute later, I was crossing Borough High Street. Above my head was the bridge I had crossed twice in the past fifteen minutes. By following the tracks with my eyes, I was able to see the direction I should go.

The big problem was how to get up onto the roofs. The authorities would not want people to reach there with ease, obviously. I could see no stairs or ladder.

Borough Market was empty, no stalls, and no traders. I walked quickly through to the other side. My footsteps sounded loud in the high space. A dirty light came down through the Victorian glass.

On the corner of Stoney Street was the Market Porter, a nice old-fashioned pub. I had been there with Skelton for a drink of real ale.

A train came past, up in the air, coming from the right direction. Hurry up, I thought.

I walked down Stoney Street, under the rail bridge. And then the house with the green window upstairs was directly in front of me.

It did not look very loved. The front door was painted dull black. In the windows, instead of curtains or blinds, were flattened cardboard boxes – and some of the panes were broken. The faded print said the boxes were once for Sony videocassette recorders.

I thought about calling Skelton on his cellphone. He could find this house if I described it. Maybe he knew it already, by sight. But I was more and more worried about the crow, so I immediately knocked on the door.

No-one answered.

I knocked louder.

Still no-one answered.

'Hello!' I shouted. 'Is somebody there?'

I banged hard on the door with my fist, and it opened – a little. On the inside was a chain. It would be easy to reach around and unhook it.

'Hello!' I shouted through the dark gap. 'I need to speak to you.'

I listened but could hear nothing.

I reached my hand inside, and felt somebody grab it. Nails went into my wrist. What I was most afraid of, although I do not know why, was that the hidden person would bite one of my fingers off.

'Hey,' said an old woman's voice, very rough. 'Let go.'

'No, *you* let go.'

My hand came free. I pulled it out of the dark slit, very glad to have it back in one piece.

The chain clicked against the wood, and the door opened on a very sad face. I am not very tall, only 150 centimetres, but the young girl in front of me was half a head shorter. There were purple circles under her eyes, which had absolutely no life in them.

'What d'you want?' the girl asked. Her voice was still that of an old woman. It seemed to come from a long distance away, like a historical radio broadcast.

'I need to get up onto the roofs.' I pointed up, to make myself clear. 'I saw something on them.'

The girl looked to my left and right. 'You alone?'

'Yes,' I said. 'But I have a friend who may come in a minute.'

For a second time she looked around me.

'You sure you don't want nothing else? You don't have to give me some story about the roof. What d'you want?'

'No. I need to get up there. Quickly.'

She stepped back into the dark, pulling the door open. 'Be quiet,' she said. 'Don't wake them.'

I followed her across the room. My feet kicked hard things out of the way.

'Stairs,' she said. 'Be careful. They're rotten.'

There was more light on the first landing. We kept going up. Another floor, and then the green window with scaffolding around it.

'It's safe,' said the girl.

It felt strange to climb out onto the roof I had seen from the train.

I saw a crow try to take off, the heart hanging from its beak. The girl must have spotted it too.

'No!' I said.

The girl understood what I meant because she jumped across to the train tracks.

At first I thought she was fleeing, but then I realized you had to go the long way round.

I got onto the tracks and ran after her. She was fast. I was faster. We went over the high bridge. My feet splashed in the spaces between sleepers as I overtook her.

The crow lifting the heart only got about a metre into the air before the other crow attacked it. Black feathers beat against black feathers, beak tried to peck eyes, and the heart fell down.

The girl showed me how to get onto the roofs of the market. We climbed over a low place in the wall.

I was still maybe ten metres away from where I needed to be.

The two crows descended together. Both beaks caught hold of the heart. Together, they took off vertically. They had seen me and were scared.

I jumped up to try and grab the dangling heart. My fingers felt the touch of it, but then the crows went higher.

The girl joined me.

We watched helplessly as the two crows flew up and up, five metres, ten.

Then one of the crows tried to pull away, stealing the heart from the other. It failed – beak lost its grip.

For a moment, I thought the other crow would now just fly away. But the heart was too heavy for it.

As it began to fall, I knew it was out beyond the edge

of the roofs. I was desperate to catch it, though, so I ran without thinking.

My hands were above my head when the heart fell into them.

I tried to stop, and almost did, but my momentum was tipping me forwards, over the edge.

If the girl had not grabbed the belt of my raincoat, I would have fallen fifteen metres onto wet pavement – or onto the head of Skelton, standing there, looking up.

2.

Her ultra-pale skin, Kumiko's, I can't compare with anything else. She was thirty-three around the time of the heart, so despite being perfect her face wasn't flawless – near the corners of the eyes, sadness had caused it to pucker. Her father and her mother were recently dead, of cancer and a stroke. We made two visits to Osaka to bury them. When I touched it, Kumiko's skin, I could sense in its smoothness and give both coming age and gone youth. Perfect. Her lips were full, her eyes heavy-lidded and her hair – her hair was like black oil flowing over a stone.

As we travelled up from my parents', we sat in a kind of exhausted but not uncontented silence. Weekends like that, however well they go, always put some kind of strain on a relationship. I thought we'd come through pretty well. My father and Kumiko obviously enjoyed one another's company. With my mother it was a little more difficult, but then it had always been like that. I was her only child.

Whatever she or my father thought, it didn't really matter. Kumiko and I had been going out for three years, living together for two; I loved her, and was planning to ask her to marry me – on Christmas Eve. Of course, all my plans were disrupted by the heart.

When I first saw it, lying on the glass roof of Borough Market, I have to say I felt deeply unnerved. I'm not claiming to be psychic, or to have foreseen everything that happened afterwards, but I knew it was very bad news. I got that pricking-of-my-thumbs feeling. Part of me hoped that Kumiko hadn't seen it. Her dark eyes, though, miss almost nothing – and I'm prepared to admit that it may have been a slight turn of her head that caused me to focus my hazy early-morning gaze.

She was convinced, right from the first moment, that what we had both seen was part of a person. When I suggested it was far more likely something from one of the butchers' stalls in the Market, she just shook her head. 'No,' she said.

With Kumiko being so definite, I put up little resistance to the idea of us going back and investigating. Undoubtedly there was a thrilling element to such a discovery. No-one else in the compartment, the one or two dozing people, seemed to have noticed.

I did wonder, even then, how the heart could have got there – always assuming it *was* a heart. Perhaps someone had dropped it whilst making their escape across the roofs. Or perhaps it had been thrown from one of the late-running trains. Or perhaps, as I suggested, rats or pigeons had carried it up from street level.

As we crossed the Thames, I was distracted enough to look at the faded red pilings sticking out of the water. These, visible from the left-hand side of the train, are all that remains of the original Blackfriars Bridge. Whenever I saw them, I always imagined myself leaping from piling to piling – then sitting down on the one furthest out and waiting for London to take notice of me. It might take a desperate act such as that; nothing else, so far, had worked.

We ran across to a train just about to depart from the southbound platform. Being lumbered with a suitcase full of Kumiko's clothes, I wasn't as fast as I might have been – so Kumiko made it onto the train and I didn't. She held up her left hand to wave, then was shunted out of sight.

I have to say, I expected her to wait for me at London Bridge. As the train clattered past where we'd spotted the heart, I'd looked for but couldn't see it. Kumiko wasn't standing there on the platform. I could only assume she had gone straight to Borough Market in the certain knowledge that I would swiftly follow.

It took a couple of minutes to get out of the station, London's oldest, but soon I was under the roofs of the Market. I looked up, hoping to see the dark silhouette of the heart or Kumiko's shadow.

What I didn't expect to see was Kumiko herself, leaning impossibly out, with the heart in her hands – and two crows flying off in opposite directions above her.

Somehow, she pulled herself back from the edge.

I stepped into the street and could see the back of her head. Then she turned around and shouted directions to me. A house. Further along. Black metal door. Not locked.

It was easy enough to find.

There were holes in the floor and no light to see them by. The windows had been filled in with something completely opaque. I could hear glass crackling underfoot. It felt ridiculous, carrying my suitcase into there. But I didn't want to put it down.

The stairs were just about visible. I stumbled up one flight of them, onto a landing, then up another flight.

There were doors I was scared to go through. It got lighter, towards the top of the house. And then there was a window out onto scaffolding. It seemed the only way.

Once on the roof, I saw Kumiko immediately – her black hair. She was standing with another woman, both looking down at what she held in her hands.

'Hey,' I shouted. 'How?'

'You have to come along the tracks,' Kumiko replied.

Seeing she meant what she said, I put the suitcase down.

There were no trains coming. I sprinted as fast as I have in years.

When I got to Kumiko, she introduced me to the young woman.

'Becky,' she said. 'This is Skelton.'

'Good morning,' I said, and quite ridiculously we shook hands.

'Let me see,' I said.

The heart was too small for a cow's, too big for a dog's. There was no blood – in fact, the muscle looked quite anaemic. This reassured me that we weren't going to find a head round the next corner.

The rain was falling and Becky was shivering. She looked like she was very good at shivering.

'Are we calling the Police?' I asked.

'No,' said Becky. 'You can't.'

'Why not?' I asked. 'This might be a murder.'

'Skelton,' said Kumiko. 'Calm down. We're not stupid.'

'But …' I said. 'You should probably put it down. Forensic evidence …'

'We don't want the Police,' said Becky. 'Not in that house.'

I couldn't stop looking at the heart. Kumiko held it gently in cupped palms.

'How else are they going to get up here?' I said.

Kumiko's eyes told me quite definitely to shut up. 'Maybe someone died,' she said to Becky. 'It's important. If you need to tidy the house, or hide anything –'

'They'll want to ask questions,' said Becky. She swore a lot, but I'm leaving that out. 'We'll be arrested.'

'Then we won't call until you have gone,' said Kumiko. 'I'm sure the Police won't be interested in you.'

'It's our house. We're living there two years.'

'Look,' said Kumiko, and held out the heart. 'Imagine it is your best friend. What do you want to do? You can decide. If you say, "Go away," we will go away – and we won't call the Police. I promise. But if you do nothing, then it is your responsibility.'

A train went past, heading for London Bridge. I wanted to signal to them, 999, call the Police!

Becky tried to find a fingernail to bite, without success.

'I have to ask them,' she said, and nodded to the house.

'Good,' said Kumiko. 'We will wait. There is no hurry.'

I knew I'd be in serious trouble if I said anything, so I waited until Becky was over the tracks and back inside.

'You're leaving it up to *her* and her friends to decide –'

'Yes,' said Kumiko. 'I trust her. She won't do something wrong.'

'But we don't know who else is in there.'

'She will explain,' said Kumiko. Her confidence was astonishing.

'We should call the Police now,' I said. 'While she's away.'

'We will wait,' said Kumiko.

So we did. A half-dozen trains went past, but I avoided looking to see if anyone saw us. Kumiko stood facing away from the tracks.

Becky returned with a skinny-hipped man. He wore only a pair of jeans. They were not clean. 'That it?' he asked, as if there might be another human heart somewhere else on the roof.

'Call the Police now, if you like,' said Becky. 'The others have gone.'

Kumiko introduced herself then me. 'Jonesy,' said the man. He was about twenty years old. There didn't seem to be any trackmarks on his arms. 'Give us a bit to get our stuff together, okay?'

'You didn't see anything?' Kumiko asked Becky.

'No,' Becky said, too quickly. 'Saw nothing.'

She glanced at Jonesy. 'She saw nothing,' he confirmed.

I felt like the Police.

'We'll wait here,' I said. 'How long do you need?'

'Give us ten minutes,' Jonesy said.

We watched them go back through the door. 'Ten minutes,' Kumiko said. 'Just ten minutes.' She seemed to be thinking how sad this fact was.

'Let's go and stand inside,' I said. 'It makes no difference.'

'The crows might come back.'

I'd forgotten the crows.

We waited in the rain. By the time Kumiko let me call the Police, we were damp. By the time they arrived, we were soaked.

Then the questions began, the same ones, over and over again from different Officers – at first on the roofs and then down at the Police Station.

We were told, quite sternly, that we should never have gone trespassing on Private Property. If we had suspicions, we should have called the Police from the train. I didn't bother saying that, in those circumstances, they probably wouldn't have come, or not for hours, and by then the crows would have eaten the evidence, and they would have been left with no investigation.

They kept asking me if the heart had been still when I saw it. 'It made no movement at all, so far as you were aware of observing?' Then they would go away, only to return and ask me the same thing again. 'Are you one hundred per cent certain?'

'No,' I said. I thought about saying, 'I'm not one hundred per cent certain about anything.' And I thought, 'Except Kumiko.'

I had to wait another two hours before they were finished with her. It wasn't clear why they were more interested in what she had to say.

Meanwhile, I called my agent, to explain that I couldn't make the day's session. She said I hadn't really been needed, but that I should turn up bang on time tomorrow.

'It's a big break,' she said.

I bought some sandwiches and sat down on a wooden bench in reception, watching people come in to report crimes or ask for directions. I had the suitcase with me, and sometimes I put my feet up on it.

The first thing Kumiko said to me was, 'It *is* human.'

'Can we go home now?' I asked.

She nodded.

We walked slowly back to London Bridge. The Police had loaned me a blanket during the questioning but I hadn't dried out completely. Even though I'd have looked stupid, I wished I still had it with me.

Kumiko ate her sandwiches as we waited on the platform. I knew better than to ask her what she was thinking.

When a train arrived, we got in and then stayed beside the doors on the left-hand side.

As we passed by the glass roofs, we could see that a small white marquee had been erected over the place where the heart lay. Two crows were perched on the edge of it. A Policewoman was looking in the opposite direction.

We got off the train at King's Cross Thameslink. Our flat was only about five minutes' walk. Kumiko didn't speak until we were up the stairs, through the front door and into the living room.

'I'm sorry, Skelton, but I am leaving.'

I didn't disbelieve her, even though it came as a total shock. All of a sudden, I felt very tired, and sat down on the sofa.

'Look, I'm sorry about my parents.'

'It's not your parents. I like your parents.'

'Can I at least ask why?'

'I don't want to say it. I don't want to hurt you more than I have to.'

'Is it because you think I didn't want to go back, this morning?'

'Yes, but not really,' she said.

Kumiko went into the bedroom and started to put things in her overnight bag. She moved confidently, as if she had already compiled a mental list of what she would need.

I went to the door to watch her. She was really doing this.

'Can we talk about it?' I asked. 'Can't we at least talk about it for five minutes?'

She looked once more around the bedroom, then came towards the door carrying the bag. I stepped out of her way, and she went into the bathroom. Kumiko wore no make-up. Kumiko didn't need beauty products. She took only a spare tube of toothpaste, some floss and that was it. Her toothbrush was already in the bag.

'Someone will come round for everything else,' she said. 'Perhaps Grzegorz. It's your decision to pack it up or not.'

'No,' I said at last. 'Don't go.'

But then she was gone. And all in less than ten minutes.

The police did not believe me when I said I saw the heart sliding down the roof. They kept going away and coming back to ask me if I was sure. Skelton was probably telling them something different or opposite. But Skelton didn't see the heart as soon as I did. He was facing the wrong way. It only slipped down a few centimetres and then it was in the guttering.

After the police let me go, we took the train straight home. I thought about Becky and Jonesy – about how we had stolen their home. It was their decision to call the police. I believe it was the right decision.

I did not know I was leaving Skelton until we were inside the flat. On the train, I was thinking about a nice hot shower and cup of good coffee to get rid of the taste of the bad coffee from the police station. But as soon as I saw where we lived I had a strong instinct inside me: *I will not sleep here another night.*

Skelton did not seem too surprised. I was hurting him very deeply, but in the end it might be good for him – and he might one day see that. He did not cry. Not while I was there.

Soon, I was out of my old life. Then I had to decide how to start again. I did not want to explain myself to anyone, not yet, and I did not want to go anywhere Skelton would find me, so I checked into the Travelodge hotel overlooking the Thameslink station.

The room was very blue, curtains, carpet, wallpaper. The double bed had a light-blue counterpane. I took a shower. My cellphone rang. It was Skelton, I knew. I let it go onto voicemail, then when I finished in the bathroom, turned it off before he could call again.

I had not enjoyed leaving Skelton, but it felt like absolutely the right thing to do, and so there was a little satisfaction in me, along with all the sorrow.

I put on a change of clothes, and with them came a new feeling of energy. The time on the bedside clock was 12.15 p.m.

Skelton had bought some horrible wet sandwiches for lunch, but I was still very hungry. If I ate in a café in King's Cross, he might come and find me. So, I put on my coat, walked quickly to the underground and took trains to Bond Street.

There was a cellphone concession in the station, so I filled in some forms and got a new account and a new handset.

I went to a sandwich bar and ordered the full English breakfast. The fried eggs tasted very good with salt on them – perhaps they tasted like the new life. I finished everything, bacon rind, crusts of toast, and the last leafy sip of tea and sugar-sludge at the bottom of my mug. Sometimes I love London life so much.

I needed to copy some numbers onto the new phone. When I turned the old phone on there were two new voice messages from Skelton, and he had also sent several texts. I didn't listen to them or read them – I knew what they would say. After a few minutes going through my address book, I switched the old phone off and zipped it up in my jacket pocket, feeling free.

It was not busy in the sandwich bar, so I sat there for another fifteen minutes. I thought about the heart. Who could it belong to? The original person was probably dead, the person born with that heart, but there was a very small chance they might have had a transplant and still be alive with someone else's heart in their chest. Maybe they had thrown the old heart from the train to say goodbye to it for ever. If so, it was a very poetic gesture. I did not feel disgust.

After eating, I really desired a cigarette. Skelton had successfully begged me to quit, although he said that the first time he saw me I was smoking, and he found it very sexy.

In the newsagent's I said, 'Ten Marlboro Lights, please.' Then, after a moment, 'No. Wait. Sorry. Twenty Gauloises, please.'

The man behind the counter paused, waiting for me to change my mind back again, then smiled. 'Just not the same, are they?' he said.

'No,' I said. 'And a lighter, too. Thank you *very* much.'

Outside, I did not light the first cigarette straight away. I wanted to be somewhere special. The only place I could think of was the roof of Borough Market.

I checked the time. 1.30 p.m.

The rain had not stopped. I decided to wait for the cigarette, until I could be somewhere special.

For the next few hours, I went to the cinema. First, I bought an *Evening Standard* and checked the listings. I wasn't being choosy, I just wanted something that started immediately. It was an awkward time. 2.30 p.m. was the next proper screening. So I just walked down to one of the gay porn cinemas in Soho. It didn't matter to me. The film itself was not important. My eyes weren't even open for most of the time. I sat very still and thought about what I was going to do. The men came and went but did not object to me. Cinemas are, for me, good places to concentrate.

When I returned to the street it was evening and a little darker. This made me feel better about returning to London Bridge.

I took the tube to Blackfriars, then waited for the right train. I was returning.

As we passed the roofs, I saw that the marquee had gone. The green window was wide open.

Then I looked up, and as if for the first time I saw it, the place where the heart must have come from.

Guy's is the tallest hospital in the world. Thirty-four floors. It looks very brutalistic, like the watchtower of a prison or a gulag. Seen from the side, the gray concrete shape is like a huge number 1.

I don't know why, but I was sure the heart once belonged to someone there. It was the obvious place.

The train got closer and closer.

I liked the building, because it was strong and without compromise. Things like that, I find easy to admire, even if I a little disagree with the detail of them.

The hospital would be a good special place for my first freedom cigarette.

There were a few smokers outside the main entrance. I joined the edge of the group, close enough to hear what they were saying.

A police car was parked there with an officer in the front. They did not look familiar. I was not thinking about them.

It was a pleasure to see the flame touching the end of the cigarette. But the first drag was something else altogether. It was far more than a joy.

I did not even have time to take a second pull before I saw two officers coming through the doors. Between them was a muscular young man with dark hair. He was wearing a white lab coat. The young man was not putting up a struggle. In fact, he was laughing. 'This is ridiculous,' he said.

The two officers, both men, guided him towards the patrol car. Then one of them opened the nearside door whilst the other kept hold of his arm.

'My God,' said a young woman beside me, also wearing a lab coat. She had long dark hair and was very pretty. 'That's Paul.'

'Just bend your head down,' the second officer said.

The young man stooped to get into the back seat of the patrol car. His hands were held behind his back by plastic cuffs.

'Paul!' the young woman shouted, but the young man didn't hear.

The first officer went and got in the passenger seat. The second joined the prisoner in the back.

Just before they drove off, the young man looked around all the faces he could see. For a moment, we stared at one another. Then he saw the young woman, shrugged and tried to smile.

The turn of the car whipped him out of sight.

'My God,' she said again. 'So we're questioned all day, and finally they arrest him.'

'What's that?' asked a man in his forties, just arriving. A doctor.

'Didn't you hear?' said a slightly older woman dressed in blouse and skirt. She was a secretary-type. 'About them finding body parts lying all over the place?'

'It was one body part,' said the doctor. 'A kidney, I think.'

'Didn't belong to King Death, by any chance?' said the older woman.

The young woman laughed.

'No,' said the doctor. 'It would have been fossilized.'

'You are terrible,' said the older woman. 'Still, I better get back. No doubt we'll soon find out what's been going on.'

'It wasn't a kidney,' I said, moving closer to the group. 'It was a heart.'

'Then it definitely wasn't King Death's,' said the older woman, and laughed. The other two didn't join in.

'How do you know that?' asked the young woman. 'No-one's supposed to know that.'

I didn't see why I shouldn't tell them. 'I found it. I called the police and told them where it was.'

'And where was it?' the young woman asked. She was slender and had very good skin.

'On the roofs of the market.'

'How did it get up there?' asked the older woman.

'I don't know,' I said. 'Who is King Death?'

The three of them looked confused.

'So you don't work in the hospital?' asked the doctor.

'No.'

Then there was a sort of hurry – all of them put their cigarettes out, said goodbye to one another and went inside. None of them looked at me.

I was annoyed with myself. To ask such a direct question was a stupid mistake. If I had waited, perhaps I would have learnt much more.

As my first cigarette had been so helpful, I thought I should smoke my second one at 'the scene of the crime'.

The market was deserted. I did not feel scared. There were no lights in Becky's house.

A new padlock was fixed to the door. Someone had smashed it already.

I pushed the door open. It was so dark inside that, if I hadn't been there before, I would never have found the stairs, or even known they were there. But I stumbled as I crossed the room, and when I put my hand out to break my fall I felt it cut by something sharp. I think it was a broken bottle.

Already as I stood up there was warm wetness on my palm. I continued towards the stairs, more cautiously. The bleeding I could deal with when I got onto the roof, into the light.

Once my feet found the rhythm of the staircase, I went up without any problem. But as soon as I climbed out onto the roof I felt myself being knocked to the floor. My hands were held behind my back and a female voice began to read me my rights. She said I was being arrested for trespassing on private property.

'Okay,' I said. 'I'm not going to try and escape.'

'Stand up,' the voice said. 'Put your hands against the chimney and stand with your feet apart.'

I obeyed. The policewoman frisked me then told me to turn round. 'Are you bleeding?'

'I cut myself.'

'What are you doing here?'

I tried to explain.

'You mean you're trespassing here for the *second* time today – and they let you off with just a caution the first time?'

'Yes,' I said.

The policewoman laughed, then she spoke into her walkie-talkie.

A patrol car was downstairs when we got there. I expect it had been waiting nearby. The policewoman had guided us through the house with her torch. I saw the broken glass on the floor.

'You don't live here, then?' the policeman in the driving seat asked.

'No,' I said. 'I've only been here twice.'

'Twice too often, if you ask me,' the policewoman said. Then she apologized and put plastic handcuffs on my wrists. 'They'll see to that cut when you get there.'

The male officer drove me to the police station while the female one went back inside the house. I doubted that anyone else would be stupid enough to return there so soon.

The police station was much busier than in the morning. They put me in a cell.

The bleeding of my palm stopped by itself.

4.

I was completely destroyed.

For I don't know how long I just sat there and wept.

Then I calmed down – enough to speak to Kumiko on the phone. Speed-dialling her number started me off again.

I hung up before it connected, closed my eyes, got my breath back, dialled a second time.

She didn't answer. A woman's voice asked me to leave a message.

I said something that came out as a wail. Even I couldn't understand what I was saying. Then immediately I rang off and sent a text. Please phone me. I love you. Skelton.

Why had she done this to me? In our bedroom I looked through her notebooks for some sort of clue, but of course they were all in kanji – which I can't read. The only thing I found was a drawing from a couple of months previously. There I was, asleep, mouth hanging open.

Half an hour later, I tried her mobile again. This time, however, it went straight to voicemail. Kumiko must have switched it off. I left another message anyway, and couldn't stop myself sending another couple of texts.

It was clear Kumiko wasn't going to speak to me unless I was right there in front of her. And so the only thing for me to do was find out where she was.

The most likely thing, I thought, was that she would go and stay with Grzegorz, her best friend. He had a flat up in Camden. Most of the day, he worked in his studio. He was an artist, like Kumiko. Not as good, though.

When I called him, Grzegorz sounded preoccupied. I didn't try to keep the distress out of my voice.

'Has Kumiko called?'

'Today? No. Are you alright?'

'Please tell me the truth.'

'Look, she hasn't called. Is something wrong?'

'If she does call, could you let me know? It's really important.'

Grzegorz was probably thinking that it couldn't be to do with either of Kumiko's parents, since they were both already dead.

'Is it an emergency?'

'Yes,' I said.

Well, it was.

I rang off.

There were another couple of London-based friends she might also try, though Grzegorz was by far the likeliest. I called them, too. One was away on holiday, as her answerphone told me, the other picked up and, down a very bad line, assured me she was halfway up a mountain in Cambodia.

If Kumiko hadn't already spoken to Grzegorz, then there was a possibility she had decided to stay somewhere else that night. The only other option I could think of was a hotel. King's Cross has dozens of them, from narrow Georgian terraces to glassy towerblocks. It would take the rest of the day to try all of them – and what if Kumiko had gone to another area of London altogether? What if she were heading for one of the airports?

I rushed into her study and pulled open the bottom drawer of her desk. Kumiko's passport was still there.

Unable to resist, I turned to her photo. She looked great.

I put the passport back, but then I decided I could at least stop Kumiko leaving the country. There was a row of about twenty large art books on her shelves. I hid the passport inside Matthew Barney's *Cremaster*. Then I changed my mind and retrieved it. I couldn't keep her affections by doing stupid things like that. I replaced it in the bottom drawer, then changed my mind again. If she did come back for it, I wanted to know she had. So I placed it on a piece of blank A4 paper right in the middle of her desk.

Back in the living room, I sat for a while on the sofa, trying to think what to do. I gazed at the grey screen of our television. It was probably this that reminded me where Kumiko always went whenever she wanted to be alone: the cinema.

Almost before I knew it I'd grabbed that week's *Time Out* and was heading for the underground. Once on a Piccadilly line train, I checked the listings to see what was playing.

There followed a bizarre, humiliating and very expensive afternoon. I went to all the cinemas around Leicester Square and up Shaftesbury Avenue. At each one, I bought a ticket for whatever was showing, even if the feature had started an hour earlier. Then I went in and searched for Kumiko. This involved a lot of shuffling along rows of seats, peering at flickering faces, and being told to sit down. A couple of places threw me out, quite aggressively, when they caught me trying to sneak into films I hadn't paid for. My explanations weren't listened to.

Around six o'clock, I gave up. The evening showings would be crowded – too many faces to check.

I bought a Final Edition of the *Standard*. Commuters jostled past me in the street as I looked to see if the heart had got a mention. It hadn't.

Then my phone rang.

'Mr Skelton?' I didn't recognize the voice. A young man.

'Yes.'

'We've arrested your girlfriend, Kumiko Ozu.'

'Arrested?'

'For trespass. Can you come down? We're about to release her.'

She was in the same Police Station we'd been taken to that morning, Southwark.

Luckily, I was able to hail a taxi almost immediately.

As we drove through Trafalgar Square, I began to think about what Kumiko had been up to, going back to the house. Surely it wasn't to sleep there?

Then I realized it was probably her new project. Play at being a detective. Investigate the crime.

In Japan, Kumiko is very famous – which is one of the reasons she moved to England.

Her breakthrough work was called 'Whisperings'. It involved her sitting in a small Tokyo gallery for a fortnight, inside a kind of self-built confessional. Whenever anyone came and sat in the other seat, she would whisper something to them. But – and this was the point of it – she couldn't see them because there was no grille, just a mouthpiece, and she only knew they were there because they pressed a red button.

For the first few days, almost no-one visited. Kumiko sat waiting. She wasn't unhappy, she said. It was just part of the piece. The gallery owner thought the show was a failure and was angrily thinking about closing it.

Then, at the end of the first week, a party of schoolgirls happened on the gallery, sat one by one in the confessional, giggled, cried and decided they absolutely loved it. They told all their friends to go, and they had a lot of friends, and these friends had friends, and one of the friends' friends' mothers was a TV news reporter who did a short report on the queue of girls outside the gallery.

The next day, the queue was a mile long. Some girls had been waiting all night to ensure they would get in and hear their whisper. Others rejoined the end of the queue as soon as they'd heard what Kumiko said.

Celebrities came, and were turned away if they refused to join the queue. Many of the girls claimed to find great wisdom in what Kumiko said to them, even if it was as simple as 'Coca-Cola' or 'Hallelujah' or 'No'.

On the final day, Kumiko refused the gallery owner's request that she continue another week. 'I'm exhausted,' she said, 'and I have no more to say.'

One fan had been collecting and collating the whispers like a pollster outside a polling station. She posted them on her website. What became clear was that Kumiko had repeated herself to nobody.

Inside her black box, Kumiko had been writing down everything she whispered. This became a book, and the book became a sensation. 'A new I-Ching,' the media called it, although Kumiko made no such claims. She was twenty-three years old.

From then on, Kumiko was a superstar, particularly among thoughtful teenagers. She fled when the pressure of expectation became ridiculous.

Without needing to worry about money, she took her time over her next project. She wrote a book of stories, all told from the point of view of a Persian cat. It was another bestseller. The title was, in English, *Peregrine Falcon*. When Japanese critics asked her why, she said it was because the words were beautiful. Kumiko could do deadpan with the best of them.

Next, she recorded an album of her own songs, accompanying herself on the piano, which she couldn't really play. Need I say that it too was a hit?

We met at an art launch where I was playing in a pick-up jazz trio. I had no idea who she was. This, I now realize, was my main attraction for her, my ignorance.

Kumiko was twenty-nine years old. She had already had three successful artistic careers. But, she said, she didn't want to repeat herself, ever. 'I need to do something different – something new. Maybe be a doctor or something.'

Kumiko was the most absolute person I had ever known. There was an interview with her in an old copy of *Art Quarterly*. I knew it by heart.

> Perhaps I will make no more art. Perhaps I will do one more piece. Perhaps I will do a thousand. What is certain is that I will do nothing before I should. I will do nothing before the moment is right for me. And I will do no more interviews.

She had done no more interviews.

As the taxi neared the Police Station, I began to realize something: the discovery of the heart might be the beginning of her next project. I couldn't see, for the moment, what she might make of it – perhaps she couldn't see, either. But it had all the right elements. Beauty. Mystery. A kind of simplicity. And most tellingly, she already seemed to have become obsessed by it.

The Officer behind the glass in the reception area didn't have a clue who I was. 'Kumiko Ozu,' I said. 'She's due to be released.'

He checked his computer. 'No,' he said. 'She's already been released.'

'But someone called me,' I said. 'I was told to come down here.'

'Wait a minute,' he said, and picked up a phone.

A few minutes later, a very young Officer came out to talk to me. I recognized him from earlier in the day. He had been one of my interrogators.

'It was my mistake,' he said. 'She'd put you down as next of kin this morning. So when she absolutely refused to give us a name this evening, I took it upon myself to call you. I shouldn't have done. I thought you'd just had a lovers' tiff. When she found out, she went mental. I told her you were coming to pick her up, and she couldn't get out of here fast enough.'

'Where did she go?'

'I don't know. She just walked out the door.'

Pointlessly, I looked at the door.

'Did she give an address where she was staying?'

'The same as this morning. You'd probably best go back home and wait for her.'

'What was she arrested for?'

He repeated what I'd been told earlier: Kumiko had returned to the house and 'gained access to the rooftop area'.

'Anything else I should know?'

'Oh, she'd cut herself.'

'Deliberately?'

'No, I think she fell over.'

'You mean when she was being arrested?'

'Nothing like that. She fell over in the dark, in the house.' I didn't really believe him.

'Was it a bad cut?'

'Not really. In her left hand. We bandaged it up for her.'

I didn't need to ask where the nearest A&E department was. Earlier that day, standing on the platform of London Bridge station, whilst Kumiko ate her lunch of sandwiches, I'd looked up at the vast ugliness of Guy's.

'Thank you,' I said to the young Policeman.

Outside, I set off through the rain towards the hospital. There was no point getting another taxi to go such a short distance. In ten minutes, I was there.

A&E looked busy. Kumiko wasn't in sight.

I sat down on one of the orange plastic seats.

'You have to register with the nurse, luvvie, if you want to be seen.' A kindly lady with a bandaged ankle was speaking. 'They give you a number.'

'Oh,' I said. 'I'm not here for me.'

I was determined not to cry.

'Nothing serious, I hope,' the lady said.

'No,' I said. 'Just a scratch.'

She smiled.

'I hope they fix you up,' I said.

'I'm sure they will,' she said. 'They're marvellous here – absolutely the best.'

I walked back out the door.

5.

I could hear other people in other cells.

When it was loud, they were shouting and singing, when it was quiet, they moved around and cursed and sobbed.

Once, a cell door was unlocked and an officer said, 'Mr White, could you come with me?'

'Yes,' came the reply, 'but you can call me Paul.'

'Come on.'

There was shuffling.

'I'd stop making jokes like that if I were you. This is a serious position you're in.'

'But this is ridiculous –'

I couldn't hear any more. They were taking the young man from the hospital – Paul White – to be questioned.

When it was my turn, the police said they were very disappointed. The officer I spoke to was called PC Wagner. He was very young, and quite aggressive. I had been cautioned once already, he said, so they would have to charge me with a crime. Trespass.

'Do you want us to call anyone?'

'No.'

'Are you sure you don't want someone notified?'

I shook my head.

PC Wagner said, 'It might be best if someone came to take you home.'

An image came to me: the blue walls and carpet of my hotel room, my home. I wanted another shower. I wanted another cigarette. Was the blue room smoking or non-smoking?

Once they charged me, there was very little else for them to do. They left me in the interrogation room for half an hour, and then PC Wagner came to set me free.

I was putting on my raincoat when he told me he had called Skelton. It took me three minutes to get out of there.

As I was about to turn the corner, I looked back. A taxi had drawn up and Skelton was inside, paying the driver.

Keeping out of sight, I watched him stride into the police station. Then I hailed the same taxi and asked the driver to take me to A&E at St Thomas'.

'Guy's is closer,' he said.

'I know.'

'Are you a tourist?'

'No, I live here.'

'You could walk to Guy's.'

'Please take me to St Thomas'.'

He paused, then asked, 'Is something wrong with Guy's?'

'I'm trying to avoid someone,' I said.

'Oh,' the driver said.

'My ex,' I said, and realized I hadn't thought of Skelton as that before.

'He a doctor, then?'

'No, he's the guy that just got out of this cab.'

'Him? Really?'

'Yes.'

'Is he looking for you?'

'I think so.'

The cabbie thought about this for a few moments, then said, 'I picked him up just outside Leicester Square tube. He didn't look so bad.'

'He isn't,' I said.

I saw the driver's eyes in the mirror.

'You had a fight?'

'He didn't do this to me,' I said, holding my hand up. 'This was an accident.'

'Sorry I asked,' said the driver. After that, he kept quiet.

At St Thomas', I had to wait half an hour before anyone could see me. I kept my eyes on the doors but Skelton did not come through them. The nurse cleaned out the wound, put antiseptic cream on it and then sealed it up with tape.

'Painful,' she said.

'Yes,' I said, meaning no.

I took buses back to King's Cross. That seemed the best way of avoiding Skelton.

My hotel room did not seem lonely. The emptiness of it was very full. No-one was going to call and interrupt my thinking. I took the shower I wanted. There was a soft white bathrobe for me to put on while I combed my hair and waited for it to dry. Why didn't everyone live like this?

At 10 p.m. I watched a news programme. They did not mention the heart. It wasn't there on Ceefax, either.

After a bit longer, I fell asleep.

I had no alarm-clock but woke at exactly 6 a.m. For a few seconds I felt confused – I was sleeping in a bed, not on a futon – then I remembered where I was. Yesterday did not seem like a dream. I knew that everything had really happened, including the crows.

It took me a few moments to get dressed. I went straight out to the nearest newsagent's and bought all the papers.

Back in my room, sitting cross-legged on the bed, I turned the pages one by one.

They contained nothing about the heart or the hospital or me and Skelton or Paul White.

At first I felt frustrated. I wanted to phone up the editors and tell them they had made a bad decision – such an interesting story, don't miss it! Then my feeling changed. It was like I knew a special secret. Skelton knew the secret too, and some police, but only I really understood. Unless there was one other person.

The breakfast room was empty of guests. A Russian girl took my room number. I ate a bowl of cereal. Everything else looked disgusting, most of all the hot food.

I made a plan for the day, then put it into action. First, I went upstairs, packed up and checked out of the hotel. I wanted to move away from Skelton, just in case he saw me by accident on the street. And I wanted to be close to where I saw the heart, even if I couldn't go inside the house and up on the roofs. So I took a Thameslink train down to London Bridge station. The roofs of the market were without policewomen. The green door was locked with a new padlock. And then I looked around for a hotel. I found one very near the station, the London Bridge Hotel. They had a suite I could use immediately.

I unpacked my clothes and called my friend Grzegorz.

'Hel-*lo*,' he said, as if he knew something already. 'I've been trying to call you. Why's your phone off?'

I explained. It took about five minutes. I lay in the middle of a huge double bed.

'And that's it?' asked Grzegorz. 'You're not giving him a second chance?'

'No,' I said.

'I think you're making a mistake. He's a good guy. He really cares about you. Do you want to come over? We can talk about it.'

'Maybe tomorrow. I have things to do.'

Grzegorz told me that Skelton had called him soon after I walked out – and again this morning.

'He told me it was an emergency. I thought somebody had died.'

'Maybe they have,' I said. 'If he calls again, tell him I'm okay but that he must stop chasing me. I will contact him … Say I will contact him in a while.'

'You're not going to be more specific?'

'I can't.'

We talked about other things. Grzegorz was preparing for a big show. I was interested in what he told me about it. We said goodbye.

I went and bought the first edition of the *Standard* – and there it was, page 10, News in Brief.

MEDICAL STUDENT'S SICK PRANK DISCOVERED BY GUY'S HOSPITAL

A medical student was yesterday arrested on suspicion of stealing human body parts from Guy's Hospital. He was caught after trying to dispose of them from the window of a moving train. The student, 24, had been taking dissection classes as part of his basic training. A spokesperson for Guy's said today, 'We apologize for any distress this incident may have caused. We are co-operating fully with the Police investigation.' The medical student is expected to be charged later today.

I had to find out more.

Immediately, I phoned directory inquiries and asked for a couple of numbers. First was for Guy's Hospital Press Office.

'Can you tell me who made the statement about the medical student who was arrested?'

'That would be me.'

'And your name is?'

'Maddy Nemec. And you are?'

'I am a journalist from a Japanese newspaper.'

'We have nothing more to say.'

'Can you confirm that the body part was a heart?'

'How do you know that? That hasn't been released.' She sounded upset.

'Has Paul White been suspended?'

'You must not print his name. How on earth did you get hold of that?'

'Thank you.'

Second was for the *Evening Standard* news desk. Once they put me through I asked to speak to the journalist who wrote the story.

'Burgess, yes?'

'I read the story about the body parts.'

'Go *away*, freak,' he said, and put the phone down.

I called a second time.

'Burgess.'

'Please could I speak to you for one second? I am not who you think I am.'

He did not speak but I could hear him listening.

'Paul White. Where will he be charged? In a court?'

'Yes,' he said. 'Do you know him?'

'Yes,' I said.

'Why did he do it?'

'He didn't. Which court?'

'Southwark Crown Court,' Burgess said.

'When?'

'They haven't given out the time yet.'

'Thank you, Burgess.'

'What's he like? Is he –'

I hung up.

Another call to directories got me the number of Southwark Crown Court.

Paul White would be arraigned, they said, at 3 p.m.

That gave me two hours with nothing to do. Without any real plan I headed for Guy's. Again there were a few smokers outside for me to join – different ones than before. Two were in nurses' uniforms, another was a porter and the rest were patients or visitors.

'– have done it many many times,' said one of the nurses, a Jamaican woman.

'But he only started in September,' the other replied. She was from China or Taiwan.

'It make me sick,' the Jamaican nurse said. 'To own such disrespect. Them people give they bodies for scientific, not for disgraceful student activity.'

'I know.'

'He should be imprisoned right an' proper.'

'Well, he won't come back here.'

They continued to talk but said nothing I didn't already know. All the rumours they had heard were inaccurate.

Only at the end did the porter – a black man with a white Afro – join in their discussion, although he'd listened to it closely from the start.

'He was always very polite to me. A very *helpful* young man. Always working. I think the police made a mistake – a big mistake.'

'Fool,' said the Jamaican nurse, but didn't go into detail.

'We will find out,' said the Asian nurse.

'That's not true,' the porter said. 'You never get to the truth here.'

The two nurses looked at him doubtfully.

'Don't start me now,' the Jamaican said. 'I don't have no time for your African foolishness.'

The porter and the patients were left behind. They started to talk about football.

I stayed there and smoked another four cigarettes, as people came and went, but my luck had gone and no-one else said anything interesting – although most did mention the scandal.

At 2 p.m. I walked the short distance to Southwark Crown Court. It was raining.

There were a few people waiting in the lobby. After I had gone through the metal detector, I joined them. Looking through the faces, there was only one I recognized: the young woman from the evening before, the one with the long dark hair who had shouted out Paul White's name. She was talking to another, less attractive young woman about the same age as her.

I tried to pick out Burgess but no-one seemed to fit his voice.

I went back outside to smoke another cigarette. My lungs felt like shopping bags full of water.

A court usher let us in at 2.50 p.m. Whilst waiting, I had started to worry that Skelton might arrive. But then I remembered he was working that day, a very important gig. Unless Skelton had changed character, that's where he would be.

I sat at the far end of the back row. If possible, no-one would notice me. More people came. The majority, I could tell, were medical student friends of Paul White's.

Barristers in wigs and gowns chatted about the merits of contact lenses and bifocals. They seemed unconcerned that everyone could hear them.

The arraignment started on time.

'All rise,' said the usher.

The judge made his entrance, and then we could all sit down again. He looked very English, I thought, but when he spoke he had an Australian accent.

Then Paul White was escorted in by two uniformed women. I saw him look round the gallery and recognize a few faces. He smiled once or twice but it was a very different smile to the one last night.

Proceedings began in the case of Regina *versus* Paul White. It took a while to get to the charge itself. Before this, the accused was asked to confirm his name and age. He stood up, spoke and sat down.

For the actual arraignment, he was asked to stand up again.

A clerk read the charge out in a loud clear voice:

'Paul White, it is alleged that on the evening of Monday the thirtieth of April, you did remove the heart from a human cadaver at the dissecting room of Guy's Hospital with the intention of stealing it for purposes unknown, that you did thereafter remove the heart from hospital grounds, and that, during the course of that night, in an attempt to dispose of the heart, you did throw it from the window of a northbound train onto the roofs of Borough Market. How do you plead?'

'Not guilty, Your Honour.'

'Thank you. You may sit down.'

For me, this was a very strange moment of my life. I hate speaking in public. I do not like the attention of crowds. But I had to behave correctly. So I stood up and began to speak.

6.

At twelve o'clock, I left the flat. The recording was taking place at Studio 2 Abbey Road, which was a thrill as I'd never been there before. To earn money, I am a session musician. I play guitar and I play whatever is put in front of me.

I felt terrible, hadn't slept all night.

When I arrived, the singer, a major pop star, was rumoured still to be in bed.

At home, I had already gone through the day's papers, looking without reward for some mention of the heart. But when a copy of the *Standard* was passed to me by the bassist, I glanced through it.

As soon as I read about the arraignment, I knew Kumiko would be there. This might be my only chance of seeing her. But where would it be?

On my mobile, I phoned Directories and asked for the number of the Police Station where Kumiko and I had been taken. They put me straight through.

The first Officer I spoke to didn't know what I was talking about. But he handed the phone to a woman who did.

'Southwark Crown Court,' she said. 'Three o'clock.'

It was ten past two.

Just then, the pop singer walked in. He was charismatic, that was undeniable. And he began working the room – shaking hands with everyone, including me. But I had no choice; I had to go. I asked the bassist, who

I knew pretty well, if he could look after my guitar — then I sprinted out and hailed a passing cab.

Traffic was bad. It was gone three by the time we made it across the river.

When I slipped into the Public Gallery, the first words I heard were 'Not guilty'. Then the Judge told someone to sit down. A good-looking young man sunk from sight. Then, unbelievably, I heard Kumiko.

'No,' she said. 'This is wrong. You are making a big mistake. My name is Kumiko Ozu. The Police know me. I was on the early train.'

'Silence in court,' shouted the Clerk.

But she continued speaking: 'I saw the heart moving. I saw it *sliding*. That means someone threw it from the early train.'

'You will not be warned again!'

'Not from a late train. So perhaps it wasn't Mr White. Perhaps he has an alibi. Ask him.'

'Silence!' shouted the Clerk.

'Ask him,' she said.

The Judge spoke. 'Before we proceed any further, the young lady will be removed from the Public Gallery.'

Kumiko waited, quite still. She hadn't seen me.

Two big men in uniforms came and grabbed her by the wrists and the upper arms. She did not struggle. They picked her up and began to carry her to the door, and so towards me.

Her eyes did not meet mine until we were a couple of feet apart. She looked ... It hurt me horribly, but she looked disappointed to see me there.

The two men frogmarched her out into the corridor. I followed them.

'That was a very stupid thing to do,' said one of the men.

'Not very polite,' said the other.

'Don't try to come back in.'

'*Ever.*'

They reached the exit, whispered a few more threats and shoved her out. Then they stood blocking the way.

I tried to push between them.

'Kumiko!' I said.

They parted enough to let me fall through.

Kumiko was already ten steps away.

'Hey, Kumi! Stop!'

I stumbled forwards.

'What was that about?'

Kumiko stopped with her back to me. Then she turned around and came very close. I thought she might even be about to kiss me.

'Stop following me around,' she whispered.

'I'm not following you.'

'You are here. Is that for some different reason?'

'No,' I said.

'Then you are following me.'

'I just want a chance to talk to you.'

'Why?'

That hurt. That was close to cruel.

Kumiko's left hand was quite heavily bandaged – palm, not wrist. The Police Officer had said she'd fallen over. I hoped he hadn't been lying. The idea of Kumiko putting herself in danger made me feel sick. I couldn't ask her about it, though.

'We were going out,' I said. 'We were living together. I thought we had a future.'

'We don't.'

Kumiko was her usual absolute self – and, in this case, I was sure she was absolutely wrong.

'I'd like to talk about this *not* here.'

'Here is good for me.' She had stopped whispering. I don't know why she'd started, perhaps as a reaction to having spoken so definitely in court.

'Why aren't you picking up phone messages?'

'Skelton,' she said, 'I will contact you if I want to talk to you. Until then, leave me alone.'

She turned and started to walk. I set off after her. She stopped.

'Do *not* follow me if you *ever* want to speak to me again. Stay there.'

Like a trained dog, I stayed.

She went round the corner, onto Battle Bridge Lane, towards London Bridge station. She could have been going anywhere.

I realized I hadn't told her I loved her. That probably wasn't such a bad thing, given her present mood. And I hadn't asked whether she had a forwarding address. But I knew there wasn't a chance she would have given me one.

As there wasn't anything else to do, I went back into the courts. The indictment was over, however. People were walking out of the lifts. A large group of them was gathered around the young man who had said 'Not guilty'.

I looked at him closely. Had I seen him before? I didn't think so. I couldn't remember him getting on the train at London Bridge. But I hadn't been paying much attention.

My phone rang. It was my agent. She had just heard

about me walking out on the Abbey Road gig. She wasn't angry so much as astonished.

'Are you going to tell me why?'

'Yes,' I said, 'but not right now. It was something I had to do.'

'You're not usually so mysterious.'

'I don't usually have anything to be mysterious about,' I said.

'Anyway,' she said, 'turns out the star wanted to spend some time polishing his lyrics. I begged and pleaded, and they'll have you back tomorrow if you promise not even to leave the room for toilet breaks.'

'Okay,' I said. It seemed so unimportant compared to Kumiko.

'Well, don't say *thanks* or anything.'

'Thank you. Very much. I do appreciate it.'

'Play brilliantly, like I know you can, and impress them loads. You could end up doing the whole album.'

'Wonderful,' I said. 'Really.'

'I love mysteries,' she said. 'Just as long as they don't stay mysterious for *ever*. Ciao.'

The weeks of regular and very well-paid work would allow me to devote time to my real love, improv. Improvised music. Not lounge-bar solos. Not Dixieland riffs cribbed from Armstrong and Dodds. Not even jazz at all, really. The hard stuff. Full-on plinky-plonk-clatter-bang in back rooms of pubs for audiences of beard-strokers and their long-suffering girlfriends. Before I discovered improv, guitar – jazz guitar – had always felt like a bit of a Cinderella instrument. *There*, but only just. In improv, everyone is wanted, equally. The playing that would be required for the pop singer's album didn't compare.

I wandered along the river, up onto London Bridge and then down Borough High Street. I felt very blue. There were plenty of places to have coffee, so I stopped in one of them. It was a tiny greasy spoon – pine-plank walls and little booths with vinyl seats. Just my sort of place.

How to get Kumiko back? That was the only thing I could think about. If she wouldn't let me speak to her, then it would have to be something I *did*. And if she was keeping her whereabouts from me, then the something I did would have to be something she'd hear about from other people. My romantic gestures had always tended to embarrass her. One Valentine's Day I got a small band together and serenaded her from the balcony outside our flat – bad mistake. She didn't speak to me until March.

It amazed me that Kumiko had got herself thrown out of the courtroom. She was incredibly soft-spoken. Preferred whispering to talking. And Japanese women aren't meant to shout, ever. She must have felt incredibly passionate about what she was saying. I remembered her words.

'I saw the heart moving. I saw it *sliding*. That means someone threw it from the early train.'

Kumiko didn't think Paul White was that person. I assumed the Police must have evidence to link him with the heart. Perhaps there was CCTV footage. But I felt bad that I hadn't backed Kumiko up when she told the Police she'd seen the heart moving. I couldn't, really. They'd wanted to know what *I* saw – and when I saw it it was lying still. However, that didn't mean that I didn't believe Kumiko. I trusted her eyes more than my own. So, if what she said was true, for Paul White to be guilty, he had to have been on the early train.

And then everything came together. I realized that the way to get Kumiko back, or at least start to, was to prove that she had been right – and to do that, I had to prove that Paul White was innocent.

But that was ridiculous. He hadn't even been tried yet. The court might find him innocent. But Kumiko clearly didn't want it to get anywhere near a trial. I knew her. Until this was out of the way, she wouldn't be able to think about anything else – certainly not me. If I wanted to stay in her life, I needed to be involved with her obsession, and the more involved the better.

The obvious place to start seemed to be with Paul White himself. With a name like that, though, he wouldn't be easy to track down.

Then, immediately, I realized that of course Paul White would still be around. He was a medical student. He'd just spent a night in the cells. All his mates had come to see him. He'd be in the pub. I just needed to find out *which* pub.

Luckily, it was the first I tried, the George, just a little further down Borough High Street.

The group of friends had reduced to about ten, still enough to take over one of the smaller bars. I got a pint and went to sit down at a table in the corner. There was an old paper which I could pretend to read.

Paul White was easy to pick out as he was doing most of the talking. He already seemed a little drunk. Others around him laughed a lot, making it difficult to hear what he said. I think he was telling them details of his night in the cells.

Sitting nearest me was a young woman of about twenty. She looked less amused than the rest of them. In fact, she wasn't really paying much attention to the joking and piss-ripping.

Not being careful enough, I caught her eye a couple of times. She was very attractive – long black hair.

Unexpectedly, she moved along the bench towards me.

'You were in the court today, weren't you?' she asked.

I said that I had been.

'What's your involvement?'

As I didn't have a lie prepared, I told her something like the truth.

'So you found it?'

'My girlfriend, my estranged girlfriend – Kumiko, she saw it first.'

'The one that shouted in court?'

'Yes.'

'So it's you that's got him into all this trouble?'

'We didn't mean to.'

For a moment I thought she was going to start abusing me in front of the whole group.

'He didn't do it,' she said.

'I believe you.'

'I know for a fact that he didn't.'

'How?'

She looked around her. 'I can't tell you,' she said. 'I can't speak about it to anyone.'

Her glass was empty, so I offered to buy her a drink. To my surprise, she accepted.

'I'm Skelton, by the way,' I said, when I got back to the table.

'Anne,' she said.

We shook hands.

One of the young men in the group caught sight of this and gave me an assessing look.

'I'm in Paul's anatomy class,' said Anne. 'There are four of us assigned to the same body. Ours is unusual. Not your average Gladys. We call her Pandora. Pandora's a young woman. Quite attractive. I mean, she would have been. Looks like Snow White. Or did before we started hacking her up.'

Anne seemed to want to talk about it. I did nothing but nod and sip my pint.

'None of us would ever steal anything like that. We joke around a bit while we're in there. But we respect the people for giving their bodies so we can learn. And anyway, it's not as if no-one's going to miss a heart. We're going to start dissecting them next week. It'll be really interesting.'

'I can imagine,' I said, feeling squeamish.

There was a loud burst of laughter from the other students.

'I'd like to speak to him,' I said. 'I need to ask him a couple of things.'

'Now probably isn't the best time,' said Anne.

'Could you give me his number?' I asked.

'No,' she said. 'But you could give me yours, and I could pass it on.'

We got our phones out. She dictated her number to me, and I dialled it so that she had mine. Of course, doing it this way I also had hers. Perhaps that been the point all along. I hadn't encouraged it, though. It wasn't as if I hadn't mentioned Kumiko.

'Goodbye,' I said.

'Don't be surprised if he doesn't call,' Anne said. 'He's a bit rubbish like that.'

She turned back to the group.

7.

I can't remember what I said in court. A voice that wasn't mine spoke through me, a spirit or a demon. Then someone forced me out, some men, and then Skelton was there, asking me to take him back. I tried to be polite, then left.

On the short walk to the hotel, I kept looking over my shoulder. I was sure Skelton would follow me, even though I had asked him to stay where he was.

In the hotel room, I waited and thought. Paul White was going to be put on trial. I would probably be a witness. Skelton, too. But if they already had the details wrong, they would probably get the verdict wrong.

After an hour, when I was sure Skelton would not be around, I went to the station.

I took the train from London Bridge to Blackfriars and back. I did this about ten times.

When we got to the roofs, I stood up and, if it was open, closed the window, if it was closed, opened it. My arms are quite thin, but I knew I could have reached through the narrow horizontal gap and thrown something. If I stood on the seats, it was easier for me.

I tried to imagine Paul White doing the same thing. It was silly. The truth was clear. A man trying to get rid of the heart would have chosen another place to throw it. Or put it in a plastic bag and dropped it into a bin.

The person who threw the heart on the roof wanted people to see it. They were making a kind of advertisement. Perhaps the person who wasn't Paul White had a reason for this. Perhaps they wanted to be punished. I did not know.

In the evening, at about the same time as the night before, I went back to the Designated Smoking Area. I was hoping to see the young woman who knew Paul.

When she turned up, she was not on her own – a young man and another young woman were with her – but I approached her anyway.

'Excuse me,' I said. 'You are a friend of Paul?'

'Yes,' she said. 'You know I am. I don't want to talk about it.'

'Leave her alone,' said the young man. He was tall with orange freckles and ginger hair.

The other young woman was the one from the courtroom, the one who had been with her there.

'But I want to help him. I want to tell the police they are wrong. So he isn't found guilty.'

'That won't happen,' said the young woman with the long dark hair. 'There isn't going to be a trial. The whole thing's been dropped.'

'But that is wonderful.'

'No, it's not. The hospital just didn't want a big scandal. Paul has been expelled. He's never going to be a doctor.' Her eyes were red around the rims.

'Oh,' I said.

'I saw you in court. I mean, I heard you. What was that about?'

I told her my reasoning.

'Well,' she said, 'it doesn't mean anything, now. So, you'd best leave it alone. The authorities have made their decision.'

'What do you mean?'

'I can't talk about it.'

'Come on, Anne,' said the ginger-haired student. He put his arm around her and they went back inside.

The other young woman looked at me for a second then followed them.

I immediately phoned the police who, after lots of delays and passing me to different officers, confirmed that the charges had been dropped.

I felt angry with Paul White. If he was innocent, why didn't he fight? I needed to talk to him.

Back in my hotel room, I went online. The internet access went through the television. It was slow but worked.

First, I looked up the hospital. Then I tried to find some listings for the students there. Paul White had played left back for the Guy's Hospital Football Club. Paul White had appeared in a comedy revue to raise money for the hospital.

After a while, I saw that all the email addresses for the organizers of these events were the same, name dot surname at kcl.ac.uk. This stood for King's College London, with which Guy's and St Thomas' were linked.

I composed a short email to Paul dot White, explaining who I was. The courtroom. The protesting woman. I asked him to call me on my new mobile number, as soon as possible. I copied the same message, and sent it to several variations of his name.

Then I wrote a simpler email, asking for help in

contacting Paul White, and emailed it to each member of the football team and everyone who had been in the revue.

It was half past twelve. I went to bed.

I did not expect this approach to be successful. And I really did not expect to find an email from Paul White in my Inbox when I woke up. It had been sent at 4.34 a.m.

> please leave me alone and stop bothering my friends,
> I appreciate your concern really but you cant help now so
> just drop it, thank you, p

I replied, asking if we could meet to talk about it.

When I got back from breakfast, there were a couple of responses from his friends. One told me to go away, in obscene language. The second said the same thing but in legalese. 'This matter is now sub judice. I advise you to leave it to the due process of the courts.'

Another arrived as I was sitting there. One line.

'Are you the Japanese woman who spoke to Anne last night?'

I replied that I was. To confirm this, I described what I was wearing.

'What do you want with Paul?'

Just to talk, I said. To try to help him.

'Can you meet me in the Smoking Area at twelve?'

Yes.

I used the morning to go into town. I bought a new laptop and some clothes from agnès b, my favourite shop. All my old things were stuck in the flat with Skelton.

I bought every newspaper. There were one or two small reports that the charges had been dropped, nothing else.

*

'Hello,' said a blonde-haired girl at 12.05 p.m. As I'd expected, it was the one who had been with Anne the night before.

'Shall we go somewhere?' I asked.

'Let's just walk,' she said.

We strolled towards Borough High Street then turned right over London Bridge.

I waited for her to begin.

'I'm Jo,' she said. 'I'm one of the other students in the anatomy class. The body I work on is next to Anne's. Warren, Lesley and Paul share hers, too. Warren was there last night. Tall with red hair. Lesley hasn't been seen since the police questioned her. I think she's hiding out at her parents'. None of them is going to talk to you. They've all been told that if they even so much as mention it again, that will be it. Expelled. The hospital has made up its mind. Keep things quiet.'

'Keep what quiet?'

'You know that Paul didn't steal the heart.'

'Yes.'

'Someone else did.'

'Of course.'

'No, you don't understand. It was very strange. The day before all this, Paul and the others came in to work on their body. We were doing major arteries. We'd already started on the heart – separated it from the body. That's how it could be removed so easily. And Paul started to ask questions. Not to the lecturer. He was saying, "Come on. Who's got it? Is it you?" I asked him, "What do you mean?" And he held up the heart and said, "This isn't Pandora's."'

'What do you mean?'

'I mean that he thought someone had gone in early and swapped the heart from their body with one from their own. As a joke. They called their body "Pandora".'

'Oh. So, someone stole her heart …'

'All of them knew the heart we had removed the week before. They knew what it looked like, felt like. The heart of a young woman is very different from that of an old man.'

'Did they report this?'

'No. Perhaps if they had, they wouldn't have been in so much trouble. They just asked around for a few minutes. And then, after class, Paul confronted a couple of people. He got quite angry. They got quite angry, too.'

'So, no-one admitted to stealing it.'

'No-one knew anything about it. And then, on the day Paul was arrested, we all came into class and our bodies were there as usual. But when they opened theirs up, the heart was missing.'

'Really?'

'Yes. So Paul told the lecturer immediately. Which is hardly what he'd have done if he'd chucked it from a train the night before. Everyone in class was asked to check their body. But only their heart was missing. I don't know what happened next. At some point during the afternoon, the police phoned the hospital to ask about stolen body parts. Naturally, they were put through to the pathologists, and that trail led them straight to Paul.'

'Why was only he arrested? Why not Anne?'

'Because he was the only one to be left alone with the body. All the rest of us went home at the usual time, the night before. But every day one student has to stay behind to help clean up. That evening it was Paul's turn. He would have been alone in there, at some point. The demonstrator usually leaves us to get on with it. Paul would have had enough time to do what he wanted. The lecturer, Dr Speed, saw everyone else go. Paul was the only one it could have been. The police questioned them one by one. Then they arrested Paul.'

She started to cry, then stopped herself.

'He's so good,' she said. 'He's the best out of all of us. He'd have made a great doctor. And now it's ruined.'

I waited. It was as if I had asked the right question.

'I think one of the other students did it. They were jealous or something. They swapped the hearts over the day before. Then they threw Pandora's where everyone would see it. And then, somehow, they took their heart out of Pandora's chest and put it back in their body. That's the only way it could have been done.'

'Did you tell the police this?'

'Yes. But they weren't interested. They just thought I was trying to cover for Paul. Everyone knows I've got a bit of a thing about him. I'm not reliable.'

'Can you give me his address?'

'No,' she said. 'If he talks to you, he'll get in real trouble. As long as he keeps quiet, he doesn't get a criminal record. That's the arrangement.'

'Then tell me whether he lives north or south of the river.'

She thought about this. Was it giving away too much?

'South,' she said.

'So when he goes home, he doesn't take the train to Blackfriars?'

'No,' she said. 'Not at all.'

We had turned round and were now walking back across the bridge.

'One more question, please,' I said. 'Who is King Death?'

'How do you know about that?'

'I overheard someone talking. They were saying the heart could not be his, because he doesn't have a heart.'

Jo looked around as if someone might be listening.

'King Death teaches us anatomy. He's our lecturer. King Death is Dr Speed.'

'Thank you,' I said.

We parted outside my hotel.

'Are you staying here?'

'I'm going to move quite soon,' I said. 'Do you know anyone looking for a flatmate? I will pay more than a student.'

'Perhaps,' said Jo. 'See you.'

I had a lot to think about.

8.

I waited a day for Paul White to phone me, then I called Anne. That was the Friday.

'Yes, I gave him the number,' she said. 'I don't know if he lost it. He had a pretty big night.'

'Let me phone him directly.'

'No.'

'Then how about a drink?' This was Plan B.

Anne accepted, without hesitation. We arranged to meet in town, at seven o'clock, outside Leicester Square tube. Anne was bored, she said, of the pubs around Guy's.

I took her to the Coach and Horses. Then for a meal at Balans. It reminded me very much of a date. Anne had made an effort, wearing a slinky black dress, quite short. Perhaps a little too short. I couldn't stop being aware of her perfume. She seemed very young.

To start with, we talked about anything but the heart. And then, when I tried to bring the subject up, she was evasive. Sparkling water, please. How long have you been playing guitar? Look at *her* over there. Eventually, she became a little angry. 'I don't want to talk about it, alright? I just want a nice night out with someone not connected to the hospital in any way, and not a student, either. I need a little fresh air.'

Having established the nature of my rôle, I tried to fulfil it. Anne paid for nothing, not drinks, not food. Instead, Anne was paid compliments. Her looks, her intelligence, her sense of humour.

Over coffee, as if to reward me for good behaviour, she said this: 'No-one understands what it's like to work in a hospital. I'm only just starting to. It's terrifying. It's like this huge monstrous place. But it's not random. It's quite disciplined, once you work out what the rules are. Even patients, if they spend enough time there, can learn to live with the monster. I'm not sure if I love it or hate it. What's happened to Paul is so cruel, but it's also quite logical.'

'It doesn't seem that way to me.'

'That's because you don't know anything about it. And the only way for you to learn would be to live there, for it to become your whole world.'

What I said was, 'Really?' But what I thought was, 'Alright, then. I *will*.'

'But you won't,' said Anne.

I held out my hand and we shook on it.

'You won't,' said Anne.

We went on to a bar for another couple of drinks. Anne was still of an age to think more alcohol was always a very good idea.

The only other thing she said about Paul was a stray comment, apropos of nothing. 'He'll be alright. He always lands on his feet.'

I walked her to the tube station and when she began to lean towards me I didn't back away. The kiss went on for about a minute. I was shocked. It felt so strange, a different scent all around me, and a mouth that wasn't Kumiko's, one that tasted of cigarettes.

'Call me,' said Anne, then tap-tapped down the stairs in high heels, only slightly awkward. She didn't look back.

Strolling home, I started to feel bad. This wasn't exactly being unfaithful to Kumiko. But it was only a few days since we'd split up – and I was supposed to be doing everything I could to get us together again. The kiss had been one of those random things that happen when you're no longer securely in a relationship. I must have seemed like I wanted it, or else Anne wouldn't have offered herself. My only excuse was that kissing Anne *was* intended to get Kumiko and me together again. In the long run. Anne was my way to get to Paul. Once I'd done that, I could quit the job and get back to normal life. It would feel painful, dropping out of the Abbey Road sessions. But it was necessary if I wanted to do absolutely everything I could to change Kumiko's mind. Like Anne said, there was only one way to know the monster.

I soon worked out a plan.

On Saturday morning, I put on my third-best suit and caught the Thameslink to London Bridge, then walked down Borough High Street until I came to one of the employment agencies there. They always had advertisements in the windows for jobs as Hospital Porters. I had noticed these before – mainly because the wages seemed to be so painfully low.

I stepped inside and up to one of the desks. A version of the truth was what I was planning to tell them: I was an out-of-work musician who was desperate to earn some money.

I had brought a CV – although I didn't really think one would be necessary. In it, I emphasized the three summer holidays I spent working in the local mental hospital. If they wanted a reference, the manager there would have to do.

In the event, the jolly woman behind the desk took my sincerity for granted – but almost nothing else. Name?

Are you eligible to work in the UK? Do you have a permanent address? Do you have a National Insurance number? I filled in a couple of forms, one of which was to check I didn't have a criminal record.

'You seem like a people person,' she said, with a beamy smile. 'That's very important. "Look out, there's a bump coming up." That kind of thing.'

She made a wheelchair-pushing gesture with her hands.

'How long will all this take?'

'About a week,' she said. 'If it goes through without a hitch, you can probably start Monday next.'

And then I was back out on the street. The whole efficient process had taken just over half an hour.

Not having planned for this, I didn't have anything to do for the rest of the morning. I walked over to Borough Market, thinking I might buy some food for the weekend. But then I saw the black metal door of the house on Stoney Street. The lock was broken again.

I had no thought of going inside. Just then, my phone started to ring. I didn't recognize the number.

'Hello,' said a male voice. 'Is this Skelton?'

'Yes.'

'I'm Paul.'

'Paul – fantastic,' I said.

'Yeah,' he said. 'Great.' He sounded drunk or stoned or both.

'No, I mean, thanks for calling. I really need to speak to you.'

'Someone told me the Japanese woman in court was your girlfriend. That right?'

'Sort of,' I said.

'Well, is she or isn't she?'

'We've split up.'

'So you've got no control over her?'

'No, and I never did.'

'Thing is, she's pestering all my friends. And I want you to tell her to stop.'

'She wants to help you.'

'Tell her I don't want her help.'

'I can't,' I said. 'I don't have her number any more.'

'Well I do — about five hundred times. Here it is.' He gave it to me. 'So, can you call her, and tell her to just fuck off and find something else to do?'

'She won't listen.'

He didn't reply.

'Will you talk to me?'

'I suppose you want to help me, too,' he said. 'Everybody suddenly wants to help.' He laughed. 'Well, it's a bit bloody *late* for that.'

He put the phone down. I immediately called back. It was a landline, not a mobile. The phone rang and rang — and, finally, someone answered.

'Paul?'

'No.'

'Is Paul White there?'

'No.'

'Who am I speaking to?'

'None of your business, mate.'

Whoever they were, they were even more drunk than Paul had been.

'Can you tell me where you are?'

'No.'

I had an inspiration.

'What pub are you in?'

'The Porter and Sorter.'

'Where?'

'No, no. Not so easy.'

The line went dead. But I had what I needed. I called Directories and got them to tell me what area the number was in. East Croydon. I would go there –

'Hello,' said a female voice.

I turned round, half expecting to see Kumiko. And at first I didn't recognize who it was.

'You got us kicked out of our house. Don't worry, though. We got somewhere much nicer now.'

It was Becky.

'I'm glad about that,' I said.

'Yeah, I just come back for some of my stuff. If the polis didn't nick it, that is.'

'I hope not,' I said.

'You're very polite,' Becky said. 'You were well brought up, I can tell.'

I was flummoxed – a very middle-class thing to be.

'You got a cigarette?'

'Sorry, I don't.'

'Your girlfriend did. Give me half a pack.'

'You saw her?'

'Yesterday. She come looking for me.'

'She did?'

'Yeah, she did.'

'How was she?' I asked.

'Oh yeah,' she said. 'I remember. She said she dumped you.'

'She just walked out,' I said.

'Shame. You make a nice couple.'

'Thank you.'

'"Thank you,"' Becky mimicked me, then said, 'Nah, she was fine. Little nervous to be in a big scary crack-house, know what I mean?'

I said I did.

'Not as nervous as you'd be.'

'Why was she looking for you?'

'Wanted to ask me questions about what I seen.'

'You saw something?'

'I was up on the roof. I like it up there when it's not winter. I was sitting there in my sleeping bag, all cosy. But I saw everything.'

'If I buy you some cigarettes, will you tell me, too?'

'Sure.'

She led me to the nearest newsagent's. I bought her a couple of packs of the brand she asked for.

Outside again, she took her time lighting up. Then she said, 'I saw a hand. Latex glove on. It chucked the heart out. I couldn't see nothing inside the train. The face was hidden. He was standing on the seats. It was a man.'

'White, black, what?'

'Couldn't tell.'

'Did you see what he was wearing?'

'Something dark. I couldn't see properly.'

'Anything else?'

'He wasn't fat.'

'Tall?'

'Couldn't say. But he wasn't fat.'

That seemed to be all the information that Becky had. Politely, I walked her back to the door of her old squat.

'Where are you living now?' I asked.

'Just round there.' She pointed down Redcross Way.

69

'Under the bridge. On the right. Can't miss it. Very desirable location.'

'Do you know where Kumiko is staying?'

'No,' said Becky. 'See you.'

Before I could reply, she slipped behind the metal door and into the darkness of the house.

I was pretty sure that I could get to East Croydon directly from London Bridge. And a glance at the departures board, once I got there, showed me I was right. That first train left while I was buying a ticket, but the next was only a couple of minutes behind.

Once in East Croydon, I planned to ask around for the Porter and Sorter. However, I came across it almost as soon as I got out of the station. It was on Station Road.

Although outside was nothing special, inside was even less impressive. A sign said 'Happy Hour, 6–7 p.m.' I didn't believe it. Happy and this place had nothing to do with one another. Which was probably why Paul had ended up drinking here.

I looked in both bars for him. The youngest person in there, apart from the bar-staff and me, was an off-duty postman in his late forties. A payphone stood beside the toilets in the public bar.

I went to get a drink.

As I was paying, I said, 'I'm meant to be meeting someone in here. Paul. He's a medical student. Tall. Dark.'

'Don't know him,' said the barmaid. She had no eyebrows, only drawn-on lines.

'He was using that phone about half an hour ago.'

'I said I don't know him,' said the barmaid. Her eyelashes were false, too.

'Thanks,' I said.

I took my pint over to an empty table. The lager tasted of ketchup. My stomach swore at me.

'No,' I said, out loud. 'Not drinking that.'

I was out of the Porter and Sorter in a couple of seconds.

Over the next hour, I visited all the pubs I could find around the station. Paul seemed to have gone home. Or maybe he'd just stopped off for a quick one before heading into town.

On my way back along Station Road, I looked in at the Porter and Sorter again. The barmaid remembered me – enough to shoot me a very dirty look.

9.

I spent Thursday afternoon researching King Death, Dr Speed. He seemed a very respectable man, married for twenty-four years with three daughters.

In the evening, I went to look for Becky and Jonesy. Perhaps they had returned to their house, now that some time had passed. But the padlock on the door was still there.

The market was very quiet, except when trains passed overhead. Then I heard the sound of knife-grinding.

Jo called me around 7 p.m. to say that a room had come free in her shared house. This was in Camberwell, a quarter-hour bus journey from the hospital. If I wanted to, she said, I could take a look at it immediately. She gave me the address, and I caught the number 35 bus. I found the place quite easily. It was a large Victorian house which could not have looked more solid or respectable.

I rang the bell and Jo answered. The carpet in the hall looked very new and clean. There was a proper shade on the light-bulb.

'It's all girls here,' she said.

I tried to think of myself as a girl.

Anne was in the kitchen. She was eating spaghetti with garlic and olive oil. Jo introduced us properly, almost like we hadn't met before. Another of the girls, Molly, was out on a big date. We talked for a few moments about that. Anne made a face and Jo laughed.

'Your room's on the top floor at the front,' said Jo. 'If you want it, that is.'

She led me up two flights of stairs. The room was small with a single bed, a desk, a wardrobe. Everything was oatmeal-coloured. A square window looked out towards a similar window in the house opposite.

'I've talked to the girls. They're a bit suspicious of you, but I told them you're okay. I want to help you help Paul. I'll do anything I can. Plus, we can't afford for the room to be empty.'

'Who was here before?' I asked.

'Lesley,' replied Jo. 'Lesley who was in Paul's anatomy group. She's moved back in with her parents. They're only in Crystal Palace. After what happened, she felt that's where she wanted to be. It's a bit extreme, isn't it? But I don't think anyone in her family's ever spoken to the police – except to ask directions. Her mum and dad came and got her that evening. All protective.'

I looked around the room again.

'Can I move in tomorrow?'

'We'll need to talk about rent.'

She mentioned an amount. I agreed to pay it. Jo disappeared for a few moments then returned with a set of keys.

'Welcome to the house,' she said.

'Thank you.'

I said goodbye to Anne in the kitchen and was having some final words with Jo on the doorstep when a taxi drew up and a hunched-up figure got out.

'Molly!' said Jo.

The young woman was crying into her fist.

I stepped aside to let her pass. She went into the kitchen and I heard a high wail.

'Don't worry,' said Jo. 'Quite a few of Molly's dates end like this. Either that or she doesn't come home at all.'

On Camberwell Green I hoped to catch a taxi, but none went past. So I went to the bus stop to wait.

I no longer expected Paul White to call me. Perhaps I would be able to find out his address whilst living with Jo. I did not like the idea of sneaking into her room and finding her address book, but if it was the only way …

The hotel suite seemed very extravagant compared with the small room I would be moving to. I ordered a burger and a gin and tonic from room service then ran myself a hot bath.

For the first time since leaving, I wondered for a moment what Skelton was doing.

On Friday morning, I returned to Becky and Jonesy's house. At first it looked exactly the same, but then I saw that the padlock had been removed. The door was slightly open. I called through the dark gap. No-one answered. I became conscious of the wound in my hand. It was healing very well.

Beneath the railway bridge was a flower stall. I asked the man working there if he had seen anyone go into the house.

'Uh-huh,' he said. 'First thing – I'd just got here. Couple of guys. They came out carrying a chair. Didn't look worth stealing.'

'Where did they go?'

He pointed round the corner onto Redcross Way.

'Thataway.'

I bought some deep-red tulips with white trim around the edges.

'Did you see a young woman?'

'I seen a lot of young women,' said the flower-seller. 'But none of them went in there.'

Redcross Way went along for about twenty metres then turned right under another railway bridge. Beyond this, it bore left. Across the road there were some houses. One of them had metal grilles over the windows.

I went and knocked on the hanging-loose door.

A man's voice shouted something I didn't understand.

Again I knocked.

Loud footsteps came down the stairs, bringing an angry man with a wrecked face.

'The fuck you want? This time of day.'

He had not threatened me with it, but in his hand was a Stanley knife.

'Is Becky here?'

'There's no Becky here. There's no-one here. Fuck off, why don't you?'

I think he was Irish or Scottish. I find it hard to tell the difference.

'I'm sorry,' I said, and started to back away.

Just then, Becky's pale face came floating out of the front room.

The angry man was in her way. She poked him and he moved.

'Hello,' she said. 'What do you want?'

I gave her the flowers.

'I apologize about your house.'

'No probs,' she said. 'These are lovely. Come in.'

I followed her down the hall and into a kitchen. She turned the tap but no water came out. A plastic Coke bottle was on the floor. Becky picked it up and, with a knife from her pocket, cut it around the middle. She put the flowers into the bottom half. I had a bottle of mineral water in my bag. When I gave it to her, she poured a little into the new vase.

'They're nice,' she said. 'From the market?'

'Yes.'

'They have nice things there.'

She was very melancholy.

'You got any fags?'

I gave her my pack and told her to keep it.

We lit our cigarettes. Then I asked her about the morning the heart was thrown from the train.

'You saw something, didn't you?' I asked.

She said she sometimes went up on the roof, when the weather was warm. She had a sleeping bag but she didn't sleep. 'I just smoke,' she said. She told me about a man, neither fat nor thin, tall nor short, and his hand sticking out of the train window.

'Which carriage?' I asked.

'The front one,' Becky said. 'Then I saw you – your face right there. I knew you seen something but I didn't expect you to come back and do anything.'

'Did you see what the man was wearing?'

'They were dark clothes. Couldn't say more.'

I paused.

'He was white,' Becky said. 'He was wearing latex gloves, like they use in hospital, but I could see his wrist. His hand was white.'

Then she seemed to lose interest in the subject and in me.

'I'm moving,' I said. 'I was living in a hotel. But now I'm going to be here.'

I started to write down my details on a piece of litter.

'Just tell me,' Becky said. 'I won't forget. If it's on paper it'll just get burnt.'

I told her my address. She repeated it back to me.

'If you remember anything else. Or you need help.'

'Thanks,' she said, as we walked out past the flowers. 'You didn't have to.'

'Becks! Becks!' A man was shouting from the front room. Not the angry man. Perhaps Jonesy. He sounded scared.

'See you,' said Becky, then went to him.

On the way back to the hotel, I went to the market and found some small presents for all the girls in the house. Then I stopped at a luggage shop and bought a shoulder bag. Getting my stuff together took me five minutes – old clothes, new clothes, laptop. I paid the bill with my credit card, then went to the station and caught a number 35.

Molly was in the kitchen of the shared house, wearing a dressing gown and eating white toast thick with marmalade. Jo and the others were at Guy's. I had let myself in with my key.

'Don't worry,' said Molly, before I had a chance to explain. 'I know who you are. Please excuse me – I'm not in a very good state today. Would you like some tea? I was going to make fresh anyway.'

I accepted her offer and sat down. It was gone twelve before I finally carried my bag up to my room. For most of that time, I had been listening to Molly's analysis of Molly's life and exactly what Molly needed to do to improve Molly's life. The conversation turned around for a while, after I mentioned that I had just split up with a long-term boyfriend. But then Molly began to draw parallels with situations in Molly's past.

She had blonde ringlets and was very English in her pear-shape. Slowly, her dressing gown came loose, revealing full breasts which really needed a bra. She didn't seem aware of her body at all.

'Her problem,' Molly said, meaning herself, 'is that she sleeps with men to find out what they're like.'

'What about Paul White?' I asked.

'How do you know –?' But then she stopped. 'Oh, of course. That's how you ... Well, just between you and me, there's only one girl in this house Paul hasn't slept with. And that's you.'

'What is he like?'

'In bed? Enthusiastic. A little lacking in technique. And patience. Not the best I've had but not the worst. Quite a decent size.'

'I meant as a person,' I said, slightly shocked at the ease with which she'd composed her review.

'Oh,' said Molly. 'You see – there I go.'

She described Paul at length. He sounded like a very normal young man.

'Did anybody hate him? Did he have enemies?'

'Jo told you her theory, did she?'

'Yes.'

'I think a few of the men were jealous of his looks and his success with girls – me, for example.'

'Enough to do something like steal the heart?'

'I don't think so. But then I haven't slept with all of them. Yet.'

She laughed with her head thrown far back, laughed loud. Japanese girls try to be like this, sometimes, but it's

78

a harsh, unsuccessful pose. Molly was like a jellyfish, a nasty sting but really very gentle.

In my new room, I unpacked carefully. There was a phone point, so I was able to collect my email. Some more of Paul's friends had replied. None of them had sent me his address.

Although Molly was so completely open, I had not asked her for Paul's details. I would be in trouble with Jo if she found out I had been prying. And if I asked and told Molly not to mention it to Jo, she would. Jo didn't want me contacting Paul directly – because that might get him into even more trouble.

I decided the best way to make progress was to make a good impression in the house, so I spent the afternoon buying and preparing a feast. Molly had gone back to bed. I didn't see her again until five thirty, when Anne returned in a hurry. She smelled the food.

'I'm sorry,' she said. 'I'm going out this evening.'

'Another time,' I said.

'Who?' asked Molly.

'Not saying,' replied Anne.

'Someone different?'

'Yes.'

She went out wearing a little black dress which seemed much too short for a first date.

Luckily, both the other girls were in, for the first part of the evening, anyway. I had cooked yaki udon, suki-yaki, miso soup, and there were pickles and sake.

Jo proposed a toast.

'To our new housemate.'

They both smiled.

Much of the conversation had been about Anne.

Neither of them knew who her mysterious date was with. There was deep speculation.

Around ten, Jo and Molly started to get ready for a party.

'You can come, if you like. It's just a student thing.'

'We're getting a taxi,' said Molly, as if that might change my mind.

'I don't have any clothes,' I said.

'We're about the same size,' said Jo, who was at least two sizes bigger than me. 'You can borrow something of mine.'

'Thank you,' I said.

We trooped upstairs with much laughter. I was a girl, like them.

In her wardrobe, we found a black silk cheongsam which Jo said she had never worn. She didn't say because it was too small.

When I put it on, I was disappointed to see how short it came. But I decided to wear it all the same. *I* wasn't going on a first date.

Jo's feet were the same size as mine, and she had some high heels that went well with the dress.

Molly insisted that I use her make-up. Out of politeness, I went into the bathroom and put on some foundation, mascara and some bright-red lipstick. It felt wonderfully strange.

'You look delicious,' said Jo, when I entered the television room.

As I sat and waited there with her I felt both very young and very old.

The party was in a house very like the one we had just come from. There were about fifty people there, and another fifty arrived soon after us.

Molly disappeared almost immediately. I stayed close to Jo, waiting for her to get drunk whilst trying not to drink much myself. We had stopped at an off-licence on the way, and Jo had bought six alcopops. I carefully drank white wine.

There was loud music in the basement. Jo wanted to dance so I left her there and explored the house. Perhaps, I thought, Paul White might turn up.

In one of the upstairs rooms, a young man started talking to me. He complimented me on my cheongsam.

'I love Japanese things.'

I told him it was Chinese.

'Yeah,' he said. 'Great. I love the horror films and everything.'

He smelled very drunk. He was too close.

'I like English things,' I said.

'What things?'

'I like the light.'

The young man looked at the shade hanging from the ceiling, then realized. 'Oh,' he said. 'Outside. Yeah, I like that, too.'

When I went downstairs, he followed me.

'Come on,' he said. 'I've always wanted to kiss a Japanese girl.'

I turned around and shouted in his ear, 'If you don't leave me alone, I will do something nasty to you, just like from a horror movie.'

He laughed and leaned closer.

I lifted my high heel up and kicked it down between the laces of his shoes.

He fell to the floor. A few people cheered. Another man poured beer on his head.

I found Jo, still dancing in the basement. I shouted in her ear that I wanted to leave. She persuaded me to stay a bit longer. We danced together to songs I knew from when I was twenty. It was fun for a while but being sober made the drunken party seem like a nightmare.

At one o'clock, Molly reappeared. She didn't say where she had been. Her lipstick was gone.

All three of us danced until the music changed to hip-hop. Then we left.

It took us half an hour to find a taxi.

A light was on in Anne's room, when we got back.

The other two sat down to watch TV, but I said I was going to bed.

I couldn't sleep. I was thinking about the alcoholic stench of the young man's breath. It reminded me of so many things I had been glad to escape when I got together with Skelton.

It had been many years since I lay in a single bed. With my hands out to either side, I could touch two edges of the mattress. The space was limited but there was no-one else to take any of it.

I woke up late on Saturday morning. Gray light was coming through the square window. I had forgotten to close the curtains but slept long and well anyway.

As I went downstairs, I could hear voices in the kitchen, loud whispers.

'– be so stupid? She's only just moved in. You *knew* that.'

'He asked me out. It's nothing serious.'

'But if she finds out she'll probably leave.'

'Oh, come on. She's not going to stick around here, is

she? She's got her Save Paul investigation. She'll be gone in a couple of weeks.'

'Well, she *paid* for a *month*.'

That voice belonged to Jo.

'Makes no difference. She's got lots of money, you can tell. Look, she *won't* find out – as long as you don't make a big issue of it. I'll keep it very quiet.'

And that voice was Anne's.

'So you're seeing him again.'

'I'm pretty sure I am. He kissed me.'

Then she really whispered something.

'You little –'

I didn't hear what Jo said Anne was.

Silently, I retreated upstairs.

I didn't know what I felt. Perhaps I should have walked into the kitchen. That would have forced me to confront my emotions. I tried to sense my heart, but it was incommunicado. My breath was fast, and so my body seemed to be excited. I was excited. This was something happening. My life was changing.

Did I feel betrayed? I thought about this for a quarter of an hour. In the end, my answer was, No.

Still, I couldn't believe that Skelton had gone on a date so soon after I left. It made him seem a different person, stronger and more independent.

I wondered for a while if, in the end, he had become bored with me as I had become bored with him.

Then I went downstairs and had breakfast while Jo and Anne talked about going shopping.

Anne was a good actress.

IO.

I tried to convince myself that I had kissed Anne because I loved Kumiko so much I would do anything to get her back. It didn't work. I'd kissed Anne because I'd wanted to kiss Anne – I'd wanted to confirm that she wanted to kiss me, and I'd wanted to know what it felt like.

If Kumiko heard, it would completely ruin my chances of getting back together with her. She would think I didn't love her any more, which was so far from the truth.

Once, I met up with an ex-girlfriend a few months after she dumped me. I was about twenty-five and somewhat brokenhearted. It was in Presto, an old-fashioned Italian restaurant on Old Compton Street. I used to go there quite often but never back again after this, and now it's been refurbished to death. Halfway through our meal, my ex looked into my eyes and asked me, 'Have you kissed anyone yet?' I told her the truth, that I hadn't. 'You should kiss someone,' she said. 'It helps.' By then, I was no longer in love with her – but I'd wanted her to treat me as if I was.

What I found most difficult now was that I could easily imagine having the same conversation with Kumiko, perhaps in a few months' time – her telling me to kiss someone else. Only this time I might choose to say, 'Yes. I have.'

I decided I wouldn't call Anne, or see her again. I doubted there was anything more she was going to tell me about Paul White. There were things she could have said but didn't, of that I was certain.

My mobile went off at half five on Sunday morning. I had been deeply asleep but I instantly recognized the voice, Anne's, it had been speaking all night in my dreams.

Was she going to berate me for not calling her? At this time?

'I thought you should know,' she said. 'Paul White tried to kill himself last night.'

'My God. So, he's alive?'

'Yes.'

'How?'

'He jumped in the river – off London Bridge. Within sight of Guy's. Luckily someone saw him do it and called 999. The River Police picked him up downstream. His coat kept him afloat.'

'Is he alright?'

'Mild hypothermia, I think. Might have picked up some infections from the water. Look, I've got to go. Speak to you later … I enjoyed Friday night.'

'I did, too.'

What else could I have said? This wasn't the time to be letting her down gently.

I wondered how long it would be before Kumiko heard. Something told me she probably knew already – she was always better informed than I was.

At ten o'clock, I called the hospital. They put me through to the ward, and the Nurse told me that Paul White was still asleep.

'We sedate him last night, quite heavy. He wek up soon, though.'

She was Jamaican. Probably middle-aged.

'Can I come and visit?'

'No. Doctor say no. Maybe tomorrow. Today he needs ress.'

'Is anyone allowed to see him?'

I was thinking of Kumiko and her powers of persuasion.

'Parents and family members only. But I don't think they come. He sure got a lot a friends, him.' She chuckled.

'Have other people called?'

'Plenty,' she said, allowing a little of her impatience through. 'Plenty women – you the first man.'

'Was one of them a Japanese woman?'

'Now, how I know that?'

'Her voice – her accent?'

'One say she muss come today. It was very urgent, y'know. Maybe that was her.'

'Did she sound Japanese?'

'Like I saying, I don't know. She phone back twice, see if someone else say different.'

That was Kumiko, surely, couldn't not be.

I thanked the Nurse for her time.

'Oh look,' she said. 'I think he a-wakin' now. Muss go.'

It might be worth hanging around the hospital to see if Kumiko turned up with the intention of sneaking in. But I doubted she would see any particular urgency, not if Paul White were out of danger – which it sounded like he was. She would go there first thing tomorrow.

A little later, I phoned Grzegorz.

'Can I come round and see you?'

'Ye-e-es,' he said, taking about three seconds over it. 'Yes, but not until this evening.'

'Why? Have you got company?'

'You could say that.'

I knew who. 'Kumiko?'

'She's not here now. But she's coming later. And she won't want to see you here.'

'When shall I come?'

'Seven. She should be gone by six. Don't take the tube, though. You might bump into her going in.'

'Are you trying to keep us apart?'

'Quite the opposite, actually. See you later.'

I did a couple of hours' guitar practice. Hard scales and obscure chords. I felt better afterwards. Then I emailed my agent to say that something had come up and I wouldn't be able to make it to Abbey Road on Monday.

Around half six, I started walking to Camden. I'd decided to be deliberately a little late, just to show Grzegorz I took his advice seriously.

Grzegorz's flat was an apartment which was really a huge warehouse like no-one gets to live in, these days. To make a bit of extra money, he rented it out for fashion shoots and videos. I could never step over the threshold without becoming tearful with an envy I didn't really feel. Our – my – flat suited me much better, small rooms, low ceilings, cosy.

We embraced.

'You don't look so bad,' he said. 'I expected much worse – unshaven, red-eyed.'

'I feel terrible,' I said. I had decided not to tell him about kissing Anne, but that was one of the things I was referring to.

'Come in, come in.'

We went and sat down on either end of his vast sofa. I could smell cigarettes; Grzegorz didn't smoke. There was an ashtray down by my feet. I was sitting where Kumiko had been sitting only a few minutes before. I tried to imagine her posture: feet curled up under her bum or propped up on the table? I couldn't be certain. It depended on how she had been feeling. Could I still feel a trace of her warmth in the soft black leather? Surely that was wishfulness. But, despite the cigarettes, I was sure I could pick up traces of her sweet scent in the air – her scent, not her perfume; Kumiko never wore perfume. I breathed in, trying not to be too obvious. It was like smelling the nape of her neck. If I closed my eyes, it was easy to imagine her there beside me on Grzegorz's sofa, just as she'd been dozens of times. Then I thought, 'She really has taken up smoking again.' Perhaps that was a sign of unhappiness, of loneliness?

Grzegorz, I realized, had been talking about his work. He must have noticed that I wasn't listening. It was out of sensitivity to my distraction that he'd kept on. I crossed my legs and, by accident, kicked the ashtray so that it flipped upside down.

'Sorry,' he said, 'I should have tidied up. But she didn't actually leave until ten minutes ago. In fact, I had to tell her you were coming to get rid of her. Until then I'd managed to keep it quiet.'

'I bet she left fast enough when she heard.'

'Yes, I'm afraid she did. Out the back way – down the fire escape.'

'Well, that makes me feel great.'

'That was a joke, Skelton. Would you like some coffee? Or a beer?'

Sometimes Grzegorz seemed very Polish.

'Coffee, please.'

He picked two espresso cups off the magazine-laden table. The one nearest to me had been Kumiko's — but they didn't look any different, Grzegorz's and hers. No left-behind lipstick. Kumiko never wore lipstick.

'Espresso,' I said, as Grzegorz walked away.

'Of course,' he said. 'Double?'

Kumiko would have had a double.

'No, just a single, thanks.'

Grzegorz didn't try to make conversation at the same time as coffee. I lay back in Kumiko's recent presence and watched him wash her traces off the cup and saucer. His industrial-style kitchen was at shouting distance from the sofa. While his back was turned, I pocketed one of the spilt cigarette ends.

It was pathetic. I had almost all Kumiko's possessions in the flat. I could bury my head whenever I wanted in her woman things. But this was different. This was a clue to Kumiko's post-me life; it had another aura altogether.

Grzegorz put the cup and saucer in front of me. Then he sat down, a pained look on his face.

'This is the message, my friend. "Don't try to see me." That's what she says. "Don't try to find me."'

'Did she tell you to pass that on?'

'No. But it was pretty clear from everything she said.'

'So, she didn't give you a message for me?'

'Not directly.'

'Do you know where she's living?'

'Does that make a difference?'

'Yes,' I said.

'Then, yes, I do know where she's living.'

'Will you tell me?'

'No. She wouldn't want me to.'

89

'So your loyalty is to …'

'Look, my friend, the one way to ensure you never get her back is to go rushing after her. She wants time alone, you give her time alone.'

'It's not about that. It's about me. She doesn't want me.'

'I think you're wrong. I think she still does, she just doesn't know it.'

'When she makes a decision, that's usually it – finito.'

I hated the word 'finito'. My suave uncle Derek from Wimbledon used it.

'Be patient. Trust her. She hasn't forgotten you. Not at all.'

'Did she tell you about Paul White?'

'A little. It sounds like a mess.'

'We're trying to sort it out,' I said. 'She is, and I am, too.'

'You see,' said Grzegorz. 'You're still together, really.'

On Monday morning, I made sure that I was stationed outside Guy's for the start of visiting hours, ten o'clock.

I wanted to go in and see Paul White, but not until I was sure Kumiko wouldn't suddenly arrive – so I had to wait until she'd come and gone.

Standing back out of sight, round some hoardings, I kept an eye on the main doors.

At ten past ten, Kumiko arrived, accompanied by a young woman who looked vaguely familiar. She was of student age, so maybe I'd glimpsed her in the Public Gallery at Paul White's arraignment. For certain she hadn't joined us in the George afterwards. Her hair was mousy blonde. She had a very square jaw. The two of them went into the hospital.

It was only after she'd gone from sight that I realized Kumiko had been wearing new clothes. An elegant black coat. Dark trousers. They weren't that different from her old clothes, probably still from agnès b, but I knew I hadn't seen them before. Her palm was still bandaged.

For the next twenty minutes, nothing out of the ordinary happened – apart, perhaps, from the arrival of a big black limousine that drew to a purring stop and then deposited a very beautiful young woman dressed as if for a funeral. I had never seen a chauffeur get out, walk round and open the door for someone. The funeral girl looked completely out of place, walking through the smokers in their wheel-chairs.

At half past ten, I saw something horrifying: Anne walking towards the entrance.

'Oh crap,' I said, out loud.

Beside Anne was another probable student, a statu-esque blonde.

This was, without doubt, the worst-case scenario.

If I was very lucky, Kumiko and her friend would have finished with Paul White a few moments ago, and so would end up taking the down lift whilst Anne was travelling up.

I wasn't very lucky. Just then, Kumiko and her friend came out of the hospital.

Oh fuck.

I couldn't watch but I did. Perhaps they would simply walk past one another. But, of course, no.

The students stopped to talk to one another – that was how it seemed to me. Kumiko stood as an equal member of the group of four, not hanging back. At this point, she might have been quickly introduced to Anne.

But they didn't shake hands. And I didn't even see Kumiko make one of her instinctive, unstoppable *ojigi* head-bows. (Her Osaka upbringing remained with her in these little ways, although from five to fifteen she'd lived in England.) There was some smiling – all of them smiling, including Kumiko. If I hadn't known better, I would have thought Kumiko and Anne knew one another already.

Finally, although it had only been a couple of minutes, the two pairs separated: Anne and the blonde going in, Kumiko and mousy student heading off.

Almost unable to believe I was doing it, I started to follow Kumiko. She and the mouse made their way to London Bridge, where they caught a southbound number 35 bus. Kumiko sat upstairs, at the front, on the left side – her favourite spot.

When she was safely out of sight, I checked the time-table. Elephant & Castle. Camberwell Green. Loughborough Junction. Brixton. Clapham Common. Clapham Junction. Kumiko was heading to one of these places, or to one of the request stops in between. Did she live in South London now? That was a change.

I went back to my spying point and waited until Anne came out of the hospital. To speak to her in front of a fellow student was more than I could do. But before she came out, the black limousine drew up again and the funereal young woman got in, with assistance. She had been crying, I could tell.

Paul White was in a general ward on the seventeenth floor of Guy's tower. It was eleven fifteen when I walked out of the lift.

I made my way to the Nurses' Station and asked where

I could find Paul, Paul White, saying it as if he were a good friend.

'No more visitors today,' said the Nurse, probably the one I'd spoken to on the phone.

'But –'

'The bwoy already exhausted. You bess leave him be.'

She jerked her thumb towards the far end of the ward. The curtains were drawn around the last bed on the left. All the other patients were obviously not Paul White.

'I just need to speak to him for five minutes.'

'He aks me no more visitors. He waan sleep.'

I wished I had thought to bring something for him, something to let him know I'd been there.

'Okay,' I said. 'Okay.'

11.

At 3.10 a.m. on Sunday, Jo's cellphone went off. And so, a few moments later, did Anne's. Molly's was turned off. But she was woken by Jo, who told her to go down to the kitchen. I had not been sleeping very deeply, so had heard some commotion. Jo came in and told me that the others were gathering downstairs.

'Don't worry,' she said. 'It's serious but not *that* serious.'

The sequence of events, as they emerged over the next few hours, went something like this. At 12.25 a.m., Paul White had jumped off London Bridge. At 12.27 a.m., the emergency services were called. By 12.50 a.m., Paul had been rescued by the River Police. Around 1.20 a.m. he arrived at Guy's Hospital, where he was handed over to A&E. One of the nurses here recognized him immediately. His wallet was still in his pocket, and this contained his watery student union card. With his identity confirmed, the nurse wanted to contact Paul's next of kin. Once it was clear his life was not in danger, she tried to find him on the hospital computer system. But his details had already been removed. And so, not knowing what else to do, she called King Death at home. He gave her permission to go into his office and through his teaching files. There the nurse found Paul's parents' number. But the phone rang and rang. His parents were not at home. They were on holiday in Australia. It was now around 2.50 a.m. In frustration, the nurse now began calling the students from Paul's anatomy class in alphabetical order, from the top of the list down. A couple didn't answer. However, the third or fourth was Martha Berkowitz, who took it upon herself to text everyone in class with the news.

For the rest of the night, we sat in the kitchen, drinking sugary tea and discussing what might have happened. Was it an accident or a suicide attempt? Was Paul the sort to try and kill himself? I learnt a lot about him – mainly that no-one could agree what he was like.

This was the first time I heard the name Monica Norfolk. She was mentioned as something important that everyone knew about. It would have been awkward to ask who she was. It would have reminded everyone that I was an outsider.

Occasionally one of the girls' phones would ring, and they would go into another room to take the call. Anne excused herself for a while. I wondered whether she was phoning Skelton. There seemed a special awkwardness about the way she behaved towards me when she came back. She wasn't not talking to me. That was my exact statement of it.

Towards daybreak, we decided that we would go and see Paul in hospital as soon as we could. But Jo found out around 9 a.m. that no visitors were allowed until Monday.

Gradually, the kitchen emptied, girls going off to sleep, until only Jo and I were left. She had been borrowing my cigarettes. We smoked the last two. With this emergency, some barrier was broken between us. Jo wanted to talk.

'I really loved him,' she said. 'But he was just screwing around. He went with everyone. He'd been like that ever since Monica stopped seeing him. It was a kind of revenge.'

'Is she a medical student?' I asked.

'Ah, no, no – she's just the love of Paul's life. Or she was. I think she still might be. That's what Molly was saying, that it all started with her – all started to go wrong with her. Paul met her at a party in King Death's house. King Death was her father. Not the King Death we have now, Dr Speed – the previous one, Dr Norfolk. You know about him, don't you? Everyone knows about him.'

I said I knew nothing.

'He disappeared. At the start of last term. October. He disappeared, and no-one has ever seen him again.'

'I'm confused.'

'Whenever there's an anatomy lecturer, the students call him King Death. If one leaves or dies or, well, disappears, he's replaced by another. Dr Norfolk had been there for years. Most of them usually are. He was a very rich man. Not from medicine. His family was rich. I don't know why I'm talking about him like he's dead. He's probably sunning himself on a beach down in Goa or wherever disappeared people go, these days. It caused such a complete breakdown in the place. Dr Norfolk was a legend. If he didn't know it, about anatomy, I mean – if he didn't know it, it wasn't worth knowing. Anyway, Monica is his daughter. And every year he used to have a party just before term started, for all the first-year students, and all the teaching and support staff. In September. We all went to his house, which is this massive Georgian place on Wimbledon Common with private gardens out the back. And that's just his London residence. It was a nice party. The sun was still out when it started. And Paul was there, and he met Monica. I think they fell in love straight away. I know they started seeing one another. That lasted a couple of weeks. Then Dr Norfolk found out, and he came down hard. Paul wasn't what he had in mind for Monica. She was only sixteen. Still in the sixth form. So, he banned them from seeing one another. But they kept on, behind his back. Monica never seemed like she was that young. They kept on seeing one another right up until he disappeared. I think they met about once, after that. Monica stopped it.'

'Did she love him?'

'Oh yes,' said Jo. 'I've never seen anything like it. She made him better than himself, you know what I mean? She made him *try*. Since then it's all been about cracking jokes, getting drunk and screwing around. I wanted to see if I could fit where she had been, but I couldn't, of course. Who could?'

Jo's voice had become dreamy with sadness.

'Monica is very beautiful. One of the most beautiful women you've ever seen. And I'm something else.'

I tried to be supportive, but Jo wasn't beautiful. It would have been insulting to tell her she was.

'There will be someone for you,' I said.

'Probably,' she said. 'But he was the first. Not *the* first, you know. The first first.'

'I understand.'

Jo decided to follow the others to bed. They slept until the afternoon.

I got dressed and went for a walk in the thick rain. To hear the story of Paul White's love for Monica Norfolk had reminded me of when I first met Skelton. I had not thought about those days for at least a year. It made me feel some sadness and some relief.

On Sunday afternoon, I went to see Grzegorz.

We sat on his sofa and drank coffee and talked about Paul White. I explained why it was so important to me.

'Is it because this is your new art-piece?' Grzegorz asked.

'No,' I said, 'this is about real life. I don't want any art this time. I want to do good.'

'Oh, Kumiko, you make the most complex things sound so simple.'

'It is simple.'

'You know it's not. What about Skelton?'

'I feel bad.'

'Are you going to call him?'

'No. Not yet. When I finish with this, maybe.'

'So you can only speak to him when you have proved you are a good person.'

'I don't like you when you are sarcastic.'

'It's surprising we're friends at all, then.'

'Sometimes it is,' I said. Then I changed the subject, because I did want to continue being friends with him. I spoke about the house of girls. Grzegorz was surprised I was prepared to live in South London.

'For how long?'

'As long as necessary.'

'But you will come back?'

'Of course.'

'We can't lose you down there.'

He tried again to make me talk about Skelton. I refused.

'If you want to see him, he's coming here at seven.'
I left just before half past six.

Once I was out of Grzegorz's building, I walked away very fast. It was almost running, sometimes. But then I started to slow down. Curiosity had made my feet feel heavy: was Grzegorz mischievously lying, to see how I would react, whether I would leave, or was he telling the truth? I decided I would find out.

I went back. It was 6.40 p.m.

Opposite to Grzegorz's front door was a pub. Most of the windows were made of dark-green glass, but in each corner was a diamond of yellow. It was the only place.

Inside, I bought a drink and went where I could look out. I am sure some people stared at me strangely.

For half an hour, I looked. I did not touch my drink. Then Skelton walked into my vision, pressed the buzzer and a couple of seconds later the door opened for him.

I hurried out of the pub.

Grzegorz had been truthful.

Skelton looked just the same as always.

We took the bus to the hospital on Monday morning. Between us, we arranged to go in pairs to see Paul White. I was with Jo.

A strange feeling came over me, as we approached the hospital entrance. I suddenly felt very safe. This was a place where I would be looked after. But once we got inside, I felt different – I wanted to leave. It had just been the area around the entrance that was reassuring. I didn't know why.

Paul White, when I finally met him, was sitting up in

bed. His ward was high up in the building, and pale light came through the window to his left. I saw him very clearly, the stubble on his chin, the bruise on his forehead.

'Hello, Jo,' he said, and looked embarrassed.

Jo embraced him for a long time, silently. She was crying. Then she stood up and said, 'Don't ever do anything like that again. I'll never forgive you.'

'Sorry,' Paul said. 'You must be Kumiko.'

'Don't try and change the subject, Paul White. How could you do anything so stupid?'

'I was drunk.'

'That's no excuse.'

'I wasn't trying to kill myself,' he said.

'Really?'

'No, I just didn't care any more. It was something I've always wanted to do, so I did it.'

'You might have died.'

'But I didn't.'

'You caused a lot of trouble.'

'Which I'm sorry for.'

'There are easier ways of getting back in the building.'

He laughed. His smile was charming. While they talked, I observed him. He was a handsome young man, in a very straightforward way. In English they call this 'hunky'. It was not difficult to imagine him playing rugby. Harder was to see him acting on a stage.

Jo sat down on one of the visitors' chairs.

'Are you really alright?' she asked, taking Paul's hand.

'I'm fine.'

He looked towards me. I could tell he wanted me to speak about something else.

'You know I want to help you,' I said.

He nodded.

'Will you let me help you now? If you don't care about jumping off a bridge, you must be happy to speak to me.'

'I'll speak to you. Not now. When I've been home for a couple of days. Jo can give you my number. Let me know when you're coming.'

'Just tell me one thing,' I said. 'Why didn't you tell the police it wasn't you?'

'I did. To start with.'

'Why didn't they believe you?'

'Because it couldn't be anyone else. And I didn't have an alibi.'

'For the morning or the evening?'

'For either.'

Just then, a young woman's voice said, 'Paul.'

I turned round and looked at a film star. I didn't know who she was, but she couldn't be anything other than a film star. She was young, beautiful and charismatic. All her clothes were black as if for mourning.

'Monica,' Paul said.

They looked at one another. His eyes started to shine with love and to sparkle with tears.

'We can go,' said Jo. 'We don't want to tire you out.'

'Come and sit down,' said Paul.

He had forgotten that we were there, and soon we weren't.

Outside the hospital, we saw Anne and Molly.

'How is he?' Molly asked.

'Fine,' said Jo. 'Considering. He's a bit ashamed, but not enough.'

This made everyone laugh.

'We can work on that,' said Anne.

'Monica's in there right now,' Jo said. 'I think you should give them a little time.'

'We can dawdle on the way up,' said Molly.

They went inside and we caught the bus back to the house.

I intended to research the disappearance of Dr Norfolk for the rest of the morning, but there was little information online.

A number of newspaper articles had appeared, including one in a Sunday paper. They all contained the same few facts. Dr Norfolk had been last seen leaving the building on a Friday evening in October. Such a disappearance was completely out of character. His friends and colleagues were increasingly concerned for his wellbeing. Anyone with any information should call ...

The hospital had succeeded in keeping the story quiet.

Frustrated, I typed 'King Death' into the search engine. The first things that came up were about the death of Martin Luther King. Then there was a book, *King Death: Black Death and Its Aftermath in Late Medieval England*. And also a novel by Nik Cohn.

I looked up the Black Death. Between 1348 and 1350, bubonic plague killed between a third and a half of the population of Europe. It was transferred by fleas on rats and other animals. Once bitten, a person usually died within a week. A horrible death. The first symptoms are headache, fever, chills, exhaustion and vomiting of blood. Most typical, though, are the 'buboes', swellings at the neck, groin and armpits. These ooze blood and pus. The skin becomes covered in dark blotches. The victim dies in unbearable pain.

With my head full of horror, I came downstairs. Molly was in the kitchen making a sandwich.

'Would you like something?'

'No.'

'He was okay this morning, wasn't he?'

'I can't compare him with before.'

'Of course.'

I asked her why the students called their anatomy lecturer King Death.

'We just do,' she said. 'Jo might know more about it.'

I did not get a chance to speak to Jo alone until Tuesday evening.

'The story is, and it's probably apocryphal, that the poet Keats gave the lecturer that name. He was a medical student at Guy's, and would have taken dissection – so I suppose it's possible. Have you seen that blue plaque on St Thomas Street? That's the one leading from Borough High Street to the hospital entrance. It's on a Georgian building on the right. "Poet John Keats lived here with his great friend so-and-so whilst attending Guy's." Eighteen twenty-something, I think.'

It was 1815–16.

I checked.

12.

'You'll never believe it,' my agent said, 'but that bloody singer is in fact a saint who is prepared to forgive you, yet again, for going AWOL. Apparently, because they didn't have a full band today, thanks to you, they decided to go with string arrangements only. And he *loved* it. They may do the whole album like that. Apart from the single. But what he says is, he hates working with bored session musicians. So, he's actually interested in someone who's got a life outside music. That means he's interested in *you*. Because you've been so mysterious about why you couldn't be there, and because you left me without a decent explanation, he wants to know why. He probably thinks it's drugs. It isn't drugs, is it? I didn't think so. But you are officially now an object of fascination. Which all adds up to, be there tomorrow morning at nine. Or. I. Will. Kill. You.'

I was there on Tuesday at nine – for one of the most embarrassing hours of my life.

The moment he arrived, the pop singer was my new best friend. Whilst the producer, the engineer and all the other musicians waited, he took me off to a nearby café and started quizzing me. What was so important that I couldn't make the gig? A woman? She must be pretty special, huh? What happened? This, of course, was dangerous territory – but more for me than him. Out of shame, I hadn't really confided in any of my friends, apart from Grzegorz, who was Kumiko's friend as much as mine. Even my parents still didn't know about the break-up.

The upshot of this, however, was that I was fit to burst – and I did. Tears, snot, choking, the lot. Perhaps him being so famous made a difference. I felt like I knew him already. His ballads (which I secretly quite liked, in an Elton John way) had invaded me. And so I ended up telling him just about everything. He was a really good listener.

'Man,' he said, putting his hand on my shoulder. 'You're doing the right thing. You'll get her back.'

'Do you think so?'

'I'm sure of it,' he said. 'I'm never wrong about things like that.'

Two Japanese girls came over and asked for his autograph. I spoke to them a little in Japanese. The pop singer was dead impressed.

We walked back to the studio. He told me about his last but one break-up.

'I loved her *so* much. I knew she wasn't worth it, but I couldn't help myself.'

The last time I'd seen his *her*, she was on a billboard advertising overpriced underwear.

'Sorry, lads,' the pop singer said as we re-entered the studio. 'Session's cancelled today.' There was a half-comic groan. Glances sharp as nunchucks were hurled in my direction. 'Don't worry, you poxy fuckers – you'll get paid.'

Everyone hesitated for a moment then saw he was serious, laughed, and began to pack up.

The singer went over to the studio piano and started to pick out a sequence of descending minor chords.

A little gospel. Quite catchy. I thought nothing of it – at the time.

As I left he shouted over his shoulder, 'See you, mate. Good luck.' Then said to the producer, 'You got any paper? And a pen.'

With the rest of the day unexpectedly free, I went back to my flat and dropped my guitar off. There was a message on my phone from the cheery woman at the employment agency. Everything was looking great. If nothing horrendous came up in the Criminal Records check, I would be starting on Monday morning at six sharp.

I headed out again, thinking it was just for a walk. But my feet took me to the Thameslink station. From there it was just a train ride to London Bridge. And once at London Bridge, Guy's was only three minutes ...

'He gone home,' said the Jamaican Ward Sister, in response to my question. 'He gone firss thing.'

The bed where Paul White had been, last on the left, was already occupied by someone else – a white-haired old woman.

'He a lot better, y'know. He a fit bwoy.'

I went back towards the station. And then I saw the buses lined up outside and thought it wasn't so far to the stop for the 35 ...

I wasn't looking for Kumiko – that wasn't why I got on. All I wanted to do was see what she had seen, sitting upstairs, at the front, on the left-hand side.

As we surged round Elephant & Castle, I began to think about Anne. I felt quite bad about what had happened. I had phoned her at half two on Monday afternoon. She didn't answer straight away, but had called back a couple of hours later.

'Sorry,' she'd said, 'I was in a class.'

I couldn't believe I was sort-of going out with a student – going out enough to be forced into *de facto* dumping them. First, though, I'd needed to find out about Paul White.

'Did you see him?'

'Yes. We went this morning. He's fine.'

'Who's *we*?'

'Me and a friend. She's called Molly.'

'Was anyone else there?'

'You sound very suspicious. Are you still playing detective?'

'Was there?'

'No.'

I'd wanted to be subtle but couldn't see how.

'So you didn't bump into Kumiko outside?'

There was a silence.

'You did,' I said. 'I know.'

'You were spying,' she said. 'That's so cool. Where were you?'

'That doesn't matter.'

'Don't worry – she doesn't know about us.'

'What was she doing there?'

'Visiting him, too, I think.'

'So she spoke to him?'

'Probably, I don't know.'

'Who was she with?'

'Another student.'

'Called?'

'Called Jo. Why do you want to know?'

'They went off together. I think they might be friends.'

'Jo's in the anatomy class. She knows Paul quite well.'

'Why did you say Kumiko doesn't know about us?'

'Well, she doesn't. You sounded paranoid.'

'Look, Anne, there isn't an us. I just wanted to find out about Paul.'

This was the wrong thing to say.

'Oh, that's great.'

'No, I didn't mean that. If I could –'

'If you could what?'

If I could finish that sentence without getting myself in even deeper shit.

'I'm trying to get Kumiko back. Doing everything I can.'

'And I'm just something that you *did*? Thanks.'

'I didn't think you'd take it this seriously.'

'Don't flatter yourself,' she said.

The line went dead.

I'd really messed up. I minded.

The 35 had reached Camberwell Green, and I had hardly noticed the Walworth or Camberwell roads.

On Denmark Hill, a woman with Kumiko's oil-black hair disappeared into a newsagent's. This was too much. I was seeing her wherever I went.

The bus continued on to Loughborough Junction. Kumiko wouldn't live here. Not under any circumstances.

Brixton. Far more likely.

Clapham Common. Maybe.

Clapham Junction. No.

At the end of the line, I went downstairs and asked the driver whether he was turning round. He said he was, but that I couldn't stay on.

I crossed the road and waited at the stop. When the bus came back, I caught it.

If Tuesday's recording session was *one of* the most embarrassing hours of my life, Wednesday's was *the* most embarrassing.

Again, I was singled out by the pop singer as soon as he arrived. And, again, he took me off by myself – but this time, it was only the short distance over to the studio piano. The other musicians were just a few paces away. They could hear everything.

'Listen, mate, what you said, yesterday. It's an amazing story and ...' The singer's fingers seemed, almost accidentally, to find one of those minor chords. 'Look, listen to this and tell me what you think.'

He closed his eyes and began to play. The verse was simple, chunky, sincere. After a single run-through, I could have hummed it back to you but, more importantly, you could have hummed it back to me. It was *that* catchy. Then he opened his mouth and began to sing ...

About me and Kumiko.

By now, all the musicians – some of whom I knew pretty well, on a professional level; seen day in, day out for several years – were listening. They couldn't help themselves.

The lyrics were vague enough, about finding, losing, loving, needing. If they had just heard it on the radio, no-one would have guessed exactly who it was about. Or that it was exactly about anyone. But, given the circumstances, there wasn't a person in that famous room who didn't know the song was about me.

'I haven't quite finished this bit,' the singer said, shockingly, halfway through the middle eight – which went up into the subdominant and was sung in a fragile falsetto.

'Then there's a guitar solo,' he said.

The chords reached a climax. I could feel the musicians looking into my face, trying to gauge my reaction. Back came the chorus:

'Dah-dah duh-dah-dah
still need to finish these, too
has ripped us apart ...
the heart.'

The song stopped.

'So, what do you think?'

It felt like I could hear the stilled breathing of every musician in London.

'Do you like it?'

I could tell that the singer was nervous, too. In a few moments, he might be back to supercool, but right now he was as fragile as the middle eight.

Leaning close to him I whispered, 'It's lovely.' My voice cracked. This wasn't acting – I wasn't skilled or confident enough to pull that off. He'd written a sweet strong song about me and Kumiko. I was genuinely touched.

'You really like it?'

'I do.'

'We'd like it to be the first single.'

'Really?'

'And I'd personally like you to play the solo.'

That word *personally* brought us back into the world of him being famous and me being approximately no-one.

'I think you could bring something really special to it.'

'Sure,' I said. 'I'd be honoured.'

Only afterwards, when the singer had hugged me and then gone to tell the producer the good news, did I realize what I was letting myself in for. The scene at the piano had been bad enough – musicians being what they are, I could be fairly sure of having that melody line quoted at me every time one of the sarcastic bastards was tuning up within earshot. However, if I took the offer of a solo, my credibility within the free improv scene would be lost and gone for ever. Yes, they understood that a guy had to make a living; that's what I'd been up to, vamping away in the chorus, fattening up the sound. But playing conventionally poignant lead guitar on a hit record? That might very well finish me off.

I was just about to go over and make my excuses to the producer when he called the musicians to order.

'New song,' he said. 'You heard it just then. No written charts. We'll just wing it to start with. We want it to be –'

'Intense,' said the pop singer. 'As intense and pure and fucking meaningful as you cynical bastards can make it.'

We all played the song through a couple of times, roughing out an arrangement. Then they started the tapes rolling.

When the spot for the solo arrived, I took it. Why? Because it was a solo and I was a musician. Because this was something my parents would understand. Because I still secretly wanted to go on *Top of the Pops*. But most of all because this song was for Kumiko, and I wanted to tell her I still loved her in the best way I could.

'Fucking astounding,' said the pop singer, afterwards – and he wasn't talking to the bassist.

'Great harmonics at the end,' the producer added. 'I think we can keep most of those.'

The band had another go at the song. By this time, the singer's falsetto was getting a little ragged, so the producer asked us to take five. The keyboardist played the Dave Brubeck riff as the horn section headed outside for cigarettes and a grumble.

I went up to the control booth and listened to a playback.

'That's it,' said the singer, leaning forwards into the mixing desk. 'Nailed the bastard.'

He turned round and caught sight of me. For a moment, I was sure, he had no idea who I was. Then he said, 'Number one or what?'

I knew I was expected to say something totally positive, emphasized with swearing, but I'm not used to talking so directly. That was probably the secret of the pop singer's success: transparency. He really was just the same in person as on stage. The moment was passing, so I said, 'Yes, probably.'

'Yes fucking definitely,' said the singer. 'Or my arse is made of brass.'

When I turned my phone back on, after the session was over, I saw I had a voice message. Of course I hoped it was from Kumiko but the name that came up was ANNE.

'Hi,' she said. 'Look, I'm sorry I got so annoyed. I think you can understand why. You weren't exactly tactful. But I'd like to meet up. If only just to say goodbye and end it properly. How about Thursday afternoon? I've got no classes. Oh, and I found out a little about Kumiko and Jo. Give me a call.'

I left it until eight that evening before I phoned. I hate people being angry at me, so was glad she had calmed down. We didn't speak for long, just enough to arrange coffee at Bar Italia in Soho. Five o'clock.

The next day, Thursday, at Abbey Road was thankfully low-key. We recorded some retakes and overdubs for 'The Heart'.

I was a little late getting to Frith Street. Anne was there already, but at first I didn't recognize her, I just saw a very attractive young woman. Anne seemed to have ditched the party-girl look for something much more understated. She was wearing black lace-up shoes, opaque tights, a medium-length suede skirt and a black poloneck sweater. A suede coat hung from the chair she was sitting on. Apart from mascara, she didn't seem to be wearing any make-up.

I kissed Anne awkwardly on the cheek, then joined her at a table in the window.

'What were you up to today?' she asked.

Embarrassed, I told her about the session, the song. She was astonished.

'About you? He wrote a song about you?'

'Kumiko and me.'

'And it's going to be released and everything?'

'They say so.'

'Wow, that's so cool.'

I downplayed it. 'Yeah, well ... Sometimes these things happen.'

'But that's not the sort of music you really like, is it? I mean, that's not what you got into it for.'

And I found myself telling her about how I fell in love with the guitar, through Syd Barrett, Zoot Horn Rollo, Charlie Christian, Django Reinhardt. And then how I discovered improvised music, Derek Bailey and all.

Anne seemed very interested – and when I mentioned in passing a gig that I had coming up on Saturday night, she asked where it was going to be. I named the venue, Sound 323, a record shop up in Archway.

'D'you mind if I come?' Anne asked. 'Of course, I won't if you do. But I'd really like to see what it's all about.'

'Um,' I said. I hated to remind her that this was meant to be the last time we met. She'd been so enthusiastic and listened so closely to what I said. I think it was the clothes that persuaded me. Although I found them sexy, I knew they weren't the kind of thing Anne would have worn if she were trying to get me back. She wasn't that attuned to my tastes.

'Okay,' I said.

We agreed to meet up beforehand – but only at Archway station. I didn't want her wandering alone into the world of weird that is improv.

By the time she mentioned Kumiko and Jo, I'd almost forgotten that she had something to say about them.

'I asked Jo yesterday,' she said, 'after class was finished. She said Kumiko emailed everyone in Paul White's year – got the addresses off the internet.'

'Did she email you, too?'

'Yeah, but I binned it – didn't reply. Jo did. They met up, and Kumiko told her all about what she was trying to do. She wanted Paul's details, but Jo wouldn't give them to her. Paul had asked everybody not to pass them on.'

'But now he's met Kumiko.'

'Yeah.'

'She always gets her way in the end. So, Jo was taking her to the hospital to introduce them?'

'Yes.'

I didn't believe her. There was something she wasn't telling me, probably quite a lot.

When she said goodbye, outside Bar Italia, I kissed her, but only on the cheek.

13.

After visiting Paul White in hospital and making the discovery about Death, I felt relaxed for the first time since I saw the heart. My investigation was making progress, and it would make more when I saw Paul later in the week.

Feeling free and happy, I went into town where I had a late lunch at Harvey Nichols.

I got on the bus with Jo, but then I had a better idea. I explained to Jo and then got off at Borough Station.

Feeling free and happy, I went into town, where I had lunch at Harvey Nichols. I am not a sashimi snob. The YO! Sushi outlet there was good enough, better than many restaurants in Tokyo. I watched the little colour-coded plates go past me on the conveyor belt and thought about nothing but what I wanted to eat next. Then I did some shopping, basics on the ground floor, indulgences on the second. Usually I only bought very plain clothes, the kind I liked, the kind Skelton liked, so this time I chose for myself a couple of brightly patterned dresses.

The house of girls was empty when I arrived back. But Anne came home a few minutes later. It was 4.35 p.m.

We spoke for a short while in the kitchen, then she went up to her room. This was off the first-floor landing.

I made myself a cup of English tea and was taking it upstairs when Anne shouted. I happened to be right outside her door, so I heard her clearly. Her words were, 'Don't flatter yourself!' The next thing was a loud shriek followed by swearing followed by sobbing.

I suspected Skelton was the cause. He could be so infuriating. But I left Anne alone. To knock immediately on her door would be impolite. And she might have many other frustrations in her life – things I didn't know about.

Twenty minutes later, I went downstairs again. Anne was in the kitchen and her eyes were pink.

I looked at her very directly and said, 'Don't worry. I know.'

'You know what?'

'I know about you and Skelton. I know you kissed him.'

She asked how, and I told her about overhearing her argument with Jo.

'But you didn't say anything ...'

'No.'

'So you don't mind?'

I thought about this, so I could give her a truthful answer.

'No. I don't.'

'Phew,' she said. 'I thought you would hate me.'

She explained what had happened – that Skelton hadn't really been interested in her, just in finding out about Paul White, and that he only wanted to find out so as to get back together with me. I knew this already.

'But what about you?' I asked. 'What will you do now?'

'Do?' Anne said. 'I won't do anything. He said he doesn't want to see me again.'

'I'm sure he does. He's just scared.'

'He loves you very much.'

'I don't love him.'

The words felt hard in my mouth, like pebbles. I wanted to say them clearly but couldn't.

'Do you already love him?' I asked.

'No,' she said, without hesitation. 'But I like him. I'm attracted to him – I'm sorry.'

'Why be sorry? You can say anything to me.'

'He's – there's something about him. He's melancholy. It makes me want to make him better. Perhaps it's just the doctor in me.'

'You understand him well. That's what he needs, healing.'

'Lots of men do.'

We talked more generally. Anne relaxed.

'Thank you,' she said.

'Why?'

'For not making things difficult. Jo thought you would.'

'I am too practical to do that.'

She got up and went to put her mug in the sink.

'If you want any advice, please come to me. I know Skelton very well. Better than himself. I'm sure you can see him again, if you want to.'

'I'll think about it. My ego's a bit bruised at the moment.'

By now I had thought for a number of days about the crime. It seemed to me that the motive for throwing the heart out of the train window was emotional – jealousy.

What I needed most of all was to know exactly who was in class that day.

On Tuesday morning, I asked Jo if she could help me compile a list. She said she could do better than that, and went upstairs to her room. Five minutes later she came back with a neatly printed-out page, forty names, two columns.

'I organize everything,' she said. 'Rag week. Plays. You name it. I can give you their contact details, if you need them.'

'Thank you very much,' I replied.

Later that morning I went to buy cigarettes from a newsagent's on Denmark Hill. On the way back, I thought about the logic of what happened. I decided that, working by a process of elimination, I would see who could possibly have committed the crime. This required two things, apart from having been on the 5.34 a.m. train. First, assuming that it was a student in Paul's class, the opportunity to swap the heart in Pandora's body for the one removed from their own group's cadaver. Second, the opportunity to remove this decoy heart from Pandora and replace it in their cadaver without being seen.

According to what Jo told me, Paul White had noticed the day before that the decoy heart wasn't Pandora's. However, this was no guarantee that the swap had not been made a day or two earlier than that. There seemed no way of discovering when this had happened, unless Paul himself knew.

Of much more certainty was the time at which the second swap took place. This had to have occurred between 5.38 a.m. when Pandora's heart was thrown from the train, and 10 a.m. when the anatomy class began, and Paul discovered Pandora's heart was missing.

Therefore the main suspect would be whichever student was first into the classroom the morning after.

To make this second swap seemed a risky thing to do. But throwing the heart from a train, even an almost empty train, was also reckless. This was one of the reasons I believed jealousy was the motive.

Of the forty names on the list, Jo had already crossed off two. When I asked why, she said, 'He dropped out after a week and she never turned up in the first place.'

CLASS LIST

ABINGDON, Mary
ARAN, Jill
BERKOWITZ, Martha
~~BERTRAM, Simon~~
BIRD, Jo
CASSANDRA, Emilia
CHOPRA, Raj
CHOWDHURY, Anala
CLEVERER, Molly
DERVISH, Roger
DINEEN, Lesley
ESSEX, Jenny
ETTERIDGE, Meredith
GARDNER, Tom
GAVASCAR, Mendip
GLAISTER, Warren
GOLWALA, Ashish
HANDLY, Anne
JENKINS-JONES, Mandy
KAVANAGH, Maurice

KHAN, Mohammed
LAWRENCE, Richard
LECHKOWA, Maria
LORD, Harry
MOHAMED, Saleem
MORRIS, Kibibi
NGOSA, Benjamin
O'CONNOR, Jane
PATEL, Lalita
POCO, Mia
PONNUSWAMY, Arun
PURVIS, Minnie
SINGH, Anjali
SMID, Pavel
SMITH, Samantha
TOLSTOYANA, Krystyna
WATANABE, Keiko
WHITE, Paul
WICKES, Danielle
~~YEOMAN, Candida~~

Obviously, I could also cross out Paul White.
And from what Becky had said about seeing a man on

the train, the remaining women – all twenty-three of them – could also be discounted.

That left me with a list of fourteen. This was further reduced when Jo remembered that Tom Gardner had been off ill all that week.

Then I remembered that Becky had been very definite that the hand throwing the heart had been white. In consultation with Jo, I was able to eliminate seven more of the men.

So I had six remaining suspects: Warren Glaister, Roger Dervish, Maurice Kavanagh, Richard Lawrence, Harry Lord and Pavel Smid.

Wednesday lunchtime, Anne came up to my room. She had her books with her, and was just back from class.

'I'd like to see if you're right,' she said. 'I mean, I'd like to see if he'll see me again.'

She was very embarrassed.

'Please, sit down.'

Anne perched on the end of the bed. I was sitting at the window-desk. I turned the chair around.

'I'm not really interested in him,' Anne said. 'You don't have to worry.'

'It doesn't matter even if you are. Listen carefully ...' And then I told her exactly what I thought she should say when she called Skelton.

'I'll try,' she said, sounding doubtful.

When she returned to the house at the end of the day, Anne came to find me again.

'Did it work?' I asked, but I did not need to. I could tell from her smile that it had.

'We're meeting tomorrow evening.'

'I will help you dress. I will tell you how to behave. Perhaps we can make him kiss you again.'

'Oh no,' she said.

'Well, we can make him see you another time.'

'Yes. That would be a nice revenge.'

The black taxi in the street outside honked its horn at exactly 7 p.m. on Thursday. Paul White was punctual. He had phoned me earlier in the day, to say that he was ready to talk. But only on the condition that we went out to a good restaurant.

When I got into the back seat beside him, the spicy smell of his cologne was strong but not too strong.

'Hello,' he said. 'You look very lovely.'

This comment unnerved me. 'Thank you,' I said. It had been several years since I went on a date with anyone other than Skelton. I had forgotten all about compliments – not that Skelton didn't pay me them, he always was very assiduous, just that I had recently taken them for granted. 'You smell nice,' I said, by mistake.

'Thank you,' said Paul. 'I used to wear aftershave to cover up the hospital smell. Formalin, you know. But that's over now. I expect, underneath it, I just stink of bachelor pad.'

This made me laugh. That he was flirtatious, right from the start, seemed to make the situation safe. I did not need to worry about a sudden lurch towards the sexual, late in the evening. If he flirtatiously proposed something I could flirtatiously put him off. I was wearing one of the bright dresses.

As the car drove us away from Camberwell Green, Paul asked me how I found it living with Jo and the others.

'They are very sympathetic,' I said.

'That's what I always found,' Paul replied. 'Very accommodating.'

I laughed again, although the comment wasn't particularly funny. It was easy to see why Paul was so popular with the girls. I had never met a twenty-year-old who seemed so much a man.

We drove to the restaurant he had chosen, which was St John near Smithfield Market – a large white room with very satisfyingly plain tables and chairs. It was one of Skelton's favourite places, although of course I didn't say this.

I waited until we had finished our starters before I asked Paul any questions about the heart.

'Do we have to talk about that? I thought we were having such a pleasant time.'

'We are,' I said. 'But if you want me to help you, you must confide in me.'

'Why are you so interested?'

'Because I found the heart. Everything is my responsibility. So you must help me.'

'That I'm more than happy to do,' he said. 'Later.'

So, we ate our main courses. I tried hard to order food that I hadn't eaten there with Skelton. The place itself reminded me so much of him, anyway.

Paul also reminded me of Skelton. There were many differences between them. Paul was a simpler person, and not just because he was so young. But there were also many similarities. I realized that some of the things I had come to dislike in Skelton were things he had in common with other English men. In fact, they were what made them English men: the constant irony, for example, and the wish to avoid anything too passionate.

'The day before you were arrested, you noticed that the heart in Pandora's body had been swapped.'

'Oh, *Pandora*. You're very well informed. Do you know, I actually miss her. That probably sounds a little creepy.'

'I understand.'

'If you'd given me her heart in the dark, I could still have identified it. I had removed it a week before, very, very carefully. King Death personally commended me on my work.'

There was something old-fashioned about Paul. He was trying to be a gentleman. But, in speaking about Guy's, I saw he felt great sadness.

'Could the heart have been swapped before the weekend?'

'No. I would have noticed.'

'Are you certain?'

'Quite positive.'

Then I came to my most important question: 'Do you have any idea who did it?'

'Honestly? No. Not a clue.'

'Someone who dislikes you?'

'Well, it would be that, I suppose. And, if so, they must be pretty pleased with themselves, now.'

'No-one ever threatened you?'

'I'm quite large, myself.'

'You never got the feeling someone was angry with you?'

'People are jealous, sometimes. Men get jealous.'

The waitress brought our pudding. We were sharing a Spotted Dick. Skelton had always wanted to do this, but I had always insisted on ordering something else. I didn't like to encourage his love of nursery food.

'Have you ever stolen someone's girlfriend?'

'Not since I've been at Guy's — since I *was* at Guy's. I didn't need to.'

'You wanted to be with Monica?'

For the first time in the evening, Paul became entirely serious.

'That wasn't happening.'

'But you saw her secretly.'

'What don't you know?'

'Everything,' I said. 'Other people have told me about you. I expect them to be wrong.'

'It sounds like they've been pretty accurate.' He looked at me with mock sternness. 'Jo? Is she your main informant?'

'She cares about you.'

'I'll take that as a yes. And yes, I did see Monica secretly. Although not secretly enough. King Death found out — her father, I mean. He put a complete stop to it. We were very careful. Someone must have gone to a lot of trouble to find out. I never met her near Guy's, or anywhere that people from there went. Jo only found out about us afterwards.'

'You think someone was spying on you?'

'Or steaming open my mail. Or tapping my phone.'

'Please. Be serious. This someone followed you and then told Monica's father you were still seeing her?'

'Either that or he found out for himself. Monica swears she didn't tell anyone. Not even her best friend. And she tells her best friend everything.'

The Spotted Dick was delicious, but I was not really tasting it.

'From what you say, it seems that you do have an enemy who hates you.'

Again, Paul stopped joking.

'I thought I was just being paranoid.'

There were other things I wanted to ask, for example about my six suspects, but I was worried I might scare Paul off. Instead, we started to talk about Japan. Paul said he wanted to see it for himself. I told him that parts of it were very beautiful and parts were very ugly.

When the bill came, I paid it. Paul said he felt guilty. I said that I believed he was completely innocent.

We took another taxi to the house of girls.

'Thank you for a lovely evening,' I said. 'You are not coming inside.'

'So I don't even get a kiss for letting you take me out to dinner?'

'What about Monica?'

For a moment he seemed almost angry.

'Monica says she can't see me, not like that. She's convinced herself that I deliberately got myself expelled. The hospital visit was a one-off – to see all my limbs were intact.'

'You will help me prove that you didn't.'

'Maybe,' he said, with no life in his voice.

'You can kiss me once,' I said. 'It can be now or another time, but that is it – once.'

He was young and cynical and lacking patience.

14.

By the time I met Anne outside Archway station, Saturday evening at half six, I was full of paranoia.

This time her outfit was even closer to that of my fantasy girlfriend. Under her raincoat, she wore a black smock over a white T-shirt, white tights and flat black Camper shoes with a single strap. And her black hair wasn't long, as before, but cut into a sharp bob. The effect was a little prim, almost schoolgirlish. Although it made her look even younger, I felt a lot more comfortable being with her. They were the kind of clothes I had often suggested Kumiko wear – to no avail.

I kissed her on the cheek, and her scent was delicious. Anne would fit in so well at the gig – so fresh, so youthful. I felt a wave of pleasure, she was with *me*.

Of course, this was immediately followed by a backwash of guilt.

'How was it getting here?' I asked.

'Oh, fine,' she said. 'The Northern line was behaving itself, for once.'

I had decided that I needed to find out where Anne lived. She had been a little mysterious about this, unnecessarily so. It was already clear she would rather tease me than tell me.

We went in through the CD-shelved shop and downstairs to where the gig would be – a small, dark room with space for a maximum of sixty people. No stage, as such. Just a microphone in front of a few unmatched chairs. There would not be sixty people tonight.

Part of the thing about improvised music is the breakdown of artificial barriers between performers and audience, so there was no star treatment on my arrival. Instead, I received a few handshakes, hellos and half-nods.

I had played with the Norwegian percussionist before but not the other musician, another Londoner. He didn't have an instrument as such. Instead, he made sounds by controlling the output of a number of smart black boxes with buttons and dials on. As we walked up, he was fiddling with a couple of effects pedals. Compared to this, I am pretty much old school. When improvising, rather than doing sessions, I make it a point of honour never to use anything other than my guitar, a lead and whatever amp the venue has seen fit to provide. I don't even use a plectrum.

My guitar is a 1952 Gibson ES-175, with f-holes, in Sunburst. But I no longer obsess about those details, much.

It's understood that, if musicians don't want to talk before a performance, you don't talk to them. All three of us were fairly taciturn – and to discuss what we were going to do would have been to miss the point completely.

Luckily, the organizer had seen fit to provide us with some beer. I gave one of my two bottles to Anne. She took this, quite cannily, as a signal to go and find somewhere to sit down. I was relieved to see she didn't intend to stare up at me from the front row. Kumiko always used to find somewhere off to one side, and Anne did this, too.

About fifteen minutes later, the gig began. I usually close my eyes while I'm playing. It helps with listening to what the other people in the room are doing – what the musicians are doing, how the audience is sounding. But this time, I snuck a couple of glances towards Anne. She looked, I was surprised to see, enraptured. Was this a genuine reaction, or just one designed to please me?

I thought it wasn't going so badly at all. We were very quiet indeed for most of the first number. The contributions made by the black-boxes guy were disruptive and deliberately non-musical. This was nicely counterbalanced by an implied but recurring pulse from the percussionist.

In the second number, their roles were reversed. The percussionist coaxed some beautifully chiming sounds from his cymbals. I replied to these – but not too obviously, I hoped – with some action on the upper part of my fretboard.

The third number, as often happened, even in those days of restraint, was more squiggly and energetic. At one point I put in a disguised quote from 'The Heart', safe in the knowledge that no-one would recognize it.

The final number, not unusually, was an attempt to synthesize what had gone before, whilst still breaking new ground.

Words aren't very good at conveying what goes on at these kinds of events.

'That was great,' said Anne, afterwards. 'So delicate, and every sound was so special and careful.'

'I'm glad you liked it.'

'I loved it. I mean, I'm sure I didn't *really* understand what it was all about. But there was such a lovely atmosphere in here. Very concentrated. You could really think.'

She was saying all the right things. However, with my paranoia still in place, I found it hard to believe her.

A few people came up to talk to me. They weren't exactly effusive, they rarely are, but I knew I hadn't disgraced myself.

The other musicians needed a lot longer to pack up than me, so we shook hands in a slightly embarrassed way. I knew them so well and I didn't know them at all.

Outside, I offered to walk Anne back to the station.

'You don't want to go for a drink?'

'Not really,' I said. 'I just want to go home and sleep.'

I was lying. Improvising energizes me to the point of insomnia. I could have stayed up all night.

'I understand. It must be quite exhausting.'

By the ticket barriers, I kissed her goodbye. She didn't make anything of it. Shaking hands would just have been silly, and it was clear I was going to see her again.

Sooner than she knew. And she *wasn't* going to see me. Not unless I made a serious mistake.

I had never followed anyone before, apart from those few yards I'd followed Kumiko and Jo to the bus stop. If I had, I would probably have known that a Saturday night in May wasn't the best time to be doing it. The southbound platform at Archway was long, exposed and far from crowded. And the fact I was carrying a very conspicuous guitar case didn't help, either.

I waited halfway up the stairs until I heard a train approaching. As it stopped, I walked down onto the platform. I could see Anne, much further along, waiting by the doors. They opened with a series of beeps, and we both got on.

All of a sudden, I found that I was incredibly excited. This must be what it feels like to be a spy. Everyday activities like strap-hanging become adrenalin-flooded adventures.

People who change carriage whilst the train is moving are always suspicious. But I needed to keep Anne in sight. I couldn't just stick my head out the doors whenever the train came to a station.

By the time the train reached Kentish Town, I had travelled half its length and had positioned myself where I could glimpse Anne if I moved my head a few inches to the left. Otherwise, I was hidden by vertical obstructions.

Just before Camden station, Anne stood up. It looked like she was going to get off. Perhaps she didn't live in South London at all.

I waited until she had passed down the platform, then went after her. I've never felt more conspicuous – like the Honey Monster or something.

Anne, it soon became clear, was changing from the Charing Cross branch of the Northern line to the Bank branch. Still heading south, then.

On the next train, I was able to position myself in roughly the same relation to her. There had been a few dangerous moments as I got on, when Anne might have spotted me.

Again, Anne stood up just before the station at which she was intending to get off. This time it was Elephant & Castle.

She walked right past my carriage then turned down the passageway towards the exit. As I followed her,

I remembered that Elephant didn't have escalators but lifts. Anne went straight into the one on the right. After the doors were closed, I went up to wait for the next.

It took a long time to come, and I became certain that I'd lost Anne. If she lived anywhere nearby, she would be well out of sight by the time I made it to street level.

A couple of minutes later, I exited the station. My first idea had been to check the southbound bus stops. I strolled along. A light drizzle was falling. Quite a few people were waiting around, and one of them, I saw with delight, was Anne. She was standing at the stop for the 35, 68 and 176.

My suspicions were further confirmed when a 35 drew into sight and Anne moved forwards with the damp crowd.

Obviously, it was too much of a risk for me to take the same bus as Anne. But just then, as they have a tendency to do, a second number 35 came into view.

Once on board, I stood in the downstairs aisle. From there I would be able to keep an eye on people getting off the bus in front – just so long as we stayed in sight.

We did.

All the way to Camberwell Green, where Anne got off and walked straight towards me. Her eyes seemed to pass over my face, but thank God they weren't focused. She carried on past the bus that I had completely forgotten I was on, so horribly exposed did I feel. Its doors remained open for a few seconds longer – just enough time for me to squeeze out.

The rest was easy. I followed Anne at a safe distance, away from the main road, down sidestreets. The drizzle had turned to something approaching a mist.

Around now, I began to feel immensely tender towards Anne. Someone was following her and she didn't know. It could have been anyone, intending anything. The fact it was me and I was harmless didn't make any difference to the essential situation: young woman being followed. Her slender back seemed too unbearably vulnerable. I wanted to warn her to be more on her guard.

The house Anne finished up at was large, ugly, Victorian, a tad shabby. It looked like shared accommodation, possibly bedsits. I could be fairly certain that Anne lived there because she had a key to the front door.

For a few minutes, I watched the house to see if any of the bedroom lights went on. Only one of the upstairs windows was lit up, that at the very top of the house – the attic room. However, the curtains of the bay window were open, and I could see flickering blue light on the ceiling. Someone was watching television. I checked my watch. It was ten fifteen.

As the street was solidly residential, I couldn't hang around for very long without seeming suspicious. So I walked to the far end, turned round and was going to make one quick pass before heading home. But when I reached Anne's house, I saw something through the bay window: Jo – the side of Jo's face. I was sure it was her. There was only one square-jawed Jo.

I stopped and stared.

Luckily, she and Anne were totally caught up in their conversation – which was lively and full of laughter.

Between and behind them, I could see another figure coming into view, female, black-haired.

I stepped back into the road to bring them into sight, and was almost run over by a motorbike. It swerved and beeped. The rider called me a cunt. I ducked down. No-one came to the window. What was the beep of a horn compared to what they were discussing?

When I stood up again, very cautiously, Anne had moved aside – enough to give me a clear view of Kumiko, a big smile on her face. More laughter. They were all three of them in on the joke, which was me.

I turned to begin making my slow, humiliated way home.

But someone was in my way – not a big figure, very slight. I looked into a face which, before I was halfway past, I recognized.

'It's Becky, isn't it?'

'Yeah,' she said. 'So you found her, did you?'

I hustled Becky a few steps further down the road, out of sight of the bay window.

'You knew where she was living,' I said. 'You knew, and you didn't say.'

'She didn't want you to know. What are you going to do now?'

'I'm going home.'

'It's a bit miserable, isn't it?'

I thought for a second she meant I was miserable.

'Are you going to visit her?'

'No. She gimme her address. I just come down and have a look, now and then, see what they're up to. It's a nice house, isn't it?'

Becky didn't have an umbrella. Droplets of water were standing out on her hair, which had been lank to begin with.

'Come with me.'

'Is that your guitar?' she asked.

'I've just done a gig.'

'Excellent.'

I offered to buy her some food from a corner shop. She said she'd prefer a McDonald's. We went into the one at the bottom of Denmark Hill. I was hungry, so I bought something for myself. It was delicious in a totally disgusting way.

'How did you find her?'

I thought for a second. If Becky told Kumiko when she'd seen me, Kumiko would be able to work out what I'd been up to. There didn't seem to be any point being secretive.

'I followed Anne,' I said, then explained.

'You're really getting into this detective business, aren't you?'

'Some of it's quite fun. Following Anne was quite fun.'

'Yeah. I do it all the time. Pick someone interesting at the Market and just follow them to see where they're going. They never catch me. I'm invisible, really.'

'I think Anne might have seen me.'

'Why'd you follow her?'

'The way she dressed, the things she said. It was all too spot-on. I suspected Kumiko might be involved.'

'At least she's still interested in you.'

'Interested in taking the piss.'

'And that's bad?'

I had to think about this.

'Maybe not. And now I know she's okay.'

'Not living in some squat.'

'I didn't mean –' I said.

Becky laughed.

'Sorry,' I said. 'I didn't mean –'

'Would you like anything else?' I asked.

Becky's supersized Extra Value Meal (Big Mac, fries and chocolate milkshake) had been wolfed in about a minute.

'Same again, please. And a Diet Coke.'

I bought her the food.

'I'll take it with me,' she said.

We left the restaurant.

'You couldn't buy me some fags as well, could you?'

'Come on,' I said.

A little shop over the road was open. I bought Becky a lighter, some Rizlas and a pack of rolling tobacco. And also some bananas. The newsagent looked disapproving.

'Can I have this?'

Becky had placed that month's copy of *Vogue* on the counter.

I looked at her quizzically.

'I like to keep in touch,' she said. 'It'll make a change not to have to nick it.'

'Get out,' said the newsagent.

Becky smoked her first cigarette as we walked to the bus stop. Her other things were in a green plastic bag dangling from her wrist.

'Comme des Garçons is okay,' she said. 'But agnès b's my favourite. More wearable. Kumiko's got good taste.'

I glanced at the shapeless dirty clothes Becky had on. She caught me.

'Yeah, I know,' she said. 'Bit too last season, innit?'

'I like you,' she said. 'You're a bit touched.'

'Thanks,' I said, more flattered than I'd been for a long time.

Once we were on the bus, sitting downstairs at the back, I asked her if she was going to mention seeing me to Kumiko.

'I don't never speak to her. I just watch. It's another life, innit?'

'It is,' I said.

I could smell the fast food. It was making me feel hungry and nauseous at the same time.

The bus windows were steamed up.

We talked about fashion. Becky knew far more about it than me. I was able to confirm that, as she had guessed, Kumiko bought her clothes at agnès b.

Just as the bus was coming up to London Bridge, Becky said, 'I didn't tell you something, when you came round. The man who threw the heart out the window. He was a *white* man in dark clothes. Kumiko was very interested in that.'

We said goodbye on the street. I knew I'd see her again.

15.

First thing Friday morning, I asked Jo for the contact details of my six suspects. I intended to meet them all. I felt safe. They were not murderers.

'How was ...?' asked Jo.

Molly joined us in the kitchen. She was wearing a pink dressing gown and fluffy pink slippers, with small irony.

'Last night? Paul is very charming.'

'Oh, he *is*, isn't he? He's lovely,' said Jo.

'No,' I said. 'He's not lovely.'

Skelton came into my mind. Once, I had known him as lovely. He could still be lovely to someone. Yet to call him charming would be to insult him. But Paul was different.

'Well, I think he's lovely,' said Jo. 'And I think you're very lucky.'

She went upstairs to print out another list.

'I don't think he's lovely, either,' said Molly. 'But he is definitely charming.'

When Jo returned, she had put day clothes on. Previously, she had been wearing soft green pyjamas.

The first thing I noticed from the list was that three of the suspects, Warren Glaister, Richard Lawrence and Harry Lord, lived at the same address. I asked about them.

'Big friends,' said Jo. 'Inseparable.'

'In fact,' said Molly, who was making tea, 'quite hard to tell them apart. Warren is the ginger one, isn't he?'

Jo made a noise which meant yes.

Their address was in Highgate.

'What about the others?'

'Pavel Smid is brilliant. Now Paul's gone, he's the best student in class. He's from the Czech Republic.'

'Perhaps he envied Paul's intelligence?'

'I don't know if Pavel notices anything much,' said Molly. 'He's very self-contained, very mysterious. Hardly speaks to anyone. I'm right, aren't I?'

'I think he doesn't have very much money,' said Jo. 'He just studies.'

Pavel lived in Brixton.

'Maurice Kavanagh is rich,' said Molly. 'And gay. And not very good at medicine.'

'That's unfair,' said Jo.

'But true,' said Molly.

I looked at the list. Maurice Kavanagh's address was a flat in Soho.

'Roger Dervish is –'

'Also gay,' said Molly. 'But just doesn't know it.'

'He's not.'

'He *so* is.'

'And why do you say that?'

'I *know*.'

'You shouldn't go round saying these things about people.'

'It's not a bad thing. He's just dishonest. And wasting his life trying to be something he's not, which is *straight*.'

Roger Dervish lived in Borough, very close to the hospital.

'Excuse me,' I said. 'Which of them do you think hates Paul White?'

'Roger,' said Molly. 'I've never liked him.'

'I don't think any of them …' said Jo. 'Well, maybe Pavel. He's so intense.'

Molly went to get ready for class.

Anne appeared. I had not seen her the night before, the night of her date with Skelton. By the time I got home she was already in bed.

'Well?' I said.

She put two slices of bread in the toaster, with her back to me. I could see she was pretending to be upset.

'It went … It went perfectly,' she said, and turned round with a big smile. 'Everything just as you promised.'

'Fantastic,' said Jo, who was still very relieved I didn't mind.

'We're meeting again on Saturday night.'

'How do you manage it?' asked Jo.

'He's got a gig,' said Anne, talking to me. 'I was so enthusiastic about music, just like you said. In the end he had to invite me along.'

'You see,' I said. 'And today we will go and buy you some perfect Skelton clothes. And get you a Skelton haircut, if you like.'

'Yes,' said Anne.

'And I will teach you how to listen.'

'I have class in the morning.'

'We can have lunch. I will treat you.'

'Sometimes I wish I had an intrigue,' said Jo. 'My life is so boring.'

'You have an intrigue,' I said. 'Find out everything about my six suspects.'

Anne's toast popped up and soon the kitchen was empty.

*

I waited until 9.30 a.m., then called each of the six. Their class started at 10 a.m.

Warren Glaister refused to speak to me, once he found out who I was.

Roger Dervish didn't answer, so I left a brief message, asking him to call me back.

Maurice Kavanagh's phone was off.

Richard Lawrence said he could meet me for coffee that afternoon. I suggested Saturday instead. He agreed.

Harry Lord said he'd just spoken to Warren Glaister and then swore at me.

Pavel Smid said, 'No. I don't want meet,' before hanging up.

Richard Lawrence phoned back and said, on consideration, he wouldn't have coffee with me.

'Did Warren warn you off?' I asked.

'Warren,' he said. 'Yes, he did. Warren says we'll get in big trouble with the hospital if we speak to you.'

'I am trying to help Paul White.'

'Warren saw you in the court. He says you're a madwoman.'

'Do I sound mad?'

'No.'

'I just want to know where you were on the morning of the day Paul was arrested.'

He paused, then answered.

'We were in anatomy class, of course.'

'Before that. At 5.30 a.m.'

'We were in bed.'

'All of you?'

'On the Tuesday? Yes. It was a big night, the night before. My brother's stag night. And he said I could bring along a couple of mates. So I brought Warren and Harry. We went to a club. Everything half price. Look, I have to go in, now.'

'What time did you arrive in class that day? Were you on time?'

'That's it. Sorry. I'm here now. Goodbye.'

I put my phone down on the desk.

Just then, a text came through from Roger Dervish. In it, he asked when I wanted to see him.

I texted back, suggesting Saturday morning. A few hours later, after class was finished, he replied, saying yes.

By this time, I was in town, meeting up with Anne. I took her to a good sushi place, Donzoko on Kingly Street. Sometimes it's best to give English people what they expect of a Japanese.

Anne told me more details of her meeting with Skelton. Then she digressed, and told me something I didn't quite understand. It seemed to be that a famous singer had written a song about me, because Skelton had told him to. Skelton sounded lonely. I felt it was time to send him a message.

When we went shopping, I chose a costume for Anne. She would wear exactly the clothes that Skelton finds most attractive. Anne must look subtly like a traditional Japanese schoolgirl.

Then we had her hair cut.

We finished at 4 p.m. Both of us were happy.

I called Maurice Kavanagh again, from the bus home. His phone was on but he didn't answer. I left a message.

Friday evening, Molly and Anne went out. Jo and I ordered spicy pizza and watched television. She drank a bottle of red wine by herself. Then I asked her some questions.

'Who is usually the first person to arrive at class?'

'Anatomy? I am. I'm such a boring swot. And every other class. Well, apart from Pavel Smid. He's always there when I get there.'

'Were you first on the day the heart was found?'

'I've been thinking about this. I was later than usual. The bus was slow.'

'Who was in class?'

'Almost everyone.'

'Were any of the suspects late?'

'I can't remember. I don't think so.'

'No-one will speak to me. Apart from Roger Dervish.'

'We were told not to talk about Paul White to anyone. They probably think you're a reporter.'

'No, they think I'm a madwoman.'

Jo laughed louder than I had heard her laugh before.

'They saw me shouting in court,' I said.

'So did I,' she said. 'I don't think you're mad. Apart from not thinking Paul is lovely.'

'Lovely comes from inside. He's a very outside person.'

'With a lovely outside.'

'Not lovely,' I said.

I explained why I wanted to know who was first into class that morning.

'It wouldn't be any of the Rugger Buggers, Warren, Rick and Harry. They're always late. So is Maurice. He likes to give the impression he's got somewhere much more exciting to be. And he probably has.'

'He is not good at medicine?'

'He just doesn't concentrate on it. Most of the time he's exhausted. I'm sure he could be brilliant, if he tried. That's half the problem. He knows it, too.'

'On Monday, can you talk to Richard? Tell him to speak to me. Tell him I'm not mad.'

'Will do.'

I went to bed early. Jo stayed up to watch another film.

Roger Dervish was on time for our meeting. He was a dark-haired, olive-skinned young man. It was difficult to be sure of any other fact about him, on first acquaintance.

We met at Balans, Old Compton Street. This was my suggestion. I wanted to see if he was comfortable around gay men. He wasn't. He looked at the table-top, or at me, or at his fingernails.

'I know who you are,' he said. 'Paul White wasn't exactly a friend of mine, but I've got nothing against him. If I can help, I'm happy to.'

'Can you remember what time you arrived in class on the day he was arrested?'

'The usual, I suppose. I tend to get there with about five minutes to spare.'

'You weren't early?'

'No.'

'I need to know who arrived first.'

'It wasn't me. I can't tell you anything else.'

I was being too aggressive. I didn't want to make him feel like a suspect, not yet, so I asked him some other questions to make him relax. He told me that lots of people envied Paul White for his intelligence and his success with women. But none of the students hated him enough to do something so extreme. Then he asked me, 'Why do you want to know who was first to class?'

I told him Jo's theory about the swapping of the hearts.

'It would be very hard to do that without someone seeing. One of the demonstrators is usually around.'

'But not impossible,' I said.

'No. Anything can happen in a hospital.'

I was stuck. I needed to ask him direct questions.

'Where were you at 5.30 a.m. on that morning?'

'Why do you want to know that?'

He became more awkward, looking only at his finger-nails. They were perfectly manicured, but the cuticles were ragged with biting.

'Because that's when the heart was thrown from the train.'

'You don't think I did that?'

'No. But please tell me where you were.'

'It wasn't me,' he said.

'Do you live with someone?'

'No. I have a flat.'

'No-one can say where you were at five thirty?'

'You're not the police. I don't have to tell you anything.'

'You don't,' I said. 'Thank you for meeting me.'

Roger Dervish left quickly. He was still a suspect.

I had called Maurice Kavanagh several times that morning, but his phone just rang and rang.

I decided to go and see Pavel Smid. He was the most likely person to be in. And if he wasn't there, I could get home easily from Brixton.

The flat he lived in was above a Caribbean restaurant. I smelled old greasy food all along the landing.

When I pushed the doorbell, it made no sound. I knocked and waited.

'Who it is?'

'Kumiko Ozu. I want to talk to you about Paul White.'

'I said no. Go away.'

'Why don't you want to talk?'

'Go away!'

His voice had some panic in it.

'Just for five minutes.'

'No.'

I waited, knocked again and then waited some more. He wasn't going to talk. I wrote my mobile number and a short message on a page of my notebook, tore it out and then posted it through his letterbox.

For a few moments, I thought about going to see the Rugger Buggers, as Jo had called them. But then I decided to let her speak to Richard. He had sounded friendly. Perhaps she could persuade him to help.

That night, I waited up until Anne returned from seeing Skelton. I was excited by the thought of them together. She was home quite early. I came down from my room to see her.

'No, it was great,' she said, talking to Jo in the TV room. I came through the door. Anne saw me. Her hands were in the air, mid-gesture. 'Amazing.'

I laughed with a different feeling than delight. Outside, I heard a man shout *cunt*.

'Really?' I said. 'Most people don't like that sort of music.'

'I've never heard anything like it before. It was very sad and empty. Not like pop music or jazz.'

'You liked how Skelton played?'

'I liked how one thing didn't have to connect with another. Sometimes he played like little bits of melodies, there was a beautiful one halfway through one song, but other times it was sounds like you'd hear anywhere. I couldn't believe it was all coming out of a guitar. He made it sound like a ghost train.'

We all laughed, but Anne was being serious. I felt an old pride. At what he does, Skelton is very good. I always loved his music, and for some of the same reasons Anne did, sadness, disjointedness, emptiness. I just hadn't expected her to feel this way. It was slightly annoying. Part of me was sorry not to have been there – but only to see Skelton without him seeing me.

'Did you go for a drink afterwards?'

'No. I could tell he was shattered. He went straight home to bed.'

This surprised me. After a gig, Skelton is usually full of energy and often has difficulty sleeping. Sometimes he needs to go for long midnight walks to calm himself down.

We talked for a while longer. Anne said she was wet through, and went to change into her dressing gown.

I told Jo I had a headache.

'See you in the morning,' she said.

Nothing happened on Sunday. I tried to call Maurice Kavanagh several times, but he never answered his phone.

16.

On Monday morning just before seven, I reported to the Porterage beside Guy's main entrance.

I wasn't sure exactly what I was doing there. It didn't have very much to do with Paul White any more. Or with Kumiko – at least, not in the simple sense of wanting to win her back. No, I was proving something to myself: that when I decided to do a thing, I would bloody well do it. A person like that, a determined person, wasn't silly or laughable. They were worth taking seriously.

'Morning,' said the strangely monkey-faced woman behind the desk. 'Just sit down and wait.'

As I did so, I remembered Anne's words about how the only way I could ever understand exactly what hospital was like was for it to become my whole world.

Well, I thought, *here I am.*

Entering the hospital, I had been worried that I would bump into Anne. But, of course, I could have found some excuse for being there. That would become a lot trickier once I'd put the uniform on. There was nothing much I could do to avoid her, though. If we met, I'd just have to tell her the truth – whatever it was.

Another five minutes of waiting passed. The monkey-faced woman was on the phone to someone about wheelchairs. Relaxing a little, I began to take in my surroundings. There was a noticeboard directly opposite me, covered in posters. One in particular caught my attention, mainly because it had the word CANCELLED scrawled diagonally across it. But immediately I noticed something else, a drawing in the bottom left-hand corner – a skull wearing a crown at an angle exactly halfway between jaunty and rakish. This had been added, hurriedly but expertly, in black marker-pen.

It was only after this that I took in that the poster was for a public talk by Dr James Speed, Anatomy Lecturer. His subject, if the event hadn't been cancelled, was to have been, 'An Anatomy of Anatomy: Bodies Public and Private'.

Finally, I looked beneath the scrawl and made out the date: May the second.

There was no need to guess why the talk had been cancelled. Dr Speed would have been busy dealing with fallout from Paul White and the heart – mainly, and successfully, with keeping the whole thing off the front pages.

'Mr Skelton?' asked a voice.

'Yes,' I said, standing up.

'I am August Walter. Everyone calls me Wally. You're going to be shadowing me for the next few days.'

I put my hand out and we shook hello. Wally was a short man, fiftyish, very powerfully built. His hair was either white or blonde, I couldn't tell. He spoke with a German or an Austrian accent – Austrian, so it turned out.

'Come on. We will first get you your locker and your uniform, and then introduce you to Security, so they don't have you arrested. You will see the Head Porter tomorrow. He has a meeting today. His name is Wilson. He is black.'

My uniform was meant to be hung up waiting for me in my locker, for which Wally had the key. But the locker (number 11) was empty, so we had to go along to the stores and argue for half an hour.

'Welcome to Guy's,' said Wally, when I was finally dressed to his satisfaction.

'Comfortable shoes,' he said, pointing at his own. 'Very important. You will do mostly walking. Miles and miles.'

The uniform consisted of a light-blue shirt, a navy-blue sweatshirt and dark-blue trousers. It reminded me of the school uniforms that kids wear, these days.

'Now for Security,' said Wally. 'Beware. These men are dangerous. Most particularly Mr Fine. You must stay good friends with Mr Fine. Everybody knows he killed his wife.'

As we walked down the corridor towards the lifts, Wally pointed at an upside-down dome on the ceiling.

'They have cameras everywhere. But no microphones. Luckily.'

'You say he killed his wife …'

Wally looked over his shoulder – he really did.

'She arrived for routine treatment on an arthritic hip, she left in a box after complications. Mr Fine made it complicated. He has a beautiful new wife, since then.'

'What did she die of – Mrs Fine?'

'Nobody knows. There was an autopsy. All proper. They did not find nothing. You will see Pathology.'

'Today?'

He stopped and looked me over, as if he had never seen me before.

'You do not *like* Pathology departments, do you?'

'I've never been in one.'

'You are not interested in the bodies?'

'No.'

'Good. Or I will have you sacked. We had a sex-pervert here last year. He was black.'

Wally was nothing if not direct.

We took the lift up to the Security Room. I wanted to assure Wally that I wasn't a sex-pervert, but there was a Nurse in the lift with us.

In that confined space, I could smell Wally's perspiration. He was one of those men who smell pleasantly spicy.

The lift arrived.

'Along here,' said Wally, and led me towards Mr Fine, wife-killer.

Wally knocked. We were buzzed in.

The room reeked of a very British machismo that I've never had and never wanted. Mr Fine was sitting in front of a curved wall of TV screens. I recognized a few familiar places, but didn't have time to take in much. Slowly Mr Fine turned his swing-chair around and inspected me.

'New?'

'Yes,' said Wally.

Mr Fine then went across to a desk, opened a drawer, produced a digital camera and said, 'Don't smile.'

I hadn't been planning to.

He positioned me in front of a square of white then took my photo.

'Your ID card will be ready first thing tomorrow,' he said. 'In the meantime, keep out of trouble, okay?'

'Fine,' I said, then realized he might think I meant his name. 'Sure,' I added.

Mr Fine glared at me. He had the smallest pupils of any man I've ever met.

I couldn't hold his gaze, and my eyes settled on the desk, where stood a framed photograph of an attractive young woman of around thirty.

Briefly, I had an almost overwhelming urge to ask Mr Fine if he'd killed his wife. But just then Wally, as if sensing my thoughts, said, 'We won't keep you longer. Thank you very much, Mr Fine.'

I followed Wally out of the room.

'You should have been more polite,' he said. 'That man makes your life very difficult, if he doesn't like you.'

'Why wasn't he arrested for killing his wife?'

Wally sped up, and didn't answer my question until we were in the lift. Even then, he was careful to speak with his back to the camera.

'The Police did investigate but there was no evidence. The autopsy was completely normal. His wife just died.'

'Then why do you say he killed her?'

Wally gripped me by the shoulders.

'Because he did.'

For the rest of the morning, I shadowed Wally as he performed his normal duties: wheeling unconscious patients in and out of theatre, taking blood samples to be tested in the lab, carrying pieces of medical equipment from place to place – and sometimes back again.

'This is my life,' said Wally, once, quietly.

He also told me that he had previously been a high-ranking officer in the Austrian army.

At the end of the day, he shook my hand in the locker room. 'Be dressed more smart, tomorrow,' he said.

With that, I was dismissed.

I slept well that night, and was back at Guy's almost before I'd had time to think about it.

Wally seemed satisfied with my appearance, although I hadn't changed it in any way.

First thing on Tuesday morning, he took me up to the Security Room again. Mr Fine wasn't there. Wally asked after him.

'Out for a fag,' said the pink-faced young man sitting in Mr Fine's seat.

'This is Mr Knight,' said Wally.

Mr Knight clearly wasn't Mr Knight to anyone but Wally – he was only just out of his teens.

'Kev,' he said, and nodded.

'Skelton,' I said, wishing it sounded friendlier.

'He wants an ID card,' said Wally.

Kev fetched it from a card index over on the desk. 'Welcome to the club,' he said. 'Try not to lose the bastard.'

'Put it on,' said Wally.

The two of them were making quite a big thing of it – and, I realized, just then, they were right to. This, and not yesterday morning, was the moment I changed from being a civilian to being an insider. Wally and Kev knew far better than I the nature of the world I was about to enter. Perhaps that helped explain their solemnity.

There were no congratulations afterwards, however. Kev turned almost immediately back to the screens, and Wally told me there was work to do.

And there certainly was. We seemed far busier than before. Wally strode from task to task. I tried to keep up. He always explained what he was doing, and why he was doing it, but often it went by so quickly that I didn't catch even the gist.

We had breaks.

'Are you a smoker?' Wally asked. 'I forgot to ask, yesterday.'

'No,' I said.

'If you are lazy, you should become a smoker. They have longer for their breaks, because they have to go outside the building to smoke. Although there are some secret places.'

'I don't smoke,' I said.

'Good,' said Wally. 'When you see how it affects people, you will understand. But still many doctors smoke.'

For much of the time we were called upon to push people in wheelchairs from place to place – and quite a few of them wore an oxygen mask and cradled a cylinder in their laps.

This didn't stop some of them from trying to make conversation. Wally, dentist-like, seemed to understand everything they said, however muffled. Either that, or he was very good at pretending.

Trusting me a little more than the day before, he let me take command of the wheelchairs myself. As I walked along, he pointed out obstructions or snags I might encounter. I remembered the employment agency woman's cheery words about *look out, there's a bump*. She had been right. One of the main parts of the job seemed to be warning people in advance.

The day went quickly, and I felt increasingly tired. Wally enjoyed proving that he was fitter than me, despite the difference in our ages. But apart from this, he was one of the most patient teachers I've ever known.

During his lunchbreak, he didn't talk to me. Instead, he laid out a book on the table beside him and read as he ate his leberwurst, pickled cucumber, black bread, carrot and apple.

When I asked what it was, Wally lifted the cover for me to see. It was Kant's *Groundwork of the Metaphysics of Morals*.

'Any good?' I asked, but Wally didn't get the joke. He wasn't without a sense of humour, but there was an implied exclusion zone around himself and everything he did.

Wally waited until the end of the shift before he said, 'I am going away for a funeral tomorrow, and so will not be here. In my stead will be Mr Nicholas Rider. He is a very bad Porter – very lazy. Don't listen to *anything* he tells you. He is white.'

Tuesday evening, I sat down to think about the Anne–Kumiko-laughter situation. I needed to do this formally because the job, thank God, had preoccupied and exhausted me during the past couple of days.

It was clear that Kumiko must have coached Anne, telling her the kind of thing to talk to me about. Also, and somehow more upsettingly, she had helped change the way Anne dressed, and her hair – changed it in my direction, so to speak.

I knew it hadn't been a set-up from the start: Kumiko couldn't have met Anne before Paul White's court appearance, and that was when we'd swapped phone numbers. But at some point after then, Kumiko had moved into the house and found out that I was seeing Anne. Or, worst-case scenario, she had found out that I was seeing Anne and so chosen to move in.

My reaction on Saturday night, walking away from the window, had been that Kumiko must hate me very much to do something so cruel. Cruelty, however, was unusual for her. Anything vindictive she saw as a waste of time.

She could be hurtful, but mainly as a by-product of being so absolute.

Now, on Tuesday night, as I thought about it more and more, I realized that the one thing this situation definitely *wasn't* was absolute. Via Anne, Kumiko had managed to establish a perverse kind of dialogue with me. This was unexpected and, in a strange way, hopeful. When she left me, I feared that I would never have any contact with her again – except to arrange a time for her to move her stuff out of the flat, a time when I wouldn't be around. That was Kumiko's way, in life and art: abrupt endings.

But this was a sneaky continuation – one she must have known I would discover, sooner or later.

The question now was, What to do? Kumiko had implicitly offered Anne to me. Should I accept? Was that what Kumiko wanted me to do? And, if I did accept, what message would I be sending back to Kumiko? Surely my unfaithfulness would be interpreted as just that. But was it unfaithful to refuse a gift? Or was it merely ungrateful? This was all assuming that Anne wasn't playing some game of her own. This gift, I was well aware, could reject its recipient.

By the time I forced myself to go to bed, I had far more questions than I'd begun with.

17.

On Sunday night, I dreamed about Skelton.

We were together. Not back together. We had never broken up to begin with.

I was in the kitchen of the old flat, making food. He was in the living room, practising guitar. Being with him felt much as I remembered – that is, it felt normal. Even during the dream, I expected something weird to happen. For me to look in the saucepan and see that I was cooking eyeballs or a heart. For him to come through the door as a zombie and stab me. But everything carried on pleasantly.

I have never had a dream that was so unlike a dream.

When I picked my cellphone off the chair by the bed I saw that I had a text. I had slept through the buzz of it arriving.

> OK WILL MEET U WHENEVER JST STOP
> CALLING WILL U?

It was from Maurice Kavanagh. He had sent it at 3.37 a.m.

I decided to wait until mid-morning before I texted him back. He might still be asleep.

Jo was in the kitchen when I went down, reading a textbook. I reminded her to speak to Richard Lawrence.

'Tell him I'm not a madwoman.'

'I'll do my best,' said Jo. 'Anything else?'

'You could try to talk to Pavel Smid.'

'But I've never spoken to him before.'

'Try to make friends. It might be useful.'

'Okay.'

'And have a look at Maurice Kavanagh. I expect he will be super-tired today.'

I took my breakfast upstairs, switched on my laptop and began to look up information about John Keats.

We read some of his poems at school. I thought he was quite like a Japanese poet, particularly in the 'Ode to Autumn'. His early death was one of the saddest things. A friend of mine, Michiko, used to cry whenever she thought about it.

In 1815, when he started at Guy's, Keats had already been an apprentice apothecary for five years. A few years before, this would have been enough for him to set up in practice. But because of a new Act of Parliament apothecaries were required to train at a hospital to be fully qualified.

The list of lectures that Keats signed up for is still in existence. They included Anatomy and Physiology, under the well-respected surgeon Astley Cooper. It was Astley Cooper who conducted the dissections Keats attended, and it was he, if anyone, who was probably the first King Death.

Keats did very well in his studies, at least to begin with. He quickly became a 'dresser', something like an assistant surgeon. This was an honour for him. However, he was also writing poetry. And poetry began to take him over.

At this time, bodies for the medical students were dug up by 'resurrection men'. They would rob fresh graves. Otherwise, no-one would have been able to learn anatomy.

I needed to know more about Keats than I could find out online, and so I ordered the latest, largest biography of him. The website said it should be dispatched within twenty-four hours.

Around 10 a.m., I showered and dressed. Then I sent a text to Roger Dervish asking to meet him on Tuesday for lunch. Because Jo was in the same class, I knew that his lecture finished at 12 p.m., and he was free in the afternoon. I suggested that I wait for him outside the hospital. That way I might also see the other suspects.

It was frustrating to have to be so patient.

Still online, I began to research grave-robbing. One of the things I love about England is how much history is known, even the smallest details. For example, the resurrection men who provided Astley Cooper with his bodies were called Bill Butler, Bill Barnett and Jack Crouch.

I tried to imagine the London they lived in, dirty and dark and full of crime, but much smaller than now. London waiting for Charles Dickens to grow up and describe it. He was born in 1812.

At 12.15 p.m., someone knocked loudly on the front door. I went to answer. No-one else was in the house.

As I was going down the stairs, my cellphone started to ring. When I answered, a well-bred Irish voice said, 'Hello, it's Maurice.'

'Please excuse me,' I said. 'Can I call you back?'

'Fine,' he said. 'Whatever.'

A young, red-headed man was standing on the doorstep. He was holding a motorcycle helmet and, for a second, I thought he was a courier. Then I remembered I had seen him once before, outside the hospital, smoking with Anne.

'You Kumiko?' he said. His face was very red, too.

'Yes.'

'Can you just leave it alone, alright? If you're not careful you could get the whole lot of us expelled.'

'You are Warren Glaister,' I said.

'Yes,' he said, slightly surprised.

'Would you please come in?'

'No.'

'We can talk in the living room. You don't have to shout on the street. We can be civilized.'

I was aware of the age difference between us. So was he. It gave me an advantage.

'Look, I just came to say leave us alone or else.'

'Or else what? Will you come back and hit me?'

'No. Just leave us alone. That's it.'

'I understand. Please come in.'

He looked around, as if someone might have followed him, then stepped into the hall. He wouldn't go any further.

'I want to go before Jo gets back,' he said.

'Is that how you know where I live?'

'They had a party, once. Early on. Why are you so interested in Paul White? I heard you went on a date with him.'

I explained about seeing the heart sliding.

'If Guy's hears I've been talking to you, I'll be in real trouble.'

'Why?'

'It's bad publicity. They hate bad publicity. You're probably a journalist, aren't you?'

'No. I'm just me. Can I ask you two questions?'

'You can ask. I won't necessarily answer.'

'When you arrived in anatomy class on May first, the day I'm interested in, who else was there?'

'Okay. What's the other question?'

'Where were you at 5.30 a.m. that morning?'

'In bed. I have an alibi, if that's what you mean. Richard can confirm that.'

'What about Harry? Can he confirm it, too?'

'I only need one person.'

'But Richard said you all went out the night before, to a stag party. You went to a club. You all had hangovers when you arrived in class.'

'Yeah. That's right.'

'So why can't Harry say where you were at 5.30 a.m.?'

'I'll answer your first question now. When we got there —'

'"We" is you and Richard?'

'When I got there, I can't remember who was there. Apart from that Czech bloke. He's always first. If he hadn't been there, I'd have noticed. There were maybe two or three others. And now I'm going. No more questions.'

He put his helmet on, as if to stop himself hearing any more. But I didn't say a thing.

Warren's motorbike was very large and, when he rode away, very loud and fast.

I immediately called Harry, who answered.

'This is Kumiko Ozu. I just spoke with Warren. Please don't hang up.'

His breathing stayed on the line.

'Can I ask you a question?'

'What did Warren say to you?'

'He came to see me. He gave me some useful answers. You can ask him about it.'

'We didn't do anything.'

'On April thirtieth, you went on a stag night.'

'Is that the question?'

'No. The question is: Where did you sleep that night?'

There was a pause before he said, 'That's none of your business.'

'Warren told me you didn't go back to your flat.'

'So what?'

'Warren told me you met a very attractive woman.'

He could not resist boasting. 'She was pretty fit, yeah.'

'Did you stay with her?'

'I might have done.'

'Were you with her at 5.30 a.m.?'

'Maybe.'

'Did you go home before you went to Guy's?'

'You said one question. That's all I have to say. We had nothing to do with it.'

'Where did you meet her?'

But he had already hung up.

Next, I called Maurice Kavanagh back, and he agreed to have lunch with me the following day. We would meet just outside the lecture hall.

Anne returned a little later.

'He hasn't called yet. I expected him to call.'

My dream had brought Skelton near the front of my mind. I was not surprised by what Anne said.

'He's still scared. You will have to wait. I am sure he will call you before Friday.'

'I'm not bothered,' said Anne. 'I just thought you should know.'

'He will call.'

*

Jo came back in the middle of the afternoon.

'I thought this might interest you,' she said, after knocking on the door of my room.

In her hand was an A4 poster.

'King Death's annual lecture. Rescheduled. He's just had me pinning them up all over the place.'

'Thank you,' I said, and put it to one side. 'You spoke to Richard, didn't you?'

'Tried to.'

'Warren came here afterwards.'

'He didn't?'

I explained what had happened. Jo told me that Warren had overheard her speaking to Richard Lawrence and had dragged him away.

'What about Pavel Smid?'

'I managed to get a hello out of him. That's about all. Then he rushed off to do more studying, like always.'

I asked Jo for a copy of her timetable. She was happy to give me it.

King Death's lecture looked interesting.

In the evening, Paul White called me on my cellphone. When I saw it was him I did not pick up. He left a message, sounding disappointed. 'I'll try you again,' he said.

Pavel Smid was first out of class, two minutes after the hour. I saw no point trying to speak to him. He hurried away towards his Brixton bus.

Jo came a few seconds later and confirmed who it had been.

Roger Dervish said to both of us, 'Oh, hello,' but did not stop.

I asked Jo to leave, which she did.

Warren Glaister pretended to ignore me, keeping two others who I guessed were Richard Lawrence and Harry Lord close beside him.

I made eye-contact with Richard before he was hustled away.

As he floated past me, Maurice Kavanagh looked like a dirty English ghost.

His suit was off-white but had started, once upon a time, as brilliant. Its knees were gray, and one of the legs had a rip at the bottom. The palest thing about him was his face, apart from the Panda eyes of raw red. His hands, too, were red.

I recognized him because he looked like he often texted people at 3.30 a.m. None of the other students did.

I said his name. The ghost turned around.

'We are having lunch.'

'Are we?' he said. 'Oh, yes, I suppose we are.'

I guided him towards Borough High Street.

'Is there anywhere you would like?' I asked.

'I don't care. It's not as if I'm going to eat anything.'

We went to a small greasy spoon with wooden walls. I ordered bacon and eggs. Maurice ordered a green salad – 'for appearance's sake' – and a double espresso.

'You called me very often,' he said, speaking floaty, as if he were remembering a past life. 'Why?'

I told him about the heart. He seemed almost interested.

'So you're on a quest for justice?'

'For truth.'

'Ah. That's much better. I like truth. Justice I prefer to avoid. Too much to lose.'

We talked a little. Our food arrived.

I asked Maurice where he was at 5.30 a.m. on May the first.

'I simply have no idea.'

'It was the morning Paul White was arrested.'

'No. Nothing's coming. I'm sorry. My mind's not what it was, and it was never up to much.'

'They discovered the heart was missing from a body.'

'From Pandora. Yes, I remember that.'

'Do you remember arriving that day? Were you early?'

'Sorry. I really can't help.'

I decided to try something different.

'When you arrive at anatomy class —'

'If I arrive, these days.'

'When you do, who is usually there?'

'I'm always late.'

'Pavel Smid.'

'Who?'

'He is the top student. He is Czech.'

'Oh, him. Yes, he's always there. Swot.'

Maurice drank his coffee down in one and looked around to order another.

'What about Richard Lawrence?'

'Now you've really stumped me.'

'He's friends with Harry Lord and Warren Glaister.'

'And King Zog of Albania. No. It means nothing.'

'Roger Dervish?' I asked, with despair.

'Ah, Roger,' he said. 'Roger's my specialist subject. Hang on a minute. Yes. I'm getting something. Roger wanted me to be late. I arrived, and nobody was in their usual place because they were all crowded round Pandora.'

'Why did Roger want you to be late?'

Maurice caught the waitress's attention, and gestured for another cup. When he looked back at me, his eyes were empty of meaning. I repeated the question.

'Well, because he didn't want to be seen with me, of course.'

'Why?'

'Oh, don't be coy.'

'You are having an affair?'

'I'd hardly call it that. No. He said he was curious about the sort of clubs I go to. So …' Maurice smiled more brightly than I'd seen before.

I made my look a question.

'So, I took him to some. Poor little love. Bit of an eye-opener for him.'

'You were with him at 5.30 a.m.?'

'I know where he was at 5.30 a.m. Roughly. He wasn't up to any mischief. Well, he was. But not the sort you're worrying about.'

'He didn't go home, that night?'

'No. But he scuttled off as soon as class was cancelled.'

The waitress brought Maurice's coffee.

'But I didn't order this,' he said.

18.

Right from first thing Monday, there had been a chance I'd bump into Anne at Guy's. But, taking the train down early on Wednesday evening, I became preoccupied with the thought that I must at all costs avoid her. There was no logical reason for my worry increasing – Anne was far less likely to be around overnight than during the day. Yet while I was putting on my Porter's uniform, I couldn't stop myself picturing Anne's reaction to unexpectedly seeing me wearing it. Kumiko mustn't know what I was up to – and if Anne found out then she would tell Kumiko straight off. They seemed to share a lot of things.

I went down to the Porterage to wait for Mr Nicholas Rider, who I guessed would be Nick to everyone but Wally.

The monkey-faced woman behind the desk was a bit more friendly than before – perhaps because I was wearing the uniform, or perhaps because I had the ID badge. We exchanged a few words about the coolish weather, then I decided I could risk asking about Wally.

'His father,' she said. 'Very sad. But he was almost a hundred. Wally'll be back tomorrow. Didn't want any longer.'

That was all she knew. I sat down and leafed through a two-day-old tabloid. The pop singer was featured, in the gossip columns. He had come out of a nightclub wearing a padded bra as earmuffs.

It was only when I'd lost interest in the paper that I looked up at the noticeboard. The poster with the skull cartoon had been removed, but in its place was an almost identical one advertising a rescheduled talk by Dr Speed – Monday evening at 7 p.m. The venue was the Tower Lecture Theatre on the very top floor of the main building. I wasn't on twilight shift; I could easily make it.

I thought for a while about Wally. Perhaps his eccentric manner could be explained by intense suppressed grief for his father. Although I had no proof, I didn't think it likely.

Fifteen minutes late, Nick – who introduced himself as Nick – arrived, smelling strongly of fags.

'Smoke?' he said.

'No,' I said.

'You do now. It's the only way to get a decent break around here. Right, let's go. See you, Barbara.'

That was the monkey-faced woman behind the desk.

'What-uh you done?' Nick asked, as soon as we were out of the office. He made it sound like I was his new cell-mate in prison.

I gave him a rundown of what Wally had shown me.

'Been to Pathology?'

I shook my head, not wanting to make the mistake of appearing eager.

'We'll try and sort you out, then. You're not a real Porter till you've done that.'

But we were called straight away to something else – something that was already routine for me: twisted ankle needing to be wheelchaired over for an X-ray.

I was halfway across A&E before I realized the person we were heading towards, described by the Nurse as 'young Chinese woman in the far corner', was Kumiko. I had taken her identity in only after seeing that the young Chinese woman had a really nasty bruise on her forehead – like someone had whacked her with a crowbar. My instinct, of course, was to rush over and make sure she was alright, but I had to suppress this: I couldn't let her discover I was working here. Certainly not in front of Nick, who could be anyone – who would tell everyone.

'You do this,' I said to Nick, turning my back towards Kumiko. 'I'll see you in fifteen – meet you outside.'

I meant the Designated Smoking Area.

'What?' he said.

'I'll tell you later,' I said, and hurried to the lifts.

The first to arrive happened to be empty and heading up. I pressed the button for the floor of our locker room.

When Nick met me outside, he was full of curiosity. 'Explain,' he said.

I gave him part of the truth: Kumiko was an ex I really didn't want to see.

'Seemed pretty fit to me. Why'd you dump her?'

'Oh, you know,' I said, feeling a horrifying glee. 'Got bored, didn't I? She took it really badly. Still wants me back.'

'And you didn't need any grief today. Gotcha.' Nick punched me gently in the arm. 'It's always the quiet ones,' he said. I realized that, because of my lie, we'd just bonded.

'Still,' he added. 'I'd like a bit of takeaway myself. Know what I mean. Meals on wheels.'

'What happened to her head?'

'Didn't say. Didn't really speak to her.'

I wasn't sure I entirely believed this. Nick spoke to everyone. I didn't press it, though. That would have been suspicious. There wasn't much time to think about Kumiko, however. It was a busy shift. Almost immediately, we were called to the site of a recent arrest. The curtains were drawn around the bed, halfway along a geriatric ward. Eyes followed us, although the lights were out. A Nurse appeared from nowhere to help. The old man lying in the bed was a dead old man. His false teeth were in a glass on the table. We had a trolley with us, and Nick took the head end. 'Just sling him across,' he said, making no attempt to keep his voice down.

With three of us, it wasn't difficult. The dead man was hardly anything more than dry bones. No rigor mortis, not yet. He sagged in the middle.

Nick and the Nurse covered the body with a sheet. My hands felt different, having touched the man's cold, hairy ankles.

'Off we go,' said Nick. 'See you,' he said to the Nurse. I think he winked.

Nick pushed the trolley to the nearest lifts. Pathology was in the basement.

'Go on a fag break after this, eh?' Nick said. 'Get some fresh air. You look like you need it.'

I thought I was doing pretty well. He was just using me as an excuse.

A lift arrived. We got in and went down.

There were two Pathologists in the basement room.

'We've got a new Porter for you,' Nick announced, as we rolled in. He told them my name was Skeleton; I explained that it wasn't. They introduced themselves.

The first Pathologist, Raymond France, was tall and good-looking in a slightly foppish way. It was hard to guess his age. Perhaps thirty-two. He came over, peeled off one latex glove and shook my hand. Then he put the glove back on and returned to his cadaver – which was the thing I was trying not to focus on.

Vic Goosen, the second and more senior Pathologist, shouted his own name without looking up.

'Come on,' said Nick. 'Be a bit more friendly like.'

Vic Goosen looked up and said hello. Aged anywhere between forty and sixty, he was, without doubt, the ugliest creature I'd seen outside of a horror movie. Yellow teeth and eyes. Greasy grey hair hanging down over a zitty T-zone. The most extraordinary thing was his nose, which looked just like a strawberry. At first I couldn't be sure that it wasn't actually bleeding, so red and wet did it appear. But this was just context. There was plenty of context.

'Skelton's never seen a dead one before,' said Nick.

'Really?' said Goosen, already back at squelchy work. 'How *interesting*, Nicholas.'

'Actually, I have,' I said. 'My grandfather.'

'Bet he didn't look like *that*,' said Nick, and pointed at France's cadaver. I could no longer avoid the sight of it. The face had been peeled back, revealing the shiny grey-white of the skull. France, I think, had been on the point of sawing this open when we walked in.

'You don't seem like the Porter-type,' said France.

'What's that meant to mean?' asked Nick.

'I'm a musician, most of the time,' I said, deciding not to lie too much. 'But, you know how it is …'

'What do you play?' asked Goosen, looking up again.

'Guitar.'

'Classical?'

'No.'

At which point, he appeared entirely to lose interest in me.

As it was obvious I wasn't going to be sick or faint, Nick didn't want to hang around any longer.

'Fag break,' he said. Then, to Goosen, 'Are you coming for one?'

'No, no,' Goosen replied, irritated. 'I quit.'

'Since when?'

'Since I quit,' said Goosen.

Nick stood for a moment, trying and failing to work up something sarcastic.

As we left, he said, 'Used to be the heaviest of everyone. Be out there all the time, chugging away. Don't know what's got into him.'

I could tell that Nick felt morally let down. We walked up the stairs to the ground floor and then out to what they called the Designated Smoking Area.

I was slowly getting used to the sight of men in pyjamas, but not yet to the sight of them outside, smoking, in what looked like a garage.

Also standing there was Mr Fine, wife-killer. Nick spoke to him – he seemed to know and be on good terms with everyone, though he'd only worked at Guy's for just over six months.

As we were coming outside, Nick had handed me a cigarette. I was intending not to smoke it but a patient offered me a light; to refuse would be suspicious if not bizarre.

I did my best impression of a smoker, learnt during my early days with Kumiko – before I persuaded her to give up.

The patient, wearing stripy pyjamas, started to talk to me about what was wrong with him: cancer of the eye. He was about the same age as me.

'But they're treating it,' I said.

'Oh yes,' the patient replied. 'They're treating it.'

'Is the treatment working?' I asked.

'No,' he said, then added, 'I never used to smoke before, but now I think, *why not*? Fuck 'em, you know. Fuck 'em.'

Nick eventually finished his conversation with Mr Fine.

'Come on,' he said.

We walked towards the lifts.

'If you want my advice,' he said, 'don't talk to the patients out there. It's the only break from them you have – and they're not exactly gonna cheer you up, are they?'

Like Wally, Nick had his own brand of wisdom.

Nothing much else happened. Just before we went off shift, Nick asked me if I played poker. Now, you don't spend as much time around musicians as I do without picking up a working knowledge of most vices.

'A little,' I said.

'Interested in a game, now and then?'

'Sure.'

'I'll see what the gang says.'

After those first few days working at Guy's, I realized that I had gone in without much of a plan. My general idea had been to investigate anything that seemed suspicious – anything, that is, relating to Paul White.

In this, perhaps naively, I hadn't counted on being told, at the start of my very first shift, that so-and-so was a murderer.

I didn't want to waste time on something completely unconnected to the heart. But Mr Fine was definitely suspicious. And, as Head of Security, he would have had some involvement with Paul White's case – even if only as the man whose cameras recorded many of the hospital's goings-on.

I decided that I would put most of my efforts into finding out about the heart. Who could have stolen it? Why? However, if a chance to learn something more about Mr Fine came up, I might as well take it.

Before the end of shift on Wednesday night, around 2 a.m., I asked Nick, as casually as possible, about Paul White. We were strolling down towards where the patients' records were kept. I didn't mention Paul White's name, just said, 'That thing that happened recently, with that heart getting stolen.'

'That?' said Nick. 'That's nothing. Stuff like that happens all the time. It's medical students, innit?'

'But surely you can't just walk out of here with a body part in your bag.'

'I could walk out of here with a fucking MRI scanner, mate. Any time. Just sort it with Security and you're laughing.'

'Sort it?'

'Yeah, they like a cut. But they're not greedy.'

I knew he was being serious.

'But that student didn't sort it, did he?'

'No. Probably just stuffed it in his bag, like wot you said. Pretty stupid. Must've been trying to get himself kicked out.'

'Why?'

'Well, I dunno, do I?'

Conversation over.

When Nick spoke again, it was about poker.

'Yeah, they're happy for you to join in. We play evenings, after dayshift's over. I'll let you know next time we've got a game going.'

'Great,' I said. Enthusiasm seemed necessary.

I tried to sleep during the day on Thursday, without much success.

The main thing that kept me awake was Kumiko. What kind of danger had she been putting herself in? Was she safe now? The obvious way to find out was to call Anne. But I couldn't do that without giving away that I knew Kumiko was living with her. And then I'd have to explain how I came to find out.

Also, to call Anne was to *call Anne* – and that meant deciding what I was going to do about her. If I wasn't going to see her again, I needed to tell her that. But if I was intending to accept the gift, I should make a date. Either way, I should call.

I didn't call.

I didn't call Anne – I called Grzegorz instead.

'Have you spoken to Kumiko recently?'

'Hi. How are you? I'm fine?'

'Have you spoken to her?'

'No.'

'So you don't know if she's okay or not?'

'I think I would have heard if she wasn't. How are you?'

'Oh, fine. Could you get in touch with her? I need to know she's –'

'You sound upset. Why do you think anything's happened?'

'I don't know. I just do.'

He agreed to speak to her. I was pretty sure that she wouldn't see anything but coincidence in him phoning her that night. It didn't matter. I had to be sure she wasn't seriously hurt.

'What are you up to?'

I told Grzegorz about the pop singer, then got off the phone as fast as I could.

He texted me half an hour later.

'Kumiko all okay. Don't worry.'

But I couldn't stop myself.

Wally returned to work for the nightshift. I could see no change in him, after the funeral.

'I was very sorry to hear about your father,' I said.

'So was I,' Wally replied.

'How was the funeral?'

'Short.'

During one of our trips along to collect patients' medical records, I had an idea. It might be worthwhile having a look at Mrs Fine's file, to see if anyone really had suspected murder. The Clerk down there most of the time was called Jeff Davis – although Nick, and quite a few of the rest of the staff, used his nickname: Jabba. He was quite fat. With a little long-term planning starting to emerge, I began to pay attention to the mechanics of file storage and retrieval. I also tried to become friendly with Jabba – who seemed delighted that someone had finally shown enough interest in his work to ask a question.

'Oh, the records here go back to just before the Second World War. You wouldn't believe the stuff we've got here – some of it still fire-damaged from –'

'Thank you, Mr Davis,' said Wally. 'But we must be going.'

Once we were out of earshot, Wally said, 'If you waste too much time down there, you will be disciplined.

Mr Davis is slightly mad. I think the loneliness drove him mad a long time ago.'

When it came time for our first break, Wally took me back to the locker room. Here, he lay down on one of the benches and fell immediately asleep. He snored loudly, more loudly than he spoke. I anticipated having to wake him up, so deeply asleep did he seem. But after exactly quarter of an hour he opened his eyes and asked if I felt refreshed.

'A little,' I said, although his snoring had made me tense.

'You should have a nap, also. It is the best way to survive.'

Two people died that night at Guy's – or, at least, Wally and I were called upon to take two bodies down to Pathology.

Raymond France was there, but not – I was glad to see – Vic Goosen. The idea of him alone among the corpses at 2 a.m. was not appealing.

Having failed with Nick, I now tried asking Wally about Paul White.

'It was a terrible thing,' he said. I thought for a moment he meant the wrong person being blamed, but then he continued: 'To steal the heart of someone. To throw it from a train. Terrible. That person must be mad.'

'You mean Paul White. He must be mad.'

'Whoever did it is a madman.'

'But you *do* think the Police got the right person?'

This was the first time I'd ever seen him hesitate.

'I am not sure. I know nothing about it.'

'You suspect something was wrong?'

'I suspect ... I suspect nothing. If it was not Mr White, he would make more noise of his innocence.'

'Tell me what you think happened.'

'Why are you interested?'

'I read about it in the papers, just before I applied for the job. Of course I'm interested to find out what happened.'

'Forget it. If you begin to suspect things here, you will go mad.'

Wally was mentioning madness too often for my liking. I had already shown too much interest in Paul White. Hopefully Wally would take his own advice, and not become suspicious.

When my shift ended at 8 a.m., I was free until Monday morning.

I slept in until the afternoon. It was time to call Anne, so I texted her instead. I apologized for not getting in touch sooner – been very busy, I said. Shall we speak tomorrow?

'He-*llo*,' she said, when I eventually called on Saturday.

I had dialled with the intention of explaining myself out of her life. The message was *I still love Kumiko, please tell her this, don't ask me how I know you know her, goodbye.* Instead, I found myself suggesting dinner on the Thursday. (I was on dayshift Monday and then nightshift Tuesday and Wednesday.) This was a slight retreat from our previous dates, and especially from her seeing me play live. Maybe Anne would get the subliminal message. She didn't sound disappointed, however.

'I've been thinking a lot about the music,' she said.

'That's good.'

'I'd like to hear some more.'

'I'll do some for you,' I said, not so much falling into the trap as stagediving into it. This *had* to be a trap. Kumiko knew I couldn't resist putting together compilations.

I didn't do much for the rest of Saturday, or Sunday, either. It had been quite a while since I'd done what most people would call 'a proper job'. Portering was very hard work, physically but most of all emotionally. In the past week, I'd seen more death than in my whole life up till then. I was sure it had changed me, I just didn't know how.

19.

Jo's timetable showed anatomy on Wednesday morning and physiology in the afternoon.

I wanted to speak to Roger Dervish and Richard Lawrence, but waiting for them outside class wouldn't work. They were too timid. I must get them alone, where no-one would see them talking to me. So, instead, I waited outside at 4 p.m. for Pavel Smid. I waited just round the corner, where I could not be seen.

It was a bright day but cold.

Pavel Smid hurried out through the lecture hall doors at 4.02 p.m. When he turned towards Borough High Street, I followed him.

The route he took was through a small alley. It brought him out close to the bus-stop.

He waited for a Brixton bus.

As soon as he got on, I did too. He went to sit upstairs, by the window, in an empty seat. I went and sat next to him. The upper deck was half full. I waited until the bus was moving, and then said, 'My name is Kumiko Ozu. Please talk to me. It is important.'

Pavel Smid's reaction was shocking. I felt his whole body turn to angry muscle. He looked at me with eyes of horror and then pushed me off, as hard as he could.

I fell sideways, hitting the seat opposite. My left temple struck the seatback and my ribs the corner of the seat itself.

Pavel Smid stood up, treading on my ankle. I knew he did not mean this. He was trying to escape as quickly as possible. His foot slipped to the floor, and he was away.

Two people helped pick me up.

'Are you hurt?' they asked.

I said I was fine, thank you, although I could feel a large bruise beginning on my forehead.

The bus had not gone far.

I hobbled to the stairs and began to hop down them. It was impossible to tell whether my ankle was broken or not. There was some pain.

Reaching downstairs, I saw Pavel Smid waiting beside the doors.

'Why are you scared?' I asked.

He ignored me, trying to make all the passengers think he didn't know me, and that I was mad.

I moved closer to him.

'You know it wasn't Paul,' I said, in a reasonable tone of voice.

He looked at me again. This time his eyes were full not of horror but of pity. I could not tell who the pity was for.

Next, the bus came to a halt, still not at the stop.

Pavel Smid flipped back the translucent cover of a large red button directly over the doors. When he pressed the button, the doors opened.

'Please talk to me,' I said.

But he was already running.

I stayed on the bus until the next stop. The traffic was heavy so it took five minutes. By this time Pavel Smid was a kilometre away, at least.

There was a dull pain in my ankle which got sharp when I tried to use it. I decided to go back to the hospital.

People looked at me curiously as I hopped along the street.

I took the same shortcut Pavel Smid had unknowingly shown me, and after ten painful minutes was in A&E.

The receptionist asked some questions then told me to sit down and wait.

Half an hour later, my number came up and I saw a male nurse. At first he was more concerned about my head than my ankle. The bruise was the size and shape of my little finger. It ran from my hairline to just above my eyebrow. I told him I had not lost consciousness and did not feel dizzy.

After gently touching my ankle, he said I would have to wait at least two hours for an X-ray.

He was an optimist.

I went from the examination room back into A&E.

A porter came with a wheelchair and took me to another department. He was very inquisitive, but I did not want to talk. 'Do you know anyone who works in this hospital?' he asked. A strange question. I said I didn't.

I waited three and a half hours before they saw me.

The ankle was not broken.

I took a taxi home.

'Oh my God,' said Jo, when I knocked on the door of her room. 'What happened to you?'

I told her everything.

'How strange,' she said. 'Pavel doesn't seem the violent type. He's so quiet and shy.'

'He isn't violent. He is scared to death.'

I hadn't eaten anything since lunch, and I found I was very hungry. From one of the leaflets in the kitchen I ordered a Chinese. When it arrived, I ate it at the kitchen table. My head was very full of thoughts.

Paul White called, but I let him leave a message. He said he wanted to see me again. I did not call back.

The Keats biography arrived first post on Thursday. I carried it upstairs while Jo followed with a breakfast tray.

My ankle felt worse. It had swollen, and I could not put my full weight on it.

I sat in bed and read the chapters about Keats at Guy's. There was more information about Astley Cooper, the first King Death – or so I had thought. I soon realized that I should not have trusted the internet.

Astley Cooper was an inspiring man, an 'idol' to the medical students. In 1792 he had been in Paris, where he heard Danton, Marat and Robespierre speak to the National Assembly. He was a compassionate surgeon who was very helpful to Keats. He did not sound like he deserved King Death as a nickname.

On page 86, I read about the other lecturers. One of them, Joseph Henry Green, was anatomy demonstrator. Perhaps he and not Astley brought the killing power of the plague into Keats's mind?

But then, a few pages further, the biographer mentioned another man, the surgeon William Lucas Jr, with whom Keats worked every day. He was far from being an idol. His operations were 'very badly performed and accompanied by much bungling if not worse'.

I needed to look up the meaning of 'bungling'.

After I did, I realized that Keats was much more likely to have given the name King Death to Lucas than to Green or Astley – who said of Lucas that he was 'neat-handed but rash in the extreme, cutting amongst most important parts as though they were only skin, and making us all shudder from the apprehension of his opening arteries or committing some other horror'.

To make surgeons shudder in 1816 was not easy. These were men who operated on patients who were awake and without proper anaesthetics.

It seemed possible that neither Dr Speed nor Dr Norfolk had deserved the title by which they were known.

I was reading on when my phone rang. The time was 9.32 a.m.

'This is Pavel Smid. I am very sorry to hurt you. I hope you have not broken bones.'

'No. My ankle is sore but not broken.'

'That is very good news. Please do not follow me again. I cannot talk to you.'

'Why?'

'Because I cannot. Goodbye.'

I tried calling back the number immediately. It rang for a long time before anyone picked up.

'Pavel?'

'Who?'

'Is that Pavel Smid?'

'No. You got a payphone here now.'

'Sorry.'

When I checked with directories, the number was Brixton.

Another call came straight away, from a mobile.

'Pavel?'

'No, this is Richard Lawrence. I want to speak to you.'

'Good. I am listening.'

'In person. I'll come round. You live with Molly, don't you?'

'Yes.'

'Will you be in around lunchtime?'

I told him I would be in all day.

He arrived at 12.30 p.m. I was waiting for him on the hall floor. When he knocked, I answered then hopped through into the living room. He followed.

'I have nothing to hide,' he said, sitting down on the sofa. 'Warren is all paranoid about nothing. Guy's isn't spying on us. They're never going to find out if we speak to you or not.'

'I agree. But you were frightened before. Why?'

'Warren. He gets in a total state about everything. He's such a fucking girl. Sorry.'

I asked him my constant question: Where were you at 5.30 a.m. on the first?

He told me exactly the same as Warren.

'And where was Harry Lord?'

'Him? He was knobbing some stripper he picked up at the club.'

'Which club?'

'I don't think it has a name. It's in Soho. It's just a door. Warren found out about it.'

'What's the address?'

He didn't know. But he described exactly where it was.

'Harry met her at the club?'

'Yeah. I'm pretty sure she works there. Why are you interested?'

'She is his alibi. I must prove the heart was not thrown out of the train by a student.'

'When I called just now, you thought I was Pavel ...'

'He spoke to me a moment earlier. When you arrived at class on the first, was Pavel there?'

'Oh yes. He's always early.'

'What about Roger Dervish?'

'You mean Roger-Me-Silly? Roger the Closet? Yes, now you mention it. I'm not a hundred per cent sure, but I think I can picture him there, looking furtive. His corpse is a man. I think he might be in love with it.'

'Who else was there?'

'Well, Harry. He was waiting outside for us.'

'So you did not go in?'

'No. Harry wanted to tell us about what he'd been up to. In graphic detail.'

'But you are sure Pavel was there?'

'He was when we went in. And he didn't sneak past us. We were right by the door.'

Jo returned and Richard left shortly afterwards.

'Did he tell you anything useful?' she asked.

'Yes.'

Grzegorz called to ask me how I was. He said he had been worried, it had been too long since he'd heard anything from me.

I told him I was fine, then told him I had almost broken my ankle. As soon as he heard this, he insisted on coming to see me.

'Okay. But only if you promise not to tell Skelton where I am.'

'I promise.'

'And not today. On Sunday. It will give me something to look forward to.'

'How did it happen?'

'I'll tell you on Sunday.'

Because of my ankle, I was stuck in bed Friday and all weekend. A house full of medical students told me to keep my foot elevated, and I obeyed them. But I did not waste time. And they looked after me with cups of tea.

The biography was a long book for such a short life, six hundred and thirty-six pages for twenty-five years. It is a simple thing, to die so young, that is what breaks the heart. I felt like I did after the death of my schoolfriend Toyo Sato. The book for him should have been longer. Toyo hung himself aged seventeen.

There was nothing more in the biography about Astley Cooper or William Lucas. I would have to look elsewhere. The bibliography included *The Life and Work of Astley Cooper*, published in 1846. I ordered a copy of this, but it was going to take two weeks to arrive.

Grzegorz arrived on Sunday at 12 p.m. bringing with him a wonderful selection of foods from Borough Market.

'What have you been up to?' he said. I told him it was very boring. Someone had pushed me when I was getting off a bus.

'Really?' he asked.

'Yes.'

We picnicked on the counterpane.

I described my investigations, but vaguely.

'So you still think he's innocent?'

'I am sure.'

'If he didn't do it, who did?'

'Someone who hated him.'

'Another student?'

'I am finding out.'

It was good to see Grzegorz. He made me remember the happy past. I wanted him to tell me a little about Skelton. Not much. Just that his life continued.

'Any good?' Grzegorz asked, picking up the Keats biography.

'He is now my favourite person, ever.'

Before he left, Grzegorz told me sternly to phone him at least once a week.

On Sunday afternoon, I called Roger Dervish.

'Not again,' he said.

'I am sorry but I need to ask you some more questions.'

'Why? I've told you everything.'

I could not say that he hadn't. And if he knew that I knew about him and Maurice, he might not speak to me ever again.

'I can meet you after your lecture on Monday afternoon,' I said. 'It won't take long.'

He sighed.

'Please. It will be the last time, I promise.'

'Alright,' he said.

We arranged to meet in the same little café I went to with Maurice Kavanagh. I liked this detail.

Paul White called me, for a third time, on Sunday evening. I picked up.

'You're an elusive one, aren't you? So, can I see you again?'

'Of course. But you have had your kiss, remember that.'

'Maybe,' he said. 'Maybe not.'

'Not.'

'Tonight?'

'No. I have sprained my ankle –'

'We can just go to a restaurant.'

'Yes, afterwards. First, I have a different idea. Do you know Soho?'

We were to meet on Tuesday evening. I hoped by then my ankle would be okay for short distances. It already felt better, going up and down the stairs.

I spent Sunday evening talking with Jo in her room. She was a very tidy person. I admired the way she ironed and folded all her clothes. She could live without trouble in a Tokyo apartment. These are measured in tatami mats, the word for which is '*jo*'.

Jo helped me by suggesting motives for my three remaining suspects.

'Harry Lord?'

'With him it would just be a stupid prank, nothing worse. He likes pranks. But if it got serious, I can't see him keeping silent – not if it meant someone being expelled. Especially as he liked Paul quite a lot.'

'And if he thought he would be expelled for telling the truth?'

'Then maybe, I suppose. His pranks are usually more on the level of pulling someone's trousers down. He's a coward who wants to be a bully.'

'What about Pavel Smid?'

'The enigmatic Pavel. Well, maybe being number one

is the most important thing in his life. There is a prize for the top student. They give it out at Christmas. He came second this year. To Paul. Maybe that was a good enough reason. It's hard to see. Throwing a heart out of a train window – it's a bit of an extreme thing to do. Quite macabre. And if he were caught doing the slightest thing wrong, I'm sure they'd send him straight back home.'

'And Roger Dervish?'

'No idea. Unless you go along with Molly's suggestion that he's gay.'

'Molly isn't alone.'

'Is he definitely gay?' Jo looked stunned.

'He is confused,' I said. 'But curious.'

'Well, well.'

'Did he talk to Paul much?'

'They were friendly but they weren't what I'd call friends.'

'Do you think he had a crush on Paul?'

'I'm really the wrong person to ask. I didn't even know … I didn't … If he doesn't …' Jo was embarrassed.

20.

I arrived early and took a seat at the very back of the Tower Lecture Theatre. As far as possible, I wanted to avoid being noticed by Dr Speed. The room was large, but not as large as the building's bulky exterior might have suggested.

The seats began slowly to fill – although with five minutes to go, the place remained half empty.

Then Kumiko walked in, on her own. I wondered for a moment whether this was for my benefit – that she had suspected I might be there, too, and had not wanted to be seen with any of her housemates.

She sat down in the second row, without, as far as I could tell, spotting me. It looked as if she were limping, but only slightly. The bruise on her forehead was still a harsh black stripe.

Grzegorz had called early on Sunday evening to tell me he'd seen Kumiko and that she really was fine.

'She had an accident, though,' he said. 'Fell over getting off a bus. Twisted her ankle. Had to go to hospital.'

'What about her head?' I didn't say it out loud, but I only just stopped myself. 'Which bus?' I said instead. A really stupid question.

I didn't believe it, her explanation. What was interesting was that she had felt the need to lie to Grzegorz, her best friend. She really was isolating herself completely.

'Can't you tell me anything about how she is?'

'Not really. Oh, she's reading about Keats.'

'Reading what?'

He told me about the big fat biography he had seen by her bedside.

I went and ordered it as soon as we said goodbye.

Dr Speed came into the lecture room dead on the hour, then sat waiting in the front row. He was a tall man but his shoulders were stooped, with a clearly shaven head and old-fashioned spectacles.

A few stragglers arrived, mostly students, bringing the audience up to a respectable size.

One of the senior hospital managers, Barry Waddham, took the podium in order to explain who he was and then to thank the sponsors. I recognized their company name from a cardboard box I'd helped Wally lug from one end of the hospital to another. They were big in pain relief. Then Barry Waddham began his introduction of Dr Speed. Although he had only been running the department since October, in the wake of Dr Norfolk's 'sudden and unexpected' departure, he had already made a strong impression – which wasn't in any way to criticize his predecessor's etcetera. Hopefully, Dr Speed's success had now put to rest any of the remaining controversy about the appointment of someone from outside the department. We look forward to a fascinating and informative talk.

Applause followed.

Two students, hunched over as if in a cinema, crept through the door and hurried to sit down. Dr Speed waited until they'd finished shuffling. It was Molly and Jo.

'Thank you. In 1971, the avant-garde film-maker Stan Brakhage released a film called *Autopsy: The Act of Seeing with One's Own Eyes*. And "the art of seeing with one's own eyes" is, in fact, a remarkably accurate translation of the word "autopsy". And to allow our students, some of whom are here this evening, to see with *their* own eyes *inside* the human body is …'

Dr Speed was perhaps the most charmless speaker I'd ever heard. It was as if the audience weren't there at all. When he looked up, it was over our heads. His voice was monotonous and his sentences repetitive.

I looked towards Kumiko. I was moved by the sight of her, in a way I hadn't been outside the hospital. When you're going out with someone, you rarely see them at a medium distance for any great length of time. The moment you spot them, you have to go up and make physical contact. If you don't, and you get caught spying, you can end up looking very creepy indeed. Not that I ever had …

What moved me most of all was Kumiko's vulnerability. Her injuries had exaggerated this, but there was something deeper, too. It wasn't that I was assessing her, it was that this was the distance at which others, who didn't know her, would assess her. She seemed smaller than I remembered her – smaller and less fierce. Our last scene, outside the court, had been fairly intense.

Dr Speed talked about how seeing the *Autopsy* film as a first-year medical student had caused him to specialize in the teaching of Anatomy. 'For what higher calling can there be for a doctor than to train other doctors?' No-one shouted out 'Curing cancer', though many must have thought it.

I tried hard not to tune out. My hands rooted through my pockets, searching for distraction. They brought out a folded piece of paper. It was a note I'd found wedged into my locker door halfway through that day's shift. 'Game tonight. Nine o'clock. Deal you in?' A room number and directions followed.

Forty minutes later, Dr Speed concluded: '… and these are the six main reasons we have, or, rather, *I* have, for wishing to continue the practice of hands-on dissection rather than moving completely to a computer-based teaching method. To summarize: there is simply no replacement for the act of seeing with one's own eyes. Thank you.'

There was louder applause than before.

'Are there any questions now?'

Kumiko, as somehow I'd known she would, put her hand up.

Dr Speed pointed a long finger towards her, apparently ignorant of who she was or what she was likely to ask.

'One of your students was expelled recently for stealing a body part from your department.'

Quick as anything, Barry Waddham was on his feet.

'Are you a journalist?' he asked Kumiko.

'No,' she replied.

'We have said all we have to say, on this matter.'

'Yes, but has Dr Speed said all he has to say?' Kumiko asked.

'I think so,' said Waddham, then turned round to look at Dr Speed – who was obviously furious at not being left to deal with this himself. It made it look as if he were being protected, and that made him look as if he had something to hide. He lifted his beaklike nose and asked, 'What exactly is your question?' I liked him more, immediately.

Kumiko said, 'If evidence is found that someone else stole the heart, will you let Paul White continue his studies?'

'Of course,' said Dr Speed. 'Although the decision wouldn't be mine. It would have to go through the usual procedures. But I'm sure, under those circumstances, he would be readmitted. Under those circumstances.'

'The Police are satisfied that it couldn't have been anyone else,' said Waddham. 'I was personally involved in this matter, and I can assure you a mistake hasn't been made.'

'It has,' said Kumiko, quietly but everyone heard.

Waddham looked very awkward, as if he expected Kumiko to begin a tirade. I knew there was no chance of that. She had what she wanted, a public promise on Paul White's future, should our investigation be successful. And Dr Speed's reply had been very carefully phrased. Unlike Waddham, he wasn't ruling out the possibility of a mistake. He might even have been hinting that he believed one had taken place.

'Any more questions?' asked Waddham.

Several people put their hands up, including a purple-pony-tailed young goth sitting right in front of me. During the talk, I had counted thirteen piercings in his left ear.

Dr Speed pointed at him.

'How many people puke when they first see a dead body?'

Kumiko turned round to look at who was speaking – and caught sight of me. With no time to prepare myself, I reacted just as I would have done had we still been going out: I smiled.

I don't know what Kumiko thought, but she reacted immediately: she smiled back – a very simple smile, as if to say, 'Oh, hello.'

Then, after holding my gaze for only a moment longer, she turned her attention back to Dr Speed.

I found it difficult to concentrate on his answer. The gist of what he said was, *fewer than you might think*.

Barry Waddham, shifting in his seat, was whispering into a mobile phone.

The goth asked a follow-up question about final disposal of the bodies. Dr Speed answered that, where requested, all the material was kept together so that a burial could be performed. Otherwise, they were disposed of in the way of normal medical waste. 'But by that point, the students have learnt a very great deal from them.'

Several questions came from students, trying to make sure Dr Speed noted their presence.

About five minutes before the end, I saw Mr Fine and Kevin Knight slip in through the door – obviously summoned by Barry Waddham.

When exactly one hour was up, Dr Speed – without any warmth – thanked everyone for coming and stepped down from the platform.

Kumiko left without a backward glance, closely followed by Barry Waddham and, following him, Mr Fine and Kev.

I pushed my way out of the lecture room as quickly as I could, but there was no sign of Kumiko in the lift lobby – nor of Waddham and the security guards.

A couple of the students came close. I heard one of them say, 'Good old King Death, never lets you down.'

The other said, 'He's a robot.' Then put on a synthesized voice: '*I will dissect you.*'

Molly and Jo walked straight past me, too.

I hesitated a few moments then decided to go and wait outside the main entrance, where I couldn't be seen.

Kumiko eventually came out half an hour later, escorted by Mr Fine alone. He watched her safely off the premises. Then I watched her safely onto a number 35.

She took a back-route to Borough High Street, dark and narrow — one I would have hesitated to take on my own. Clearly, she hadn't been intimidated by whatever they'd said to her. Her limp was only very slight.

I returned to the hospital, and got a little lost trying to find the poker game. I couldn't believe it was really where the note said it was — room 305, which was the Dissecting Room. Nick was surely setting a trap for me. But when I opened the door, I saw a light on in a side office.

The Dissecting Room was chilly as I crossed it. The bodies lay under plastic sheets. I wanted to take a proper look around, but that would have been suspicious.

'Aha,' said Nick. 'Made it.'

All six chairs around the joined-together desks were occupied. Two computer monitors sat nearby on the floor.

'Ladies and gentlemen, let me introduce Skeleton, the new Porter.'

'Skelton,' I said.

'Bones,' said one of the men. I couldn't see his face.

A chair was fetched and room was made for me.

'This is Sasha Distress.' Nick gestured towards a man wearing a Nurse uniform. 'That's Claire the Loon and

Sally-up-the-Alley. Also Nurses. And he's Aragon the Arrogant, who lets us play here.'

'Simon,' said the man who had called me 'Bones'.

'And these are Phil-and-Bill, Bill-and-Phil.' Cleaners. 'We are playing No Limit Texas Hold 'Em. The blinds are currently at ...' He filled in the details.

I put my money on the table, although there were counters to play with. Nick's stash was biggest, then Simon's.

This first night, I intended just to watch and learn. After about ten hands, I thought I had their poker characters. Nick joked about all the time, using nicknames, exaggerating how bad his cards were, but, beneath all that, was a serious player – probably the best at the table. Sasha folded just about everything. Claire was also very cautious. Sally, by contrast, made lots of aggressive moves and would have bossed the game if it hadn't been for Simon, who wanted to be in almost every hand.

Mostly, I let the others slug it out among themselves. But then, after a run of trash, I was dealt two kings, and another came up on the flop. Everyone but Simon dropped out. So I ended up taking him on directly. He represented aces all through – and when the river card was an ace, I folded.

Laughing, Simon turned his cards over. A three and a seven, suited.

'Welcome to the Dissecting Room,' he said, smiling for the first time.

'You've gotta watch him,' said Nick. 'We don't call him Arrogant for nothing.'

After this, my stack was low. It ran out around eleven thirty. I made my excuses and left.

Walking through the real Dissecting Room, I looked around at what I suppose was the scene of the crime – where the heart had been stolen from, where Anne spent most of her days.

I made my way to London Bridge station and took the overland train home.

As we passed the roofs of Borough Market, I looked again at where the heart had been. So many things had changed, since then, three weeks ago, but so many were just the same.

The flat seemed more empty of Kumiko than ever before. I was surprised that she had gone all this time without needing any of her stuff – she had walked out with almost nothing.

Tuesday, I was on a nightshift.

By now, Wally had decided that he could trust me with some basic tasks. One of these, as it didn't involve contact with patients, was returning medical records to the library. Jabba wasn't there, and so the job consisted of putting the files on a trolley to be sorted the next morning. But, over the course of a couple of visits, I was able to have a quick look around. Security wasn't exactly tight. However, to get in to where the records were stored would involve breaking down a locked door. It seemed I'd have to find another way.

Wally would say nothing more on the subject of Paul White, although I tried gently to steer him in that direction. His main focus was training me not to be a Porter but to be a junior version of himself.

On my own, walking the quiet corridors, I thought of Kumiko. At such a late hour, she must be sleeping. It was reassuring to think of her safely in bed, a houseful of students around her.

Towards dawn, I began to lose sense of my own identity – and one or twice found myself speaking with a slightly Hollywood-Austrian accent.

We made several trips to Pathology – together; Wally would not let me go *there* alone. I could feel him observing my reactions closely, whenever we were around the corpses. I'm pretty sure he wouldn't have seen anything but a growing indifference. Vic Goosen was present, but ignored me completely. About all that could be said of his dealings with Wally were that they were impeccably efficient and almost totally monosyllabic.

'Here?'

'Yes.'

'Yes?'

'Yes.'

Although I liked Wally, I knew that I would have learnt a great deal more about the inner workings of Guy's had I been hanging out with Nick and the smokers.

My wish was to be granted, in quite a tragic way, the following evening.

21.

Roger Dervish was late for our Monday meeting. The café was not busy. I had started to think he wouldn't come.

'I won't sit down,' he said. 'I just want to say that if it's really all you're interested in, then, yes, I was with someone on the morning in question, and, yes, that person is the person you think it is, and I know who that is because he, they, told me they'd told you. Now, I don't want anyone else to hear about this.'

'They won't.'

'Good,' said Roger.

His face had started out beetroot, as if he had been holding his breath all the way from Guy's. It was now only pink.

'Please sit down.'

The effort of his speech had tired him out.

'Whatever you may think, I am not a troubled soul. I am perfectly secure in –'

'My closet,' said Maurice, appearing behind him. 'You certainly are.'

Roger gave him a look.

'Did you follow me?'

'Well, makes a change, doesn't it?'

Roger said, 'I am leaving.'

'Running away, just as usual,' Maurice said.

We watched him hurry out.

'He's so much more of a queen than I am, that's the biggest irony. He'd be such a big hit, and he's wasting so much time.'

'Please join me,' I said.

We talked about Roger's innocence.

I saw Skelton at King Death's lecture. I wondered how he had heard about it. I knew Anne had not told him. He looked well. Quite handsome, sitting at the back. His face seemed thinner.

The lecture was a boring fifty minutes. But I was able to ask the important question, and I got the answer I wanted.

King Death assured me, publicly, that Paul White would be accepted back on his course if evidence proved him innocent.

But the hospital was not happy that I asked anything so direct. Mr Barry Waddham, a self-important manager, came up to me afterwards and said he wanted a word. Although he was polite, he was accompanied by two security guards. They took me quickly into a small room nearby.

To begin with, Mr Waddham told me that he had seen me at the arraignment, and that he had made a note of me then. He went on to say that the police were quite certain of Paul White's guilt. Then his questions began:

'Could you tell me what your relationship is to Mr Paul White?'

'No.'

'Can you tell me why you are so interested in his case?'

'No.'

He became frustrated.

'Do you have any evidence regarding Mr White?'

'Yes.'

'Will you tell us what it is?'

'No.'

After more of this, he formally cautioned me against entering hospital buildings without prior permission, in writing, from him.

'What if I'm ill?' I asked.

'Get ill somewhere else,' he said.

Then they let me go.

The security guard who took me in the lift was an older man with an ugly face. His breath smelled of sweet mint and bad breath. He gripped my wrist tight enough to leave bruises the next day. As we walked down the corridors, he pointed out the CCTV cameras.

'If you try to cause any more trouble,' he said, 'we'll spot you. Remember that. I never forget a face. Especially a pretty one.'

After all that, he was still trying to flirt with me!

On Tuesday evening, Paul White met me outside Leicester Square tube station.

He tried to kiss me, on the lips. I reminded him of his promise.

We walked up towards Old Compton Street. Dinner first, then the club.

'Why are you limping?' Paul asked.

I told him what had happened.

'That's quite bad,' he said.

I didn't take his arm, although he offered.

'Have you seen Monica again?' I asked.

Paul was evasive, but I thought that he hadn't.

He looked much worse than before. His suit was the same, but crumpled and stained. He had shaved, badly.

We ate a cheap meal at an old-fashioned Italian restaurant called Presto. The tablecloths were red gingham. Paul didn't talk much.

A narrow staircase led down to the strip-club, painted in black gloss. I descended in front of Paul. Painfully, I took it one step at a time. He still didn't know where we were going, although he must have suspected.

A very thin woman was touching herself on a small stage. Her face was bloated and she had panda-eyes. She reminded me of Elvis Presley. The music was loud and electronic.

'What's this?' Paul asked.

I could tell he meant, What is your reason for bringing me here?

'Let's sit down.'

There was a free table right beside the stage. I felt no embarrassment. The dance was boring. I sat down.

As he moved around to the opposite chair, the stripper came close. Paul's mouth was at the exact height of her sex. He glanced sideways at it, then gave me a comic look. I had forgotten he was an ex-medical student. Anatomy was something droll to him.

'Tell me about Pandora,' I said, when he sat down. 'How did she die?'

'No idea. They don't tell us that sort of thing. Not unless there's something special to look out for. A fascinoma, they call it.'

'It wasn't a violent death?'

'If you want my professional opinion —' Paul said, then stopped. He realized the irony of his words, and that it was more bitter than intended. Perhaps he never would be a professional. 'She just died. People do. Doctors don't like to admit it, but anyone here could pop off at any moment. It doesn't matter if you're healthy.'

A waiter came over and tried to sell us champagne. His English was very bad, or he pretended it was. 'Champagne, yes?' That seemed to be the only sentence he knew.

'No,' said Paul. 'Red wine. House red.'

The waiter brought us a bottle of champagne, already opened, already flat. He poured it out into two wineglasses, then demanded payment.

'You've got to be joking,' said Paul.

The waiter walked away, and a big man with dark glasses came immediately out of the shadows.

I understood.

'It's okay,' I told Paul. 'Let me pay.'

'Is there a problem?' the big man asked.

'We would like a girl to join us,' I said. 'Do you have any English girls?'

The man laughed. 'You've got to be joking,' he said. I wondered if he had heard Paul say the same thing. 'We employ blondes and brunettes, but they're all foreign.'

'Harry Lord,' I said to Paul. 'Which does he prefer?'

'What's that got to do with anything?'

'Do you know?'

'Blondes, big ones. He's such a bloody stereotype.'

'Did you hear?' I asked the man.

'All tastes catered for,' he said. 'And the girls like champagne. This is thirsty work. I'll get you a fresh bottle.'

He took the three-quarters-full one away.

Marilyn joined us a couple of minutes later. She was peroxide blonde and full breasted. But what I saw were the bruises on her upper arms.

She smiled, more at Paul than at me. Her conversation was limited.

Another song began, and another stripper was soon waving her pimply bottom over our heads. Paul didn't look at her much, though she was more attractive than the last.

'Do you go home with men?' I asked Marilyn.

'I go home late,' she said, misunderstanding.

Paul stared at me.

'No,' I said. 'That's not happening.'

Our second bottle of champagne arrived, again already opened. I had heard no pop. Perhaps the music was too loud. Paul insisted on paying, as if to prove something to me.

I had to play the detective.

'On April the thirtieth,' I said to Marilyn. 'Can you remember April?'

'April is fourth month?' she asked. 'Is my birthday. I am eighteen.'

I prayed she wasn't eighteen. Not looking like she did.

'The last day of April. Were you here?'

The girl grimaced. She didn't get holidays.

'A young man. His age.' I nodded at Paul. 'Did he pay you for sex?'

'I, not,' Marilyn said.

'Never?'

'Never.'

'He was called Harry Lord. He is quite fat. This is important.'

Marilyn made eye-contact with the big man, who was straight over. I took charge. 'We would like another girl.'

'Fine,' he said.

We talked to Nikki and Beatrice, both blonde. Each was followed by a new bottle of champagne.

Marilyn began her strip. Having spoken to her, I found myself more embarrassed than when the other girls had been on stage.

The fourth blonde was called Summer. She spoke the best English so far, and understood my questions, perhaps better than I wanted her to.

'I do not remember.'

I repeated my description of Harry Lord.

'He was probably very drunk,' said Paul, who by now understood what I was after.

Summer shook her head and pretended to sip the champagne. I could see the white marks on her shoulders where the bra-straps had been a few minutes before. Her breasts were very large.

'He is a medical student,' I said, and saw something happen behind Summer's eyes. 'April thirtieth?'

'Like a doctor,' she said. 'Like make examine. Speaking Latin language.'

'You remember?'

'He want me lie down, very still. He make examine on me.'

'Dirty sod,' said Paul.

'Were you at your flat?'

She nodded.

'When did he leave?'

'He was very boring man. All night big talking. Nothing down there.'

She nodded towards Paul's crotch.

'What time?' I held up my watch.

'Six hours,' Summer said. 'In the light. He say he come back – to club. He not come back.'

'Are you sure?' I asked.

The big man had returned. 'I hear you've been asking lots of questions.'

'We have a friend,' said Paul. 'He had a very good time with one of your girls. But he didn't know her name. We were just trying to find the same girl.'

'Have you found her?'

'I think so,' said Paul.

The man hung around a minute longer, undecided. Then he stood a couple of paces off.

'Where do you live?' I asked Summer.

'Alright, that's enough,' said the big man.

We left without giving him an excuse to touch us.

Outside, Paul White asked me, 'What exactly did that bizarre little scene just prove?'

I spoke slowly. 'The only student with no alibi is Pavel Smid. The person who threw the heart was him or some-one else not in the class.'

'Bastard,' said Paul. 'I'll fucking kill him.'

'But it wasn't Pavel. I'm sure.'

'Why?'

Paul was looking more dishevelled than before. And he had drunk a lot of the disgusting champagne.

'Trust me.'

'Who else is there to trust?' He looked very sad. I thought he was about to make a pass at me. I was right. He leaned in my direction.

'No,' I said.

'Come on. You can't take a guy to a club like that, and then just leave them.'

'You were turned on?'

'I'm twenty. They were naked. Of course I was fucking turned on. I'd probably have been turned on if it had been their grandmothers.'

'We can share a cab,' I said. There was a company touting for business just down the road.

'No,' Paul said. 'I'm staying here.'

'Don't go back to the club,' I said.

He smiled.

'Which one?' I asked.

'Summer,' he said.

'It's a mistake. But you're a grown-up.'

I limped towards the cab controller.

By the time I reached him and looked back, Paul was already through the door.

I did not go directly home. I told the driver to take me to Borough Market. There, he waited for me on Bermondsey Street, under the railway bridge, lights shining.

I went to Becky's house and knocked on the door. Then knocked again. Then shouted her name.

'Okay, okay,' I heard her say.

The door opened.

'What d'you want now?'

'An answer to a question.'

She looked shivery.

'I'll give you some money,' I said.

'Ask.'

'The man on the train. He was average, yes?'

'Suppose so.'

'He wasn't very thin?'

'I only saw his hand properly. He was wearing dark clothes, like I said.'

'Was his hand very thin?'

'I don't think so. It was just normal, like.'

'Can you meet me tomorrow outside the hospital? I'll give you more money.'

'When?'

'Nine thirty.'

'See you there.'

She held her hand out, and I put a couple of notes in it.

'Jonesy!' I heard her shout as she closed the door.

In the morning, I visited a cashpoint and a newsagent's, then took a bus to Borough. Becky was waiting for me.

I took her to the lecture-hall entrance. It was 9.45 a.m.

'I want you to look at a student,' I said. 'He comes early every day. He is dark and very thin. If you can, I want you to tell me if he was the man on the train.'

I gave Becky a cigarette and took one for myself.

We waited.

At 9.51 a.m., Pavel Smid came round the corner, head down, walking fast. His hands were not in his pockets.

'Him,' I said.

Becky watched him closely.

'No,' she said, just as he drew level.

Pavel broke his stride, looked up and saw me.

'It wasn't him,' said Becky. 'I mean, look at them.'

Pavel's hands were almost freakish, the fingers so long they seemed to have an extra set of joints.

'Are you sure?' I asked.

'What is happening?' Pavel asked.

'Sure as I can be,' said Becky. 'Now pay up.'

'In a minute.'

'I say to leave me alone,' Pavel said.

'Why are you scared?' I asked. 'Talk to me. I know you didn't do anything.'

He hesitated, then went inside.

I gave Becky the money.

'We're going to have a party,' she said. 'Do you want to come?' I smiled. 'Thought not.'

22.

When I arrived on Wednesday night, a little early, Wally wasn't there in the locker room. I waited twenty minutes, though I might as well have left after five: Wally, I knew, would never have been late without serious cause. And, as Barbara in the Porterage told me, he certainly had that.

'His mother. Apparently, she died this morning. They had been married over seventy years. It often happens.'

Wally's father had been so old that I'd naturally assumed his wife was no longer alive.

'That's terrible.'

'He seemed quite together, considering.'

'When will he be back?'

'He couldn't say. A week?'

'Am I with Nick, then?'

'Nick's off sick. Some DJ he wanted to see, I think. Only in town tonight. So, I'm afraid, you're on your own. Don't worry, I won't give you anything difficult. You can start off in A&E. Just make yourself useful.'

My first job was to take a young woman along for an X-ray. She had a suspected broken skull, from a fall in the bath.

'I feel so stupid,' she kept saying.

I thought about Nick, wheeling Kumiko down these same corridors. What had she really said to him?

It was on the way back to A&E, slightly dazed, that I finally made the connection between King Death and the drawing of the crowned skull on Dr Speed's poster.

I could easily see how the nickname suited him. He was icily regal.

When I arrived back in A&E, the atmosphere had changed completely. It was like when someone had a heart attack, only multiplied by about a hundred. At first I thought it was a joke – people were staggering about, covered in soot. There was a smell of burning. Eventually, I realized that this was the aftermath of a fire somewhere. Junior doctors were taking patients off to be examined. It seemed to be my job to keep the less urgent patients calm, and explain that it might be a while before they were seen.

First one ambulance arrived, then another. Paramedics pushed a creature of some sort past on a trolley. Half of him was the colour of rotting meat.

A voice said, 'What you doing here?'

I looked round, and saw another soot-person. She was small, slight: Becky. There were lines of pink down her cheeks where the tears were flowing.

'Can you get him treated faster?'

'I'm sure they're doing everything they can,' I said, automatically. Then added, 'I'll see what I can do.'

Together, we followed the trolley. They were taking him – I assumed it was Jonesy – straight to the Burns Unit. As we strode down the corridor, we could smell his flesh.

'We was having a party,' Becky spoke between sobs. 'He was just cooking up. Just like normal. It's that fucking house. Too plush. Too much in it to burn. Should never have moved. First it was the sofa. Then we thought it was out. But it wasn't, round the back. It came up like a campfire. And then it was all up the wall. He was trying to save them upstairs. They was all asleep. The smoke did it to them.'

I tried to calm her down.

Up ahead, the figure on the trolley had stopped moving.

A paramedic put his fingers to the carotid artery.

'Arrest,' he said.

'What?' said Becky.

I held her back as they went to work, doing CPR.

'Listen to me,' I said. 'I think he's going to die.'

Becky's eyes were those of a bewildered animal.

The paramedics gave it a minute, then another.

'Can you let her through?' I asked.

They stood aside.

'Call it,' one said.

'8.23 p.m.,' replied the other. He looked at me. 'Nothing we could do.'

Becky took Jonesy's unburnt hand.

'Make him better,' she said.

I wondered how real she thought all this was.

'They can't,' I replied. 'You should speak to him now. Say what you want to say. Don't worry, you'll see him again.'

'Do you mean in heaven? I don't believe in heaven.'

I had been thinking of the undertakers.

Putting my arm around her, I said, 'What do you want to tell him?'

'You stupid cunt,' she said. 'You stupid fucking cunt, you burnt the fucking house down.'

She turned into my shoulder.

I hugged her.

When I looked around, I saw that the paramedics had gone to where they were most needed. It would be my job to take Jonesy down to Pathology.

'I have to go,' I said. 'If you wait in A&E, I'll come back and see you there.'

Becky turned and shuffled off, zombie-like.

I had nothing with which to cover Jonesy, and he looked pretty upsetting, so I rushed the trolley to the nearest lift. Thankfully, it was empty.

'No paperwork?' said Raymond France, on receiving the body.

'His name's Jonesy,' I said.

'You look upset. Did you know him?'

'No. I met him a couple of times.'

'Horrible way to die,' said France. 'Probably the worst.'

'Thanks,' I said.

When I got to A&E, Becky was nowhere to be seen.

The rest of the shift was unremarkable.

I tried looking for Becky around Borough Market, in the old squat and near the still-smouldering remains of the new, but she wasn't there.

Back at home, there were a couple of messages on the answerphone. The first was from Anne, agreeing to my suggestion as to where and when we might meet. The second was a hang-up.

I wouldn't have paid much attention to it, but for a couple of things. Whoever it was waited a good ten seconds before putting the phone down. I could hear them breathing, and then, right near the end, sighing. I played it a couple of times. Was it Kumiko?

1471 only told me, 'You were called at 9.10 p.m. on

Wednesday the twenty-third. The Caller withheld their number.'

Feeling just slightly unnerved, I looked my flat over to see that everything was alright.

And it was then that I noticed Kumiko's passport had gone from its place on her desk. The paper that had been beneath it was slightly askew, but still blank.

Instantly, the flat felt like a different place. When had she been here? What else had she taken?

I went back to the answerphone and unplugged it – making sure that an incoming call couldn't erase the message. Then I went into our bedroom and searched through Kumiko's clothes. As far as I could tell, she had taken nothing from here – not even some extra underwear.

Next was her desk. This, too, looked untouched. Diaries, in Japanese, still there.

If I didn't stop now, I knew I could spend all morning trying to find the one significant thing that was missing.

I listened again and again to the answerphone message. Was that Kumiko's breathing? Her heavy sigh? And, just at the very end, before the phone was put down, a slight clearing of her throat?

The obvious explanation seemed to be that Kumiko had called the flat to find out whether or not I was in. When I didn't answer, and she heard that I had messages already (Anne's had been rather long), she knew the coast was clear, probably.

Then I remembered Grzegorz had called me earlier, to see if I wanted to go out. It was possible she was using him to find out the same thing. In which case, the answerphone message was from someone else.

I remained sitting on the sofa for a long time. What had Kumiko thought when she stood here? Perhaps she was all business and didn't pause to take a breath. But surely the sight of our shared belongings had made her hesitate.

I slept most of Thursday, then got ready for my date with Anne. This included burning a couple of compilation CDs for her. It felt disloyal to Kumiko, for whom I'd made dozens, but I did my best. I put a couple of extreme blowouts in to test the boundaries of Anne's taste – Borbetomagus, Brötzmann. Could she really say she liked this stuff?

Just as I was about to leave, there was a knock on the door. It was a motorbike courier with a package under his arm. He held out a clipboard and I signed my name.

The padded brown envelope contained a CD.

'The Heart (Final Mix)' was written on the surface of the disc. There was no accompanying note.

I loaded the song onto my MP3 player, and began listening to it as I walked to the station. Before the music began, the pop singer gave a brief spoken introduction.

'Hi, Skelton. This is it. Finished. Hope you like it, mate. We're all really chuffed, aren't we?' I heard a few muffled sounds of agreement. 'It'll be out pretty soon. Rush release, you know. Because I've been away far too long.' Ironic cheers. 'Maybe middle of next month. See you around.'

I doubted I'd ever meet him again.

The opening chords sounded clearer than before. Whoever did the mix had earned their money. An organ was doubling up with the piano. It reminded me of 'Let It Be', but in a good way. The lyrics of the first verse had changed completely, also for the better. When it got to my solo, I was amazed to find it intact. Not one note had been removed. The second half of the song built more powerfully than in the original mix; a gospel choir joining in for the final chorus – a gospel choir which, unwittingly, was singing about my love for Kumiko.

I had to step inside a doorway for a second. I couldn't see where I was walking. 'The potency of cheap music'. Who was it said that? T. S. Eliot? Noël Coward? Well, this music wasn't cheap. It was very expensive, and was going to make the pop singer a lot of money. I didn't mind. I could never have written anything so direct.

Anne and I had arranged to meet at St John, out by Smithfield meat-market. Again, I was testing myself. This was a place I had often been with Kumiko. I wanted to see how it would feel, going there with another woman.

Part of the problem, a minor part, was that I couldn't really think of Anne as a *woman*. She was still a girl. That made everything feel wrong – although I was aware that her wrongness was one of the reasons I was attracted to her. Kumiko must have known this, too. It explained why she was happy to use Anne.

When Anne arrived, five minutes late, she was carrying another message from Kumiko: her new black agnès b coat. I thought back to Speed's lecture. No, Kumiko hadn't been wearing it then. If she had, this would have amounted to wrapping the gift in crêpe and tying it up with a big black bow.

'You look lovely,' I said. I meant it. Beneath the coat,

Anne was wearing a stylish black and white dress – very slightly Mod. She looked almost Mary Quant-ish.

Anne sat down, and we began to talk about what we'd been up to, since our last date. I had decided in advance to lie.

'My agent got me some more session work,' I said. 'I've been in the studio.'

'Any good?'

'Okay,' I said. Then, on a whim, I decided to play her 'The Heart'. 'Hang on. See what you think of this.' As I was fumbling for my MP3 player, the waitress took our drinks orders.

Anne listened to the song, the ghost of a smile on her face.

'So?' I asked.

She hadn't cried.

'It's one of those songs – it's one of those songs you feel you know even though you've never heard it before.'

I suppressed a desire to ask what she thought of the solo.

'The guitar in the middle's you, isn't it?'

I told her yes, it was.

'I think that's the best bit – the bit that makes it a little unusual.'

Now I wanted to ask whether she thought Kumiko would like it. Instead, I gave her the compilation CDs.

'Is that song on one of them?'

'I'm afraid not. It arrived just before I came out.'

She seemed more than a little disappointed. 'I'll post it to you,' I said. I wanted Kumiko to hear it just as much as Anne did.

We turned our attention to the menus. I deliberately

chose to order dishes I hadn't eaten there with Kumiko. We shared a Spotted Dick.

All through the meal, I kept changing my mind about what to do. Accept the gift or refuse it? When Anne said something surprisingly amusing, I thought, *No, I can't.* But when she was youthfully crude, I thought, *Why not?*

To delay the decision, I ordered a double espresso. Anne had one, too.

I was still wavering when we stepped out of the restaurant.

'Thank you for that,' said Anne, and looked expectantly up into my face.

I kissed her, hard.

'Would you like to come back to mine?' I asked, slightly breathless.

'Love to,' she said.

We caught a black cab opposite Smithfield, then kissed in the back of it all the way to King's Cross.

I was thinking that if things happened in a rush, and with some passion, then they wouldn't be quite as bad. What I couldn't get out of my head, however, was the chorus to 'The Heart'.

Outside my block, I paid the driver.

We climbed the stairs and, once through the door, began to undress one another. I took off the agnès b coat. I wanted to smell it – to bury my head in Kumiko's recent scent. I wanted to do this more than to make love to Anne. And it was this realization that stopped me.

'No,' I said. 'I can't.'

'Why?' asked Anne.

I almost told her that I knew who the coat belonged to.

'It just feels wrong.' I was using all the worst clichés. 'I'm still in love with Kumiko.' It was a relief to say her name aloud, she had been so present all evening.

'But you know that's over.'

'Maybe. Maybe not. I'm sorry, but sleeping with you isn't going to help.'

What if Anne suddenly said, *She wants you to*? How would I react then?

'Then why go out with me? Why ask me back here? Why kiss me like you did?'

'Because, in other circumstances –'

'There are no "other circumstances". There's me and I'm here. For about the next minute, anyway. After that, I'm gone – and I'm not coming back. You're just lucky I haven't broken your nose.'

'You're right,' I said. 'We shouldn't see each other again.'

'Don't worry. We won't.'

For the first time, Anne looked as if she were going to cry.

I opened the door for her.

'It was just a bit of fun,' she said. 'We were never going to get married.'

I wanted to give her a message to Kumiko. But then I realized that the refusal of the gift was message enough. Plus, there was 'The Heart'.

'I can call you a taxi, if you want.'

'No,' said Anne. 'Don't.'

I listened to the echoing clack of her departing heels. What I'd done felt awful but totally right. I was sure of myself in a way I hadn't been since Kumiko walked out.

This didn't stop me lying awake brooding for most of that night.

I tried to imagine the scene when Anne saw Kumiko, back at the house – their shared disappointment.

The most deluded part of me expected Kumiko to call me straight away. Of course, she didn't.

23

After Becky left, I waited for Jo outside the lecture hall. She arrived a minute or two later.

'I need a new list,' I said. 'Everyone who might have been around the dissecting room on April twenty-ninth or thirtieth.'

'You mean it wasn't a student?'

'No. I was wrong about that. Unless I have made another mistake in my logic.'

'I'm sure you haven't. I'll do you a list when I get home.'

'No, I want it as soon as possible.'

'Lunchtime, then.'

I went and had a coffee. Then I stood for a while outside the hospital, watching people go in and out. A security guard came and stood in the doorway, looking towards me.

Just after 12 p.m. Jo and Molly came out of the lecture hall. Jo had done a handwritten list. It was very short.

'There really aren't many people allowed in,' Jo said. 'Just the lecturers and the demonstrators. I don't know about the support staff. We never tend to see them. I think all of them are women. The demonstrators do most of the prep.'

Lecturers

Dr Speed (on the 29th and 30th)
Dr France (occasionally)
Dr Goosen (very rarely)

Demonstrators

Simon Aragon
Timothy Kendall
Sazzad Muhammad
Anita O'Driscoll
V. P. Singh
May Wilders
Zhu Zhang

I asked Jo a few questions. Sazzad Muhammad was dark-skinned. V. P. Singh, a man, was also dark. Zhu Zhang was pale, but was only five foot tall.

Discounting the lecturers, that left Simon Aragon and Timothy Kendall.

'Tell me about them.'

A man brushed past us.

'Excuse me,' he said.

'Really interesting,' said Molly, interrupting loudly. 'And then we might go clubbing or to a bar. Just anything blah di blah.'

'What?' asked Jo.

'Hair extensions. Fitness club.' She looked over her shoulder. 'That was Timothy Kendall.'

I watched him walk away. He was of average height

and build. His hands looked normal. He was wearing a black overcoat.

'Let's get away from here,' I said. 'I need to ask you some more questions.'

'Can't we leave it to this evening? I'd like to get some lunch before class.'

'I'll treat you,' I said. 'Both.'

We went to Tas, a Turkish restaurant on Borough High Street. The place was well lit with plain wooden tables and chairs.

Jo went to the loo. I asked Molly what she knew about the two suspects.

'Simon Aragon – don't know much at all. Timothy Kendall – shall we talk about my biggest mistakes ever?'

'You slept with him?'

'Only once, I swear. It was really early on. I thought he was quite funny.'

'What is he like?'

'He's a joker.'

'Practical jokes?'

'Any kind of joke. Usually not all that funny. Look, I was drunk. He invited me back to his place. It was all over in about five minutes.'

'Did he like Paul White?'

'Timothy likes everyone. Or he hates everyone. His relationship with the world isn't very discerning.'

'He liked you.'

'Everyone likes me. I'm not being immodest, they just do. I make them feel safe. They think I'm not serious.'

'What about Simon Aragon?'

'He's completely different. He never flirts with anyone.'

'Is he creepy?'

'No. He's hardly there at all. And I say that even though he's my anatomy demonstrator. He's like a text-book. Some people call him Aragon the Arrogant. Maybe that's the explanation.'

'What about him and Paul?'

Jo returned.

'We're talking about the anatomy demonstrators,' I said. 'I was asking whether Simon hated Paul.'

'Not that I know about,' Molly replied.

'Does he even notice?' Jo asked. 'He seems completely cut off to me.'

'Like a psychopath?' I asked.

'Like a very boring young man,' said Jo. 'He wants to be a great surgeon. He'll be a great surgeon. That's it. End of story. In the morning, he works with us. In the afternoon, he does rounds at the hospital. I can't even imagine him having a social life, let alone a girlfriend.'

'Timothy and Simon – neither has a good motive for harming Paul?'

Jo looked at Molly and Molly at Jo.

'No,' they said, together.

I was stuck.

The waiter came over. We ordered a couple of set menus. Haloumi. Couscous. Lots of choice. And sparkling mineral water. When he had gone I tried again.

'I think the person who stole the heart was jealous of Paul.'

'I've just remembered something,' said Jo. 'Simon Aragon was away on the thirtieth.'

'Just the thirtieth? What about the first?'

'No, he was there when Paul discovered the heart was

226

missing. He took charge until Dr Speed arrived. I think he was trying to impress him.'

That was interesting.

'Who is the demonstrator for Pandora?'

'Zhu Zhang.'

Molly confirmed that Simon Aragon had been away on the thirtieth.

'Yeah. We got to work on Pandora for a change. She's so lovely. We call our one "the Yeti". He's covered in white hair.'

'But on the thirtieth, Paul thought the heart was a different one.'

'I wouldn't know which,' said Molly. 'It wasn't the Yeti's heart. That was covered in yellow fat.'

'We weren't supposed to be looking in the chest cavity,' said Jo.

'Didn't anyone make a fuss?' I asked.

'People thought it was a joke, I suppose.'

'Timothy Kendall's kind of joke?'

'Oh, definitely. But I don't think he did it. He'd get into terrible trouble.'

'Why was Simon Aragon away on the thirtieth?'

'How would we know?' said Molly.

'Was he there from the start of May first?'

Molly shrugged.

'Probably,' said Jo. 'He often answers questions for Pavel, when Pavel gets there early. He's very conscientious.'

'What about Timothy Kendall?'

'None of the demonstrators has ever been late. Not that I remember. They have to get there about an hour beforehand. It's not like they arrive when we do.'

The waiter brought our food.

I needed to speak to Paul White.

After lunch, Jo and Molly headed back to Guy's.

I called Paul from outside the restaurant. He picked up – and immediately began trying to charm me.

'I'm fine,' I said, and then asked him about the anatomy demonstrators, without mentioning any names. 'Do you think any of them dislike you?'

'You mean did they try to get me chucked out?'

'Yes.'

The line was silent for a moment.

'Timothy Kendall. He knows I think he's a prick. And I'm pretty sure he fancied Monica.'

'When did he see her?'

'I suppose at her father's party, at the start of the year.' He meant the academic year. 'She used to meet me out of class, quite often.'

'Did he talk to her?'

'He talks to everyone.' He coughed a couple of times. 'Yes, I think he talked to her.'

'I need her telephone number and her address. Can I have them?'

'Look, even I'm not allowed to call her.'

'I will explain. She will understand.'

'I don't know.'

'What happened at the strip-club?'

'Oh, nothing much,' he said. 'At the club.'

'Did you go home with Summer?'

'Maybe.'

'Where does she live?'

'A long way out. Stratford, somewhere like that. She made me pay for a cab.'

'Monica's address,' I said. 'Monica's phone number.'

'Hang on.' He came back a short while later. 'Have you got a pen?'

I crossed the road and hailed a black cab.

Monica lived on Wimbledon Common. Her father's house was Georgian, three storeys high with tall windows. Lights were on. A Range Rover, a Mini and a black limousine were parked on the gravel drive.

I rang the bell.

A middle-aged woman answered.

'You are Mrs Norfolk? Can I speak to Monica, please?'

'Not Mrs,' said the woman, with a strong Italian accent. 'Mrs not here. Mrs at house.'

'I want Monica. I am her friend.'

The woman closed the door. I thought she wasn't coming back.

Next time the door opened, it was a man. He was unshaven and carrying a paper.

'You're after Monica. Well, she's not here.'

'Can you please tell me where she is?'

'She's at the house in Italy. Went there at the weekend.'

'When will she be back?'

'Couple of weeks.'

'Where is the house?'

'Look, how do I know you know her?'

'It's okay,' I said. 'I will come back.'

Standing on the edge of the common, I dialled the number Paul had given me. An automated answer-message spoke up.

It took me half an hour to find a cab to take me home.

As it drove me, I called Paul again.

'She's not there. She's in Italy.'

'Oh.'

'Do you know where?'

'Tuscany.'

'Where exactly? The address.'

'No,' he said. 'Or maybe – hang on. I might have a postcard.'

He went away and came back.

'It's Fosciandora,' he said, then spelt the name. 'I can't tell you the address, but it's near Castelnuovo di Garfagnana. You're not going, are you?'

'I have no choice.'

When I got home, I searched for the next available flight. There was one from Alitalia at 6 a.m. the next day. I started to book it. One of the boxes to fill was for passport number. But my passport was in Skelton's flat.

I phoned Grzegorz.

'How is your ankle?' he asked, after hello.

'Better,' I said. 'I need to go to the flat. Can you phone and see if Skelton is there? If he is, can you find out when he won't be?'

'Okay,' he said, grumpily.

Five minutes later, Grzegorz called back.

'He's there. But he's out this evening. I suggested we go for a drink. He couldn't make it.'

'What's he doing?'

'He wouldn't say. I think it's something secret.'

'When will he be out?'

'I said nine o'clock. If you go then, you should be safe.'

With time before Jo and Molly returned, I decided to look up my new suspects online.

There was little information. Both men had hospital email addresses. Simon Aragon was on a committee relating to hygiene. Timothy Kendall had written an article for the student newspaper about being a demonstrator.

'Most people,' it began, 'are a bit wary of corpses. I don't know why. I've always found them perfectly accommodating. It's the living I tend to have problems with!'

He said that he intended to become a surgeon, and that anatomy demonstration was the best preparation for the exams.

'But, I hear you ask, what exactly do we do? Well, according to our job description, we, and I quote, "teach and supervise, via demonstrations, tutorials, cadavers and other classes, undergraduates in the Department of Anatomy of Human Sciences". Translated into English, that means we are the guys standing next to you the first time you pick up a scalpel in anger. We tell you memorable anecdotes and facts that you will almost certainly forget. We answer your dumb questions without sniggering. (At least, not in front of your face.) We pass on your feedback to the anatomy lecturer. (This is commonly known as "Keeping Dr Speed up to speed.") And we help set and mark your spot exams. In other words, we are the Demi-Gods of the Dissecting Room, and don't you forget it!'

Timothy Kendall was annoying.

After a little more searching, I found the minutes to one of Simon Aragon's hygiene meetings. It had been held a month ago. As far as I could tell, Simon Aragon did not speak.

Jo came back around 5 p.m. Molly had decided to go out for a drink.

I told her about the trip.

'Wow, you're really serious, aren't you?'

I nodded.

We talked for a while, then I went upstairs to pack. It didn't take long.

At 8 p.m., I set off for King's Cross.

As the train passed over Borough Road, I could see smoke rising into the air. It looked like something large was on fire.

I got to Skelton's block at 8.50 p.m., but waited until the hour before heading upstairs.

The lights were off. No sounds came from inside. I knocked. Skelton did not come.

I put my key in the lock. It still worked.

The flat felt both familiar and completely strange. I knew where everything was, in the way that a ghost might know.

I moved quietly into the bedroom. A silly part of me thought Skelton might be hiding in the wardrobe, waiting to jump out.

My passport was laid out in the middle of my desk, a sheet of blank paper beneath it. Skelton was inviting me to leave him a message. He was also telling me that, if I took the passport, he would know almost immediately that I had been in the flat.

I thought about taking some more clothes. But I wanted to keep my statement of total independence clear. The passport was all I really needed.

I went and stood in the middle of the living room. I tried to imagine that this was the last time I would be there. But it didn't feel like that. Certainly not as much as before, when I had walked out.

The red light was flashing on the answerphone. I wondered what I would learn if I played the message.

I turned to go, and just then the phone rang.

My heart moved violently in my chest.

After six rings, the answerphone went on. The caller waited a few moments then hung up.

Now I wanted to get out of the flat as fast as I could.

The moment I finished locking the door, my phone began buzzing. It was Grzegorz.

'Are you there?' he asked. 'I just tried.'

'Idiot,' I said.

'I thought you might pick up. Did you get it?'

'I got it.'

24.

The Keats biography arrived on Tuesday, but I didn't get around to looking at it until late Friday morning.

By then, I was already on a train down to London Bridge. Over the last twenty-four hours, I had become increasingly guilty about Becky. I needed to find her and make sure that she was alright.

The biography came in at over six hundred pages. Why was Kumiko reading this now? It didn't take long to find out.

I went through the index, where I saw: Guy's Hospital, London; K and, xxv, 5, 16, 49, 66, 73–4, etc., etc.

What if this was just background reading? Kumiko didn't waste time on extraneous things, however. There must be something here that meant something to her.

Quickly, I scanned the chapters dealing with Keats's time as a medical student. The biographer was obviously making the case for Keats as a committed surgeon, rather than a romantic dilettante.

I was just staring out the window, wondering about this, when I caught sight of Becky. She was sitting cross-legged on the roof of her old squat.

It took me about six minutes to make it there. I hurried, even though Becky didn't look like she was going anywhere soon.

The black metal door was open, so I made my way in.

'Hello,' I shouted, once I got halfway out the window. I didn't want just to sneak up on Becky.

'Oh, so it's you,' she said.

I clambered round until I was beside her on the crumbling asphalt of the rooftop.

'I saw you from the train,' I said.

'Saw you, too,' she said. I wasn't sure I believed her. She picked up on this, and became annoyed. 'You were reading some book.'

'Yes, I was.'

I undid my backpack and pulled it out.

'It's a biography,' I said.

'I know Keats,' Becky said, as if he were one of her mates from the squat.

'I'm sure you do.' God, I was so middle class. I just found it impossible not to be patronizing. 'I'm sorry,' I said. 'I keep saying the wrong thing.'

'He went to Guy's. There's a plaque up on St Thomas Street. He was gonna be a doctor.'

'Kumiko's reading about him,' I said. 'So I wanted to find out why she was interested.'

'Can't help you there.'

She offered me a cigarette, which I politely declined.

'I came down to see how you were.'

'Why you working in the hospital, anyway?'

'I'm trying to solve the mystery so I can win back the girl.'

'Solved it yet?'

'No, I've just found another one.'

'What?'

Becky's voice couldn't have sounded less interested, but her eyes when I looked into them were curious in a dull sort of way.

I told her about Mr Fine.

'We know him,' she said. 'He deals. Prescription stuff. Get you almost anything you want. Evil bastard. Carries a gun. Lets you know it.'

'Really?' I asked.

Becky had started to cry. 'I miss him. He was a cunt but I miss him.' Only for a second did I think she meant Mr Fine.

'I'm sorry,' I said. Burning was such a horrible way to die that all of the usual words of comfort didn't fit. 'Were you together long?'

'Few years. I should hate him. He got me onto it in the first place. But my life would've been piss-boring otherwise. Just've had a kid and got fat in some shitty flat somewhere.'

'What are you going to do now?'

'We used to climb up there, for a laugh. Onto the tracks. Then, when a train come along, we'd lie down and let it go over us. That was such a fucking rush. There's enough room under them, if you don't stick your head up. Sometimes the drivers seen us and stopped the trains, but we was long gone by then.'

'That sounds fun.'

'Want to try it?'

'No, thanks.'

'You don't believe me. I'll show ya.'

'I do believe you. Why would you lie to me?'

'Loadsa reasons for lying to cunts like you.'

Cunts was bordering on affectionate.

'Do you need anything?'

'How much money you got?'

I gave her the notes from my wallet.

'That all?' she said.

'Yes.'

It was quite pleasant sitting out there on the roof. For the first time, I didn't feel like getting away from Becky as soon as possible – as if her poverty were something contagious. We sat there for five minutes without speaking. Then Becky, after lighting another cigarette, said, 'I seen Kumiko the morning the house burnt down. She give me the money for the party we was havin'.'

'She's gone abroad. I don't know where. She took her passport from our flat.'

'Italy. Tuscany. I went round her house yesterday.'

Another train went past. It seemed particularly loud and heavy.

'When you saw her, did she ask you any more questions?'

'Just one. She wanted to know if some bloke was the bloke from the train. We was waiting outside the lecture rooms until he come along.'

'And was he?'

'Naah. Wrong hands.'

'Did Kumiko seem annoyed by that?'

'Didn't seem nothing. Just said *fank you*.'

Becky did a small Japanese bow.

'Was he a medical student? Was he young?'

'Yeah, he was a student. Bag an' all. Going to a lecture.'

I couldn't think of any more questions to ask.

'Are you living here now?'

'Got fuck all else. Other house is fucked.'

I said I would go and have a look, not mentioning I'd seen it before, still smouldering. Then I said *see you*, and for once I believed it.

Fucked was definitely the word for the second squat. I could smell it almost before I could see it. The roof had collapsed. Black soot caked the walls above the windows. These had been boarded up – as if someone might want to move in.

I stood there for a few moments, thinking about Jonesy. I had known almost nothing about him.

Then I walked up Borough High Street, across the road and along St Thomas until I saw the blue plaque.

I continued down the street until I came to the turning for Guy's. Even though it was my day off, I'd been drawn here. The world outside seemed less real than the hospital world of illness, pain, death and – occasionally – healing. Perhaps this was what Anne had meant about not knowing until you worked there. Perhaps now I knew.

'Alright?' said a voice I recognized. It was Nick. He was tugging the cellophane off a fresh pack of cigarettes, so I guessed he'd just been to the corner shop. 'You on shift today?'

'No,' I said.

'Shame. There's a game on tonight. Usual place.'

'Well, I might make it anyway.'

I had nothing else to do.

Taking the train back, I decided to call Grzegorz. He was in, and I forced an invitation to lunch.

'I can't tell you anything,' he said, even before his front door was fully open. 'I am, as always, sworn to secrecy.'

'She's in Tuscany,' I said. 'And she's been investigating the medical students in Paul White's class, trying to rule them out, one by one. And because none of the students, so far as I know, lives in Tuscany, I'm assuming that she's succeeded in ruling them out.'

'Congratulations, Sherlock,' said Grzegorz. 'I am genuinely impressed.'

'Also, I know where she lives, who she's living with, and all the new clothes she's bought in the past month.'

'Now you're sounding like a stalker.'

Not as much as I was feeling like one.

Three different salads were laid out on the long table in the middle of Grzegorz's flat. Some soup was cooking.

I sat down. He poured me a glass of water.

'When you phoned me the other night,' I said, 'that was so Kumiko would know I was out, wasn't it? So she could get into the flat.'

'I can't answer that question.'

'Which means it has to do with Kumiko. Which means yes.'

Grzegorz looked at me meaningfully. 'I can't answer that question.'

'Someone called me around that time, but didn't leave a message.'

'Did they? Is that significant?'

'Probably not. But it might have been Kumiko.'

Grzegorz brought two bowls of the soup, homemade tomato, to the table.

'This month, I'm vegan,' he said.

We started to eat, managing to talk about Grzegorz's work and not my and Kumiko's investigations.

But over coffee, I asked, 'I don't believe what you told me about Kumiko twisting her ankle. I need to know if she's putting herself in danger.'

'Would she even recognize it as danger?'

'No. You're right. Not until it was too late.'

Before I went, I let Grzegorz listen to 'The Heart'.

He closed his eyes and touched the headphones with his fingertips.

'It sounds like something else,' he said. 'Like a hymn.'

We said goodbye, and I told him to try and keep Kumiko safe.

'Who could do that?' he asked.

'Me,' I said.

The rest of the afternoon I spent at home, reading about Keats.

I made noodles for supper, then set off for the poker game. Becky was still on the roof as the train went past. I waved at her, pretty sure she'd seen me and known who I was.

As I walked through the chill of the Dissecting Room, it struck me that the place was far less secure than I'd assumed. The heart could have been stolen at any time, day or night.

The same players were sitting round the table, minus Sasha the Nurse, who was on shift.

Right from the start, my cards were better than before. I took a couple of small pots pretty much uncontested. Sally was much too aggressive with weak hands, lost all her money and went home laughing. That left Nick, Claire, Simon, Phil, Bill and me.

Because he'd bluffed me so humiliatingly last time, I kept close watch on Simon. But he seemed to be playing more conservatively, and, when he did win, he resisted the impulse to show his cards. His poker-face was strong. Arrogant was probably the right word for him – but as he looked arrogant all the time, whatever might be in his hand, he was impossible to read. After Sally left, he seemed to relax a little.

Nick chatted away, just like before, continuing to annoy Phil and Bill, and to take money off them. They accepted this with a certain grim humour.

Following a short run of trash, I got dealt two aces. So far I had resisted the temptation to bluff Simon back. This time, though, I decided I'd trap him.

The first round of betting, I was cautious. But then came the flush, bringing an ace, a five and a three, unsuited. I went in overstrong, making sure everyone knew I had a monster hand. Claire took me seriously, as did Phil and Bill, who didn't have the money to be curious. Nick stuck around, out of interest. Simon squinted at his cards as if they were the other side of a dark room, then he came out betting.

The turn was a two. The river was a jack.

Simon and Nick were still there, Simon having raised me a couple of times, Nick just tagging along.

Betting finished, it was time to turn over the cards. Simon waited until I'd shown my three aces. He smiled knowingly as he revealed ace queen. He'd fallen for my bluff.

I wanted to rake in the pile but first of all turned to look at Nick.

Deadpan, he flipped over a six and a four. He'd picked up a double-ended straight draw, and hit it on the turn. Bastard.

Both Simon and I were now very short-stacked. Phil and Bill took full advantage of this, taking turns to force us out of hands. And as the game went on, it seemed like a little more of Simon's character was revealed. He began to bluff desperately, almost every deal. None of us believed him any more, and within half an hour he was finished.

I had him now. Arrogance was indeed the key. With enough chips, he was a goodish player, confident but within reasonable limits. Back against the wall, he lost perspective and started chasing dreams. I wondered what he, in turn, could tell about me. He didn't hang around to watch, however.

'Lock up, will you?' he said to Nick, and tossed him a spare set of keys.

After such a big beat, I thought I played pretty well. I took the opportunities that came my way. In this I was helped by Claire, who seemed to be able to read Nick better than the rest of us. Perhaps because, at crucial moments, she was able to flirt with him.

At twelve thirty, we packed it in. I was down a few quid. The others left, but I stayed behind, ostensibly to help Nick put the room back in order.

As we were putting the blotter back on one of the desks, I noticed the doodles: a skull wearing a crown at an angle exactly halfway between jaunty and rakish.

'Is this Simon's office?' I asked.

'Not really. All the demonstrators share it. But he behaves as if it's his.'

'Do you think he drew that?' I asked, seeing no other way of getting the answer I wanted.

Nick came round to have a look.

'I saw it on a poster,' I said, 'for a talk by Dr Speed.'

'Might be Simon, might not. Like I said, they share the desks.'

Nick was less expansive than usual, which made me suspect the doodle might also be by him.

I waited until we were walking out past the cadavers before I asked another question.

'It means King Death, doesn't it, the doodle?'

'Yeah,' he said.

'Did you give him that nickname?'

'God, no. It's ancient. Some poet back in the sixteenth century.'

Nineteenth century.

25.

My Thursday-morning flight left on time and my hire car was ready for me at Pisa airport.

Tuscany was in a different season to London. Already the land seemed dried out and waiting for summer heat.

The roads became winding, with sharp drops to the side. I enjoyed the feeling that steering meant something.

Halfway to Castelnuovo di Garfagnana, I stopped at a village café and ordered a double espresso. It tasted wonderful, as if it had an extra ingredient, cocoa or chestnuts.

I reached Castelnuovo about an hour later. I parked the car, a little red Fiat, and went to find somewhere to stay. A vivacious lady of sixty in the tourist office directed me to the Hotel Ristorante La Lanterna. There was no problem getting a single room for two nights.

I put my bag in the room – the same bag I had packed when I left Skelton.

After a shower I went out for lunch.

I found an ordinary café on the central square. It had a waiter who was not as handsome as he thought he was. He flirted with me, because he flirted with everyone, but with me he flirted excessively, perhaps because he thought I was exotic.

The menu was mostly panini. I chose prosciutto and mozzarella. This time I had a single espresso.

'Per favore,' I said. I speak a very little Italian. 'Is there an English girl staying in Fosciandora?'

He shrugged. No idea. He began to move away.

'Is there a *beautiful* English girl staying in Fosciandora?'

Immediately, a different man stood in front of me.

'*Sì*,' he said, and with his new body language he tried to describe her. His hands in the air were his hands on her shoulders, then on her cheeks. '*Donna molto molto bellissima.*'

'Which house is she staying in?'

He put on a dejected face. It said, if only I knew, I would be howling outside it every night. Then he realized he was insulting me, and began to flirt again.

I paid him with money I had changed at Heathrow.

'*Arrivederci, bella.*'

I was *bella*, not *bellissima*.

Not wanting to waste time, I drove to Fosciandora and parked in a sidestreet. This proved difficult. It was market day.

At another café, with another waiter, not handsome, I asked after the beautiful English girl. Yes, he had seen her. No, he didn't know where she lived. But perhaps his mother did.

He went through beaded curtains into the back room. A television there became quieter. When he returned, he was smiling.

'*È bueno. La Camera Inglese.*'

He tried to direct me, then started to draw some lines on a napkin.

But, even as he did, he was distracted by something passing by. I looked up, and at the same moment, the waiter began to say, '*È lei! È lei! She is her.*'

The waiter made such a noise that Monica looked round. This was awkward. I had wanted to follow her for a while.

A woman, obviously Monica's mother, was a few steps ahead of her.

I put some money down for my glass of water.

Monica had started to walk away.

The waiter went after her, explaining that I had been asking after her.

Monica turned to face me.

'Yes? What do you want?'

'My name is Kumiko Ozu. I am trying to help Paul White. Please will you answer a few questions?'

'Oh, so you're *her*,' she said. 'You don't look mad.'

'Some people think I do.'

Her mother stood protectively at her side. 'What's this about?' she asked.

'And you've come all this way? Just to talk to me?'

'Only for that. It is very important.'

The waiter was also listening.

'Mother,' said Monica, 'this is a friend of Paul's. Kumiko.'

'Pleased to meet you,' the older version of Monica said. 'And you're here on holiday?'

'I came to find your daughter. She may have information that will help Paul.'

'What a terrible thing that was,' said Monica's mother. 'Quite horribly distressing.'

'Look,' said Monica, 'we're going to the market, right now. And this afternoon we're going to Lucca. And this evening we have some very boring people for dinner.'

'They are not,' said her mother.

'Can you come tomorrow morning?'

'To the house?'

'Yes. It's just up the hill from the railway crossing. Follow the road until it runs out.'

'What time?'

'Eleven?'

'See you then.'

She and her mother walked off, each with a shopping bag swinging from their right hand. Their arms were slender. Everything about them was slender.

The waiter looked at me.

I thanked him as enthusiastically as I could.

To keep out of Monica's way, I went and looked round the church for an hour. Then I bought a light snack at the market: focaccia, pecorino, olives.

I drove until I found a view and then sat eating the delicious things. I love Italian food.

Friday morning, I found La Camera Inglese without difficulty. It was 10.35 a.m. The day was already warm. I waited in the car, listening to Europop.

> DISASTER DATE W S! DINNER, NICE. BACK 2
> HIS FLAT. THEN S FREAKS. SAYS HE CAN'T BE
> UNFAITHFUL 2 U. I LEAVE. NO CALL OF REMORSE
> FROM HIM – YET. WHAT SHD I DO?

I replied that she should wait until I was back, probably later that day. There was no hurry.

I thought about Skelton. What did I feel? It seemed to me I felt annoyed and proud.

At 11 a.m. exactly, I made the sharp turn into the drive, and parked beside a Mini just like the one I'd seen outside the house in Wimbledon.

Monica's mother was reclining in a hammock on the

veranda. Smoke from a cigarette came out of her mouth as she said, 'She's by the pool. Just follow your nose.'

I walked around the house and up a slight incline.

There was no-one by the pool. But Monica's thin face appeared at an upstairs window. 'Down in a jiffy,' she said.

I sat in a stripy deck-chair and waited. A novel lay face down on the wall. It was a crime thriller.

'You're very lucky,' said Monica, coming out of the house. 'I wasn't going to talk to you. But then Mother persuaded me I had to do the right thing. So, I'll answer your questions, if I can. But first you have to answer mine.'

'That seems fair.'

She closed her eyes, as if she didn't want to see my face.

'Are you in love with Paul?'

'No.'

'Because, you see, I heard that you went out on a date together.'

And now her eyes opened.

'We did. We went to a restaurant.'

'And to a strip-club.'

'That was another time.'

'So, in fact, you went on two dates.'

'I wanted to ask him some questions. He insisted I take him out for a meal.'

'And to see naked women.'

'No. I needed someone to go with me to the club.'

'If you don't love him, why are you doing this?'

I thought about this for a while. 'I am annoyed when there isn't justice,' I said.

'You kissed him,' said Monica. 'True or not?'

'We kissed, yes.'

248

'Who made the first move?'

'He did. I told him he could kiss me, but only once.'

'Why did he kiss you?'

'I think he wanted to see if I would kiss him.'

'But he's meant to be in love with me!'

For the first time, Monica seemed young.

'I think he is. But I think he is also very confused. His life is a mess. He jumped in the river.'

'Stupid idiot. He could have got himself killed.'

Behind the cliché, there was love.

'You have shut him out. He needs your help.'

Monica thought about this for a while.

'Do you have any more questions?'

'No,' she said.

'May I ask you something?'

'Ask away.'

I made no prelude.

'Did you meet Timothy Kendall at your father's party?'

'Who?'

'The anatomy demonstrator from Guy's.'

'Oh. Which one is he?'

I realized I couldn't give a physical description.

'He tries to be funny all the time.'

'Right. Yes, I think so. It's quite formal. We stand by the door and welcome people as they arrive. I at least shook hands with everyone.'

'More than that. A conversation.'

'Yes. Probably. I really can't remember. But the other one …'

'Which one?'

'The creepy one. Very intense.'

I didn't want to be first to say his name.

'Zhu Zhang?' I said.

'No. English. He told me he loved me.'

'Can you remember his name?'

'Not really. I think it was something quite boring. He just came up to me and said he was in love.'

'Why was he creepy?'

'He stood too close. He was a bit drunk. I hadn't even really noticed him before. Steven?'

'Can you describe him, physically?'

'Just average. My height. Mousy hair. Not slim or fat. I didn't hang around very long.'

'You met Paul that night, too?'

'Yes,' she said.

'Did you see the creepy man again?'

'Arrogant! That's his nickname. Paul told me later. But I didn't think him arrogant at all. He hardly seemed to exist.'

'Did you see him around the hospital?'

'Sometimes. When I met Paul.'

'Did he look at you?'

'Oh God, yes. Stared and stared.'

'Was he jealous?'

'You know, I think he probably was.'

'Simon Aragon.'

'Yes, that's his name.'

Monica's mother came out a while later and asked if we would like coffee.

'Yes, please,' I said. 'That would be lovely.'

'Is Monica being helpful?'

'Very helpful.'

'Good,' she said, and went off into the house.

'So, have you solved the crime?' Monica asked.

'I think so,' I said.

'And you're going to prove Paul innocent?'

'If I can.'

'And you don't love him?'

'No.'

'And he doesn't love you.'

'He loves you.'

She took this in.

'Who told you about our date?' I asked.

'Oh, Anne.'

Monica's mother brought the coffee out, then sat down to join us. I had to say something.

'I am sorry about your husband.'

'Yes ... well ...'

'Do you think they will find him?'

'Oh, no. He's dead. I'm quite sure of that. He wouldn't just disappear off into the ether. He had no reason to.'

She was proud of their marriage.

'We've never believed he was alive,' said Monica. 'Not after the first few weeks.'

'He loved his job, as well,' said her mother. 'He was wonderful at it. All the students loved him, despite the nickname. You know what they called him?'

'Yes.'

'Not like this new man, Speed. He really is deathly. But at least they didn't appoint Goosen.'

'There wasn't any chance of that, Mummy,' said Monica. 'He's just an unqualified troll.'

'That didn't stop him applying. Repeatedly.' Monica's mother turned to me. 'Goosen works in the pathology department. My husband always had a very difficult relationship with him. Very strained. Even when they were at medical school. He was always the jealous type. Not that I'm implying he had anything to do with the death.'

'We don't know anyone who would want to kill my father,' said Monica.

'We would like to know,' Monica's mother said. 'Very much.'

It sounded as if she were talking about the provenance of a favourite painting.

I left quarter of an hour later.

'Goodbye,' said Monica, standing beside the car.

'Thank you,' I said, and then turned away.

'Is Paul alright?' Monica asked. 'I'm not allowed to speak to him.'

'He would like to see you, I think.'

She didn't reply.

I drove back to the hotel, packed up and continued to the airport.

My ticket was for the following morning, but by going on standby I managed to get on the 8.35 p.m. flight.

When I arrived back at the house of girls, everyone was out.

26.

This weekend was my first on nightshift.

On Saturday evening, Wally was still not back from his mother's funeral, so I was left to look after myself.

A couple of hours in, some medical notes had to be taken downstairs. I knew Jabba wouldn't be there. I expected the door to the library to be locked, and it was. However, the metal grille which came down over the wooden counter had a small gap at the bottom. When I looked at it more closely, I saw that the hook by which it was usually attached had broken.

I decided to wait until my break before trying anything.

Time passed very slowly. Partly because, after the chucking-out flood, we weren't very busy. Partly because I knew I would be taking a big risk. If I was caught, I'd be fired, and probably worse. But this might be my only chance.

Around half three in the morning, I returned. I had saved some notes from earlier, to give me an excuse for being there. As I went, I checked for CCTV cameras. There were a few along the corridors leading to the library. None of them swivelled as I passed.

I knew that, on this shift, there was only one guard in the Security Room. The others were either in A&E or on patrol. Usually it was Mr Fine who sat watching the screens – lazy bastard. The chances of him spotting me were, I hoped, very slight.

Once, I turned back. But I realized I would need to drop the medical file off sooner or later. It might as well be now. Then, at least, I'd get some break.

I had lifted the grille up almost before I knew it. The thing rose easily but noisily. Then I was up on the counter and over behind it, pulling the grille down behind me.

I hurried away from the light, half expecting alarms to go off.

Now to find Mrs Fine's file.

From what Jabba had told me, the system was alphabetical. I pulled a folder at random from the nearest shelf.

Burton, James.

I walked around to the next aisle. My legs were so full of adrenalin it felt like the bones were dissolving.

Drummond, Michael.

And the next aisle.

Gerson, Mary.

I moved along a bit.

Gallop, Peter.

It took another couple of minutes to get to Fine.

I went through the folders one by one. Although I didn't know Mrs Fine's first name, I knew the rough date of her death, and that she'd been in her forties.

But the file wasn't there.

I checked through again: six people with the surname Fine. Of these, four were men. And of the two women, one had been born in 1936, the other in 1975.

Perhaps Mrs Fine had been treated under her maiden name – that wasn't likely, though. The only other explanation seemed to be that someone or other had removed the file. There seemed little doubt as to who.

I had just climbed back over the counter, and was pulling down the grille, when Mr Fine himself came through the door.

'Caught you,' he said, with a harsh chuckle.

There was no way I could talk myself out of this.

'Yes,' I said. 'I suppose so.'

Mr Fine stepped close. 'And what *exactly* were you looking for in there?'

'My girlfriend,' I said.

'Your girlfriend? Oh, is that where she lives?'

'No. I mean, my ex-girlfriend. She came in for treatment the other day. I wanted to know what for.'

'You wanted to know what for. And what did you find?'

'Twisted ankle, that's all.'

'Hardly worth losing your job for.' He was going to report me. I was in the shit. 'Why didn't you just slip Jabba a tenner, like everyone else?'

I didn't know what to say.

Mr Fine leaned in close. His breath smelled of artificial mint.

'I own you now,' he said. 'I've got this whole little escapade on video upstairs. So, from now on, anything I say, you do it – understand? Anything. Or else, this gets reported. So, next time you're on a drugs run, I want some codeine. Big pack. Just to show your good will. You can bring it up whenever's convenient.'

'Sure,' I said. 'You just needed to ask.'

Mr Fine looked at the grille.

'Have to report that, won't we? Get it fixed. Can't have people just going in there whenever they like, now can we?'

He gave me a pat on the back. In a strange way, now that he'd found out I was corruptible, Mr Fine seemed genuinely to like me more.

He escorted me back upstairs, blowing minty breath all over the side of my face.

The rest of the shift gave me plenty of time to think about just how much I'd cocked up. I should have waited until the following night. But by then the grille might have been mended. I should have made certain that a disturbance in A&E meant all the security guards were in attendance, and no-one was watching the CCTV cameras. But maybe that never happened.

At first it seemed incredibly bad luck that Mr Fine had been watching the camera for the ten or twelve seconds that it took me to get into the records room. But the more I considered it, the more likely it seemed that he'd been watching out for an attempt to get at the medical files. Either that, or he'd been keeping a permanent eye on *me* – waiting until I did something iffy, and he could pounce.

Only towards the end of the shift did I start thinking again about the file. If Mr Fine *had* murdered his wife, then of course he would have wanted any evidence destroyed. In the months since it happened, and given his position, he would have had thousands of opportunities to remove the file. Or perhaps, as he said, he had just slipped Jabba a tenner.

What I needed to do now was find out as much about Mrs Fine's death as I could. It was a distraction from finding out about the heart, but it wasn't as if I had a lot to do there. And if it came down to things being stolen from the hospital, Security had to be involved somewhere.

I had seen Becky on all but one of my train journeys across the Thames. She seemed to have taken up permanent residence on the roof. On the Sunday morning, as I went home, she was sprawled-out sleeping. I thought she was dead, until I saw one of her hands move.

Wally returned for Sunday night's shift.

He seemed quieter than before, less forthcoming with advice on correct portering technique.

'I was sorry to hear –'

'It was a sad day,' said Wally, leaving the past tense to do its work.

I shadowed him for a few hours. But I got the feeling he wanted to be left alone.

After our first break, I went my own way. He didn't call me back. One reason for breaking off was that I needed to get the box of codeine for Mr Fine.

I managed to achieve this without too much difficulty.

Mr Fine was in the Security Room when I buzzed.

'Excellent,' he said. 'And now I've got you *stealing* on video, too. Want a gander? Very shifty, you look.'

'No, I believe you,' I said.

'Until next time.'

I found Wally in the locker room, when I took my next break. He was lying down with his eyes closed.

Seeing no way of introducing the subject subtly, I asked him straight out what the name of Mr Fine's first wife had been.

'Belinda,' he said. 'Why do you ask?' His eyes were still closed.

On an instinct, I said, 'Her file's missing.'

'Of course it's missing,' Wally said. 'I took it.'

'You took it?'

'Yes. Because otherwise it would have been stolen.'

I paused, then decided to follow this line of conversation as far as it would go.

'You really do think Mr Fine killed her?'

'I am sure of it.'

'Why don't you report him to the Police?'

'I have tried, anonymously. I wrote them two letters. It is obvious they are not interested. Mr Fine was once a Policeman.'

'Can I see the file?'

'Are you making investigations into this?' asked Wally.

'Yes.'

He smiled, as if I were suddenly his son.

'We can meet tomorrow,' he said. 'In a park.'

We did. In Regent's Park. At four o'clock. By the bandstand.

I didn't know whether this was Wally's desiccated sense of humour, or some allusion to a spy film, or perhaps just entirely understandable caution.

The bandstand itself was an elegant structure, like a maharajah's hat on the legs of a spider with rigor mortis.

Wally came into view at two minutes to four. His walk was military, and a briefcase was swinging from his right hand.

'Let us walk,' he said.

We headed north into Queen Mary's Gardens. After a while, we found a bench and sat down.

Wally opened the case.

'Here is the file,' he said. It was wedged into an illustrated art book about Albrecht Dürer.

'What's in it?' I asked. I couldn't remember when I'd last felt so giddy with excitement.

'Look for yourself,' he said.

I knew I looked far more suspicious reading a large hardback book than a buff-coloured file, but I didn't want to upset Wally.

The autopsy report was the first thing I came to. I read it carefully. There was nothing suspicious in it. Mrs Belinda Fine had died of a combination of pneumonia, pleurisy and what's commonly known as a superbug.

All this time, Wally had been watching me.

I was just about to pass on to another page when I noticed the signature at the bottom. It was one I had become very familiar with, a fat clot of gummy biro: Vic Goosen. He signed off on every corpse I delivered to him.

'Him?'

'Who?' asked Wally. 'I'm not going to help you. I want to see your logic is the same as mine.'

'Goosen did the autopsy.'

'He did. That is usual.'

'And you think Fine killed his wife. But that should have showed up somewhere. That's what autopsies are for.'

'Keep going.'

I knew my conclusion already.

'So Goosen lied to help Fine get away with it?'

'And?'

'Fine blackmailed him.'

'Why do you think that?'

I told Wally about him catching me down in the medical records library.

'Is he suspicious of you?'

'No. I don't think so.'

'It is possible,' he said, 'that Fine blackmailed Goosen.'

I went gradually.

'But you don't think he did. I don't think he did, either. There are no cameras down in Pathology. What could he have on Goosen?'

'Many things,' said Wally. 'Many things we don't know about.'

I thought about Jabba, and Fine's suggestion that I just slip him a tenner.

'He could have paid him,' I said. 'Paid him to say there was nothing suspicious.'

'Perhaps nothing was suspicious. Perhaps we make the whole thing up.'

'Why do you think Fine killed his wife?'

'I saw him.'

'What did he do?'

'Gave her a glass of water.'

'Why is that suspicious?'

'He made her drink it. She didn't want to. There were two glasses. She had orange juice, but he made her drink water.'

'How long were you watching?'

'Only one minute. I heard her complaining. She had a very loud voice. It was not the first time he made her drink water. She said he was cruel. He said she must drink lots of water. If I didn't hear this, I would not think him guilty. If I didn't hear this, I would not be involved.'

I sat back on the bench and looked out across the park. A feeling of unreality overtook me. It was possible that Wally was entirely mad. I wanted Kumiko there to reassure me I wasn't mad, too. After a few minutes, I found myself speaking.

'If Fine didn't blackmail Goosen, and he didn't pay him, then why did Goosen help? Did he hate Fine's wife, too?'

'I will not answer,' said Wally. '*That* you must discover for yourself. It is too much.'

We were to leave the park separately – Wally insisted on this. Just as I was turning away from him, he said, 'Be very careful. These men are dangerous.'

It was the second time he had used those words.

27.

On Saturday morning I began a letter to the police. In it, I told them why Paul White was innocent, and then why either Simon Aragon or Timothy Kendall – probably Simon Aragon – was guilty.

My idea was to deliver the letter to Southwark police station by hand as soon as it was finished.

At 10 a.m. someone tapped lightly on the door of my room: Anne.

'You're not busy, are you?'

Anne was here to talk about Skelton.

'Please come in.'

She sat down on the bed, cross-legged, with her back against the wall. Then she told me about the date. The last thing she said was, 'He still really loves you. He told me that directly. I've thought a lot about it – why he went out with me. He fancied me, I'm sure. But not enough to be unfaithful to you. That's what it was – that's what he thought it was. And the only reason he even let me as close as he did was because he was trying to prove something to himself.'

'He knows,' I said.

'Knows what?'

'Knows that I sent you to him as a message.'

'Did you?'

'Without realizing it. You were a test for him, although I was testing myself as well. I wanted to see if I could seduce him again, but as another woman – as you. It

262

didn't work. I failed the test, and he passed. Because he resisted. If I had really wanted to succeed, I would have been more subtle. I changed you too abruptly. That made it almost an insult. He couldn't have missed it.'

'But how do you know that?'

'The restaurant he took you to was our special place. He was saying that to himself, like a challenge. "You can't do this, can you?" It was like armour.'

'I don't understand.'

'I can't explain any better.'

'But what should I do?'

'Whatever you like. The game is over. I hope you didn't get hurt.'

'Of course not.' Anne wasn't speaking the one hundred per cent truth. 'Like you say, it was a bit of fun.' She was pretending to be Molly, who pretended to have a robust heart.

Anne got up to leave. 'Are you going back to him?' she asked, from the doorway.

'I don't think so,' I said.

When she was gone, I crumpled the letter up. I no longer wanted to present the police with either/or. That would not work. For my own pride, I needed to prove that Simon Aragon was the guilty one.

The best thing would be to confront him face to face. But if I tried to enter the hospital, I would be stopped and perhaps arrested. That was what Fine the security guard had told me last time.

I looked at the scrunched-up ball of paper. A letter wasn't such a bad idea. I would write Simon Aragon a letter, and Timothy Kendall, too. Just to make sure.

*

Half an hour later, I joined the girls downstairs. They were still talking over the previous night. Molly had been on a date, and hadn't returned until a few minutes before.

'Really, nothing at all happened,' she said.

'Who was your date with?'

'Pavel Smid,' said Anne. 'Can you believe it? *She* asked *him* out, and he said yes.'

'You should have seen his face,' Molly said.

'When?'

'When I asked him out, of course. He was so shocked. I had to reassure him that we wouldn't have to go anywhere expensive.'

'Where did you go?'

'A noodle bar in Brixton. Fujiyama.'

'Please don't break his heart,' said Jo.

'Stop saying that,' said Molly. 'I'm not some vixen-bitch. I really like him. He's so –'

'Don't say sweet,' Anne said. 'That'll jinx it completely.'

'He is absolutely sincere,' said Molly, more sincere herself than usual. 'He does have a sense of humour, but most of the time he's serious about everything. It's good for me.'

Anne and Jo told me they had been out for a pizza, locally, at the Sun and Doves.

'And Jo got chatted up,' said Anne.

'I did not,' Jo said.

'Well, you spent a lot of time talking to him.'

'He was very interesting.'

We all laughed.

'Who?' I asked.

'A sixth-former,' said Anne. 'Cradle-snatching vixen!'

'He wanted to know —'

The other girls shouted various phrases out to complete the sentence. Jo turned pink with delighted embarrassment.

'He's almost nineteen. He told me his name, and said I could email him if I liked.'

'Tomorrow,' said Molly.

'Wednesday,' said Anne. 'At the earliest.'

'What do you think?' Jo asked me.

'I think you have emailed him already.'

Jo managed to blush some more.

'You haven't!' Molly shrieked.

'Actually,' said Jo, 'I wasn't going to tell you, because I knew you'd disapprove, but we spent most of last night instant-messaging.'

'I thought you looked tired,' said Anne.

'So you emailed him the moment you got back?' said Molly.

'There was something neither of us could remember. About removal of necrotic tissue. I looked it up when I got back. I thought he'd like to know straight away. He wants to be a doctor.'

'How romantic,' said Anne.

'Swot-love,' said Molly.

'I am very happy for you,' I said. 'In a mature relationship, you can always be direct.'

Molly took this as a criticism of her. Correctly.

We spent the rest of the morning talking dating do's and don'ts. Kissing on a first date was mentioned. It felt good to forget my serious life for a while.

After a light lunch, Jo went to bed. The others joked

that she should make sure she unplugged her computer, in case she got pregnant.

Anne decided she would go shopping, and left in a hurry.

'I need to talk to Pavel,' I said to Molly.

'He told me,' she said. 'He's still really guilty about what happened on the bus.'

'Did he tell you why he is so scared?'

'No. Not directly. But I think, mainly, he's just terrified of losing his place at Guy's. He's worked so hard to get there. Two thousand people applied for the scholarship he's on.'

'Do you think you could persuade him to talk to me?'

'Perhaps. He's so nervous. If I push too much, he'll think that's the only reason I wanted to go out with him.'

'What is the reason?'

Molly looked over both her shoulders, not simply out of a sense of drama. 'Don't tell the others,' she said. 'I think I'm in love.'

'Yes,' I said. 'You are.'

Soon afterwards, Molly went to bed.

I called Paul White, and told him I hoped to clear his name by the end of the week.

'That's good,' he said. 'So you found Monica, then?'

'It wasn't difficult,' I said.

'And did she speak to you?'

'With a little persuasion.'

'You're very good at that.'

'Not from me,' I said. 'From her mother.'

'But she doesn't want me anywhere near her daughter. Never has.'

'She likes you. Secretly.'

'She thinks I did it.'

'Of course. You didn't fight enough.'

'They were very threatening,' said Paul.

'Who?'

'Barry Waddham.'

'If you get back together with Monica, be very nice to her mother,' I said. 'She has done much to help you, by helping me.'

I had a bath.

There was a message on my phone when I finished: Grzegorz. I called him back.

'How did you fare?' he asked.

I told him.

'Skelton came round,' he said. 'He knows almost everything you've been up to.'

'We have been in constant touch.'

'I thought you weren't speaking.'

'Not by speech.'

He didn't reply to this.

'What about his investigations?' I asked.

'Those that aren't into you? He didn't tell me much.'

'Did he seem depressed?'

'No. He was energetic. A little angry. Perhaps he is close to discovering something. What are you going to do now?'

Early Monday morning I gave Jo the two letters. She wanted excitement in her life. Her task was to place the letters where Simon Aragon and Timothy Kendall would find them. It was important that they read them before speaking to one another.

At 11.50 a.m., I was waiting in the greasy spoon on Borough High Street.

Jo and Anne arrived at 12.05 p.m.

'Wow. You certainly got to Timothy,' Anne said.

'Tell me.'

'He came into class, holding the letter up above his head. "Okay," he said, "who wrote this shit?" And no-one said anything. And he said, "Is this your idea of a joke?" Everyone was looking at one another.'

'Then he read the letter out, in full,' said Jo, wanting to be involved. 'And he said, "I'm not afraid of these allegations. 'What's your alibi?' it says. What's my alibi? Wrong question. Should ask, 'Who's your alibi?' Isn't that right, Jenny?"'

'And everyone looked at Jenny Essex,' continued Anne. 'She just said, "You bastard," and ran out of the room.'

'Timothy seemed quite happy, after that. He screwed the letter up into a ball, and chucked it in the bin – like a basketball. "You're lucky I don't recognize your hand-writing," he said. "Whoever you are."'

'What was Simon Aragon's reaction?'

The girls looked at one another.

'Nothing,' said Jo. 'He didn't mention it.'

'Did he seem nervous or annoyed?'

'Absolutely normal,' said Anne.

This wasn't unexpected.

'Are you sure he got the letter?'

'Certain,' said Jo. 'It was sticking out of his labcoat pocket.'

Just then, Molly arrived, followed by a shy Pavel. He tried to escape, but Molly pulled him towards me by the hand.

'He'll talk to you,' she said.

Pavel stood there, his body stiff with fright.

'Can you leave us alone?' I asked the girls.

Jo and Anne told me they would see me at home.

'You, too,' I said to Molly.

'Hey. If it wasn't for me, he wouldn't even be here.'

'It is right,' said Pavel. 'She should to stay.'

They sat down at my table.

Pavel began by apologizing, again, for injuring me.

'Please forget it,' I said. 'You were worried, weren't you? Because you know something.'

He nodded.

'On the morning of the first, you were the first student in the dissecting room.'

'I was early.'

'You're always early,' said Molly.

'I was early for my early.'

I waited.

'In the room, it is locked. But I look through the window, and I see Aragon with the heart. He has it in his hand. He carries it from Pandora-body and places it in chest cavity of the Clown.'

'They call him that because he has such big feet,' said Molly.

'You are sure it was him?'

'I see his face. Aragon is smiling. And then he sees me.' Pavel gave a loud laugh. 'He stop smiling.'

'What happened?' said Molly, asking my questions for me.

'He looks at me for two minutes. No lie. Then he comes unlock the door. He says nothing. But the next test I do, I get the low mark. He is the marker. And he keeps watching me. I say nothing. My marks get better. I still say nothing. More better. But if I fail in any part, I must to go home.'

Molly snuggled up against him.

'Isn't he brave?' she said.

'Very brave,' I said.

28.

When I got home from my meeting with Wally I felt extremely excited and extremely frustrated. My next shift at the hospital was due to begin on Wednesday morning, but I couldn't see how I could make any progress anywhere else.

I phoned Barbara behind-the-desk to see if I could do some overtime. She said she thought it would probably be okay, even though I was still on probation. They were short-staffed at the moment, she said.

'Let me see, and I'll call you back when I know for definite, alright, love?'

I think she liked me.

Whilst I waited, I had another look at the Keats biography – and now I knew the reason for Kumiko's interest in him, I did so with greater focus. As far as I could see, though, the text made no mention of King Death. Perhaps that was just a bit of unfounded student legend. Kumiko was still following up something, though.

Barbara took longer to get back to me than I expected. So I moved on to the computer.

Searching 'Keats' and 'King' and 'Death' brought up a load of irrelevant pages. The addition of 'Guy's' narrowed it down a little. There were a couple of student articles about Dr Norfolk – generally very affectionate, as far as I could see; even the ones written before he disappeared.

Once his name came up, I decided to pursue it further. 'Dr Norfolk' and 'mysterious' and 'disappearance' returned a few news stories, which I read. Re-entering his name, along with the date he was last seen, took me to a couple more articles. All in all, not very much or very helpful.

The final piece I came across was more in-depth, from a Sunday newspaper. In a sidebar it included a timeline of Dr Norfolk's last day. Those who spoke to him noticed nothing unusual in his manner. His office, when he left it, was tidy, and his paperwork up to date. He was last seen on the hospital CCTV system, leaving through the main entrance, by a senior Security Guard at around eight o'clock in the evening.

This stopped me dead.

I flicked back to the start of the article, found the byline. The journalist's name was Gina Flintlock. Then I called Directory Inquiries and got the number for the editorial team. When I asked to speak to Gina, Gina Flintlock, there was a moment's confusion at the other end. 'Her, she's a freelancer.'

'Do you have a number for her?'

A few moments of typing followed, then, 'I can't find her number on the system.'

'Well, do you have an email?'

More typing.

'Okay. Have you got a pen?'

I typed the address straight into my mail programme, said thank you, put the phone down and began composing a message. After rereading it, I sent it off.

Five minutes later, the phone rang.

'Skelton? Overtime's fine. Come in tomorrow morning, and you can do eight till eight.'

'Thank you,' I said.

'I understand,' Barbara said. 'Bills, bills, bills.'

At half past six, the phone rang again. This time it was my agent. 'I've just heard the song,' she said. 'Why didn't you tell me? It's simply sublime, and the biggest hit I've ever heard. Your playing is exquisite.'

'It's a little weird,' I said. 'You know it's about us – Kumiko and me.'

'Really? That makes it even more wonderful. Look, they just rang up to say you'll get a smidgin more money, but not much. And they're only doing that out of the kindness of their hearts. His heart. The star. It should bring you in loads of work, though – and I hope you're not going to be so silly as to turn it *down*.'

'I might have to,' I said. 'It all depends.'

'Still being frustratingly mysterious?'

'Yes, actually – and, right now, I'm waiting for quite an important call.'

'If I didn't love you so much, I might not forgive you for that.'

'I didn't mean –'

'It's okay, sweets. Speak soon, and you are an absolute star.'

Gina Flintlock didn't call back until after nine that evening. I had explained a little in my email.

'You wanted to ask me a question?'

'Thank you for calling. It's about Dr Norfolk of Guy's Hospital,' I said.

'Oh, the King Death article. That was a while ago.'

'Yes. Just a detail really.'

'Are you a journalist?'

'No.'

Gina didn't seem to believe me, but asked, 'What is it?'

'Can you remember the name of the Security Guard who was the last person to see Dr Norfolk alive?'

'Fine and Dandy,' she said, without hesitation. 'Mr Fine. What a psycho. Why do you want to know?'

'I'm just interested,' I said. 'I work at the hospital.'

'Did you know Dr Norfolk?'

'No.'

'You've found out something about the disappear-ance?'

The conversation was dangerously close to turning into an interview.

'Thanks for your help,' I said, and put the phone straight down.

She called back to ask another question, but I didn't pick up.

I was restless, now – I needed to think, and to do that I needed to walk.

I strolled all the way down Gray's Inn Road, then through Holborn, along Newgate, Cheapside and onto King William Street. My mind kept following through different explanations as to what I'd found out. It seemed clear that there had been some collaboration between Mr Fine and Goosen. But if Goosen had helped Fine get away with murder, what exactly had he got in return? The obvious answer was *the same*. Was it possible that he had been responsible for Dr Norfolk's permanent disap-pearance? Surely I was making that up in the enthusiasm of investigation. I remembered what Dr Speed had said, during his lecture, about disposal of dissected cadavers. Down in Pathology, anything was possible – I had seen that for myself: a body could be reduced to sludge and simply flushed away. In fact, where better to do it?

I crossed the Thames at London Bridge and turned left towards the station. Again, I had found myself heading back towards the hospital. This time, however, I had a definite aim: I wanted to see if Nick was around. He was the only person I could think of with whom I could check – subtly, of course – my suspicions.

I went into the Porterage. They told me Nick had been on dayshift, and had finished at eight. I thought, on balance, it was probably worth passing by the Dissecting Room before I headed home.

When I got there, I could see a light on in the side office. I walked down the aisle between the corpses, taking no particular trouble to be quiet. If Nick had been there, I would probably have heard his mocking voice by now.

Simon Aragon was alone at his desk, examining a crumpled piece of A4 paper with handwriting on it – handwriting that I recognized immediately as Kumiko's: black pen, superneat.

I cleared my throat, and Aragon almost fell off his chair. 'What?!' he said. 'Oh. You. What do you want?'

'I just wondered if there was a game on.'

He looked around, almost uncertain himself.

'No. No game tonight. Nothing happening here, okay?'

My eyes strayed to the letter, for that's what it appeared to be. Aragon followed my gaze.

'Do you know anything about this?' he asked.

'About what?' I asked, playing for time.

He looked at me penetratingly. Was I lying?

'Someone is taking the piss,' he said.

'Out of you?'

'Of course out of me!' he screeched, suddenly furious. 'Now fuck off! Go on. Fuck off!'

'I know who it's from,' I said.

'You know.'

'And I know what it's about.'

'You're bluffing.'

'Am I?'

'You're full of shit.'

'The heart,' I said. 'She knows you did it.'

His face lost all colour.

'Who?' he asked. 'Who wrote it?'

'I'm not telling you.'

I turned to leave. Aragon leapt from his chair. I think he wanted to grab me, but he caught his upper thigh against the sharp corner of the desk. When he carried on towards me, he was limping and swearing.

I hadn't been in a proper fight since school – and it took me a couple of seconds to realize this was just that: a proper fight. The fights I'd *almost* found myself in, since then, had both of them been stopped by someone intervening. (Don't be so stupid! Okay, enough!) That wasn't going to happen now.

Aragon tried to grab my throat. I backed away, and found myself trapped against one of the plinths bearing the part-dissected bodies.

The shock of this, of touching cold dead flesh, distracted me for a second. Aragon took advantage. He punched me in the face – on the nose. I was, strange to say, pleased to feel this shot. It was so reassuringly feeble. He leant forwards, trying for another. Bracing myself

276

against the plinth, I kicked him in the gut. He collapsed, winded.

In fantasy-fights, when I have defeated the mugger who has been menacing Kumiko, I tend to stand over them and make them promise never to attack anyone ever again. With Aragon, embarrassingly, I went across to him and asked, 'Are you alright?'

'Go away,' he said.

Blood dripped to the floor. I realized it was coming from my nose.

'You shouldn't have attacked me,' I said.

'Watch out,' Aragon said. 'I'm going to fucking get you.'

As he clearly didn't want my help, I left him there.

If my thoughts heading down to Guy's had all been of Goosen, my thoughts on the way back were exclusively of Kumiko. She had seriously spooked Aragon. There seemed little doubt that he was the guilty one. Everything in her investigation had come together. She had been single-minded, methodical, and had got her man. I, by contrast, had been randomly following whatever lead came up. This had left me with plenty of explanations based on very few facts. What we really needed to do, Kumiko and I, was meet up and talk over what we'd managed to find out. Perhaps that way we would discover some connection between Mr Fine, Goosen, Dr Norfolk and Aragon.

My main question, though, was why – knowing what she did – Kumiko hadn't had Aragon arrested? She must have had some reason for not going to the Police – and, because of that, I decided I couldn't go to them either.

It was hard to sleep that night. Eventually, around three in the morning, I got up and went through into the living room. The amber glow of London gave me more than enough light to see by. I sat on the sofa, waiting for time to pass.

On Tuesday morning, I was still desperate to speak to Nick. He was on shift, I knew – Barbara had told me that when I arrived. But I didn't see him until I went down to the smoking bay around nine thirty. Unfortunately, he wasn't the only person there I recognized.

'What?'

It was Anne. I'd almost forgotten my earlier fears of her catching me in my uniform.

'You're a Porter!'

'Yes, I'm a Porter,' I said, downplaying it. 'Why are you so surprised?'

Nick was already moving to join us.

'But you're a musician.'

'And I'm a musician, too. But when you said what you did about working in the hospital, I decided to try it out.'

'Morning,' said Nick.

'And besides,' I said, over-elaborating, 'I needed the money.'

'Introduce me, Skelton,' Nick said.

Even in the awkwardness of the moment, I felt slightly pleased to know someone from Guy's who Nick didn't.

'Nick, this is Anne. Anne; Nick.'

'You seem a bit surprised to see him here.'

'Just a little,' she said. 'We've been on three dates in the last month, and he never mentioned he was working in the same place as me.'

Nick looked at me.

'Ashamed of the job, are you? Think it's not good enough for you?' He was half joking.

'No. No. I wanted to impress her.'

I couldn't really tell whether my answers were consistent or not.

'So, what's wrong with being a Porter?'

'Nothing. But I thought if she knew I wasn't doing very well as a musician –'

'What? I wouldn't be interested? Do you think I'm *that* shallow?' She turned to Nick. 'And then he goes and says he doesn't want to see me again – after taking me back to his flat.'

This had the opposite effect to the one intended. Having already seen the beauty of my dumped ex Kumiko, Nick now gave Anne the onceover and then looked at me with something approaching awe.

'Anyway,' said Anne. 'I've got to go now. Class.'

She strode off towards the Dissecting Room. As she went I could see her pulling out her cellphone and dialling. I hadn't even had the chance to remind her of our bet.

'You bastard,' said Nick, watching Anne's arse. 'How could you chuck that away?'

'Can I ask you a direct question?'

'You're not a bender, are you?'

'What do you think happened with Dr Norfolk?'

He paused before answering. 'King Death? What does that have to do with anything? Burned out, I suppose. Couldn't take it any more. Headed for the hills.'

'He wasn't murdered, then?'

'Murdered? Nah. Happens all the time. We just never get to hear about it, unless it's someone we know personal-like. There's millions of missing persons.'

'But just supposing he *was* killed. Who do you think would want him dead?'

'No-one. He was a nice guy, from what I hear. Every-one liked him. Not like Speed.'

'What about Raymond France?'

'I think you need a lie-down,' said Nick. 'This is all a bit nuts.'

Perhaps he was right.

'What about Vic Goosen?'

'Nurse!' said Nick, to a nearby smoker. 'Nurse, this man needs seeing to – a good hard seeing-to. The sperm's gone to his head.'

The young woman scoffed and turned away.

'Look, mate,' said Nick. 'Your problem isn't Speed. It's all those beautiful honeys you keep dumping. I mean, have some fucking sense, why don't you?'

I went back inside to continue with my shift, leaving Nick behind with the other smokers. One of them, I noticed with some anxiety, was Kev the Security Guard.

Although I couldn't be certain, I was pretty sure that Anne had been calling Kumiko. Now that Kumiko knew I was working as a Porter, what difference did that make? Perhaps she would reckon I had inside information, information she needed to have Aragon arrested, and would give me a call. I could always call her: I still had her new mobile number, which Paul White had given me.

That Tuesday morning was unusually quiet – giving no hint of what was to come. I spent much of it ferrying people up from A&E. There was one arrest, and, after it had been called, I wheeled the body down to Pathology.

As the lift doors opened, I remembered Wally's final words to me – 'these men are dangerous'. I couldn't avoid them, however. This was my job.

Goosen was on the phone when I entered the room.

He looked at me, slightly surprised. 'Speak of the devil,' he said, loud enough for me to hear. 'I'll call you back,' he said, and hung up.

France came across to do the paperwork on the corpse – a young woman who had died, probably, of blood poisoning. But Goosen intervened. 'Well, well, well,' he said. 'What have we here?' He was looking at me, not the body. 'Something very *curious*.'

I held the clipboard out to him. After staring at me for half a minute, he took it. I found it hard to suppress thoughts of Dr Norfolk and what Goosen might have done to him. The possibilities, in various states of dissolution, were all around me.

Goosen put his signature on the bottom of the form – the same signature I had seen on Mrs Fine's autopsy report. I tried to avoid his eyes, in case he could see in mine what I was thinking.

I had turned to go, very relieved, when Goosen grabbed my wrist. The latex fingers were cold and wet against my skin. 'You forgot your pen,' he said.

'Thanks,' I managed to say.

Just then, my beeper went off. Goosen let me go, so I could look at it.

When I walked out, I was shaking.

The rest of the shift was uneventful. At ten to eight, I was just hanging about in A&E, trying to look useful, when Anne and Jo came through the doors from outside – with Kumiko between them, supported by their shoulders. Her black-haired head was lolling around as they carried her towards the admissions desk.

I ran across to help them, pushing a wheelchair in front of me.

'What's wrong with her?' I asked, frantic.

Their answer was given to both me and the Nurse behind the desk.

Jo said, 'Overdose. Probably of Diazepam.'

'We're medical students,' added Anne. 'She needs to be admitted, stomach pumped and put under observation.'

'Quick,' said Jo.

'Has she vomited?' asked the Nurse.

Jo began to answer her formula questions.

'Did you tell her about me working here?' I asked Anne. 'Did she do this because of that?'

'No,' said Anne. 'This has absolutely nothing to do with you. Just do your job.'

29.

Immediately after saying goodbye to Molly and Pavel, I went to Southwark police station.

'Excuse me, please,' I said to the officer behind the counter. He was high up, head above me. 'I need to speak to PC Wagner.'

'What's this concerning?'

'Please just let me speak to him.'

The officer went away into a back room, and then returned.

'Would this be regarding the earlier matter?'

'I will explain to him.'

The officer dialled a number on his phone and said, 'Yes, it is.'

A few minutes later, PC Wagner came out to see me.

'Hello, again,' he said, struggling to be friendly. 'I hear you have something to tell me.'

'Not here,' I said.

'I'm a little busy, right now.'

'It will be very short.'

He took me to the interview room.

'Will you record this?' I asked.

'Not unless, you're making a confession of something. You haven't been trespassing again, have you?'

'I know who threw the heart from the train. Like I told you before, Paul White is innocent.' Briefly, I went over the course of my investigations. Then I said, 'The person you should arrest is Simon Aragon. He works in the dissecting room, which is where the heart was stolen from. His motive is jealousy. He hated Paul White because Paul White was going out with Monica Norfolk.'

'Hang on. Let's rewind a little. You said just then you have a witness who saw something crucial.'

'Yes.'

'And what precisely did they see?'

'They saw Simon Aragon taking the decoy heart from the body they call Pandora.'

'That proves nothing.'

'It does. You are not following my logic.'

'That may be because I can't see any logic.'

'I would like to speak to a more senior officer.'

'No. You'd just be wasting their time, just as you've been wasting mine.'

'What I have done is your job.'

He looked at me with anger.

'Please don't try to tell me my job.'

Reluctantly, I said, 'There is also a witness who saw the heart thrown from the train.'

'Why didn't they come forward before?'

'She doesn't like the police.'

'And where was she when she saw all this? Flying over Borough Market in a helicopter, perhaps?'

'No. She was on a roof.'

'At half five in the morning?'

'Yes.'

'And what precisely was she doing there?'

'She sleeps there, sometimes.'

'And what is her name?' He did not have his notebook out.

'Becky. I don't know her surname.'

'Sumner. Rebecca Sumner. Know her well. I've arrested her three times in total. Once for soliciting, once for assault and once for possession with intent to supply. Supply crack cocaine, that is.'

He stood up.

'What do you do?' he asked.

I didn't know what he meant.

'What do you normally do? What is your occupation?'

'I am an artist.'

'Well, then –' He made his face ugly. 'Why don't you go and paint another picture. Please.'

He showed me out.

'Goodbye,' he said, firmly.

I took the bus to Clerkenwell.

'The police are not interested,' I told the girls.

'Why not?' asked Jo.

I repeated the conversation with PC Wagner.

'They're so stupid,' said Anne.

'What are you going to do now?' asked Molly.

'I have been thinking about it,' I said. 'I think I must speak to Simon Aragon. Perhaps if I approach him in the right way, he will collapse. We know the police won't prosecute him, but he doesn't know that. Not yet.'

'What's the time?' Molly asked. She never wore a watch.

'Half one,' said Jo. 'That means Simon will be on rounds.'

'I will go and find him,' I said.

The girls said they would skip their lecture to help me. We caught the bus back to London Bridge. Jo made a couple of calls to Administration, pretending she needed to hand some urgent paperwork to Simon. 'He's on the seventeenth floor,' she said. 'It shouldn't be too hard to track him down.'

'Thank you,' I said.

'I enjoyed that,' she replied.

At Guy's, we took a lift.

I recognized the ward. It was the same one Paul White was admitted to, after jumping into the Thames. Today it was full of old women. Molly asked one of them if they had been seen that afternoon, by a young doctor. The old lady, who had bright-yellow hair, pointed us down the ward. We carried on. And in the next ward, Molly pointed out Simon Aragon.

'Let me speak to him alone,' I said. 'It is better if he doesn't see me with you.'

I was halfway down the ward when I felt a strong hand on my arm, and smelled peppermint.

'Stop right there,' said Fine.

'Let me go.'

Fine said, 'I thought we warned you to stay off hospital grounds.'

'There is someone I must speak to.'

'Visiting your gran, are you?' Fine looked along the beds. All were occupied by white Caucasians, apart from those occupied by black Africans and Afro-Caribbeans. 'Didn't think so.' Then he caught sight of Simon Aragon. 'Him? You want him?'

'Yes,' I said, thinking there was a chance he would let me.

'Come with me,' Mr Fine said.

Simon Aragon continued with his rounds. He had not seen our argument.

Fine's grip upon my arm grew even tighter. I was frogmarched straight past the girls.

'If you don't let her go immediately,' said Jo, 'I will report you.'

'And who are you?' Fine said, without stopping.

'I'm a student here.'

'A student – ooh, I am scared.'

We were now passing the old lady with the yellow hair. She sat up in bed, looking concerned. 'Is there something wrong?' she asked.

'Nothing, love,' said Fine, over his shoulder.

Once we were inside the lift, he put me in an armlock.

'I am not resisting,' I said. 'You are hurting me.'

'This is the last time,' he said, pepperminty in my ear. 'If you persist in bothering our staff, we shall have you arrested and prosecuted.'

I said nothing.

The girls continued to ask Fine to be more gentle with me. He ignored them just as if they weren't there.

At the main doors, Fine pushed me out with a hard shove. 'The last time,' he said, and strode off.

'Are you okay?' asked Jo.

'Bastard,' said Molly.

'I know his name,' said Anne. 'He's often out here, having a fag.'

'It is Mr Fine,' I said. 'We have met before.'

He had turned round ten paces away and was now watching us.

'Let's go,' said Anne.

Back at the house, the girls became very incensed about Fine's behaviour.

'I'll write a letter,' said Jo.

'We can all sign it,' Molly said. 'We all saw what happened.'

'Thank you. It doesn't matter,' I said. 'But I still need to speak to Simon Aragon.'

'I suppose you could wait for him – try to catch him when he comes off shift,' said Jo.

'Do you know his route home?' I asked.

They did not.

'One of us could follow him, and call to let you know, so you could catch up.'

We decided to try it.

Jo phoned Administration again and, by asking indirect questions, found out that Simon Aragon would be finished at 8 p.m.

At 7.15 p.m., we left for Guy's.

I waited just off hospital grounds, along the most likely route: down St Thomas Street.

It was a damp evening but not raining. I wore my black agnès b coat.

At 8.10 p.m., Jo called.

'I followed him,' she said. 'He went straight from the ward to the dissecting room. Perhaps he's just picking up his clothes.'

Half an hour later, she called again.

'He's still in there.'

And once more, an hour later.

'I don't think he's going home tonight. Hang on. Someone's just going in to see him. A man.'

I asked her to describe him. It was Skelton.

Ten minutes later, Jo phoned to say, 'He's come out again. And he's all roughed up – bloody nose. It looks like he's been in a fight. No sign of Aragon.'

I told her to come and meet me. Simon Aragon was either staying very late or spending the night in hospital. Clearly, my letter had scared him.

But what about Skelton? Why was he visiting Simon Aragon? Had he also found out that he was guilty? How did he even know who Simon Aragon was? Or where the dissecting room was?

Back once more at the house, we debated what to do.

I felt strongly that I must speak to Aragon as soon as possible, while the impression of the letter was still strong.

'What if he attacks you, too?' Anne said.

'We don't know that is what happened,' I said.

'His schedule tomorrow is exactly the same,' said Jo. 'Anatomy class from ten till twelve, then in the hospital from one until eight.'

'You could wait for him outside the lecture hall,' said Anne.

'But we already know that Fine watches there,' said Jo.

'I need to be inside the hospital. And I need to be there in a way that means I can't be removed.'

'A disguise,' said Jo. 'We could steal you a cleaner's uniform.'

'How many cleaners are Japanese?'

'Alright, a nurse's uniform. There are several Asian nurses.'

'No,' I said. 'Someone might ask me to save a life, and I could not do it. It would be easier to be admitted as a patient.'

'Brilliant,' said Molly.

'Now what can we give you?' asked Jo.

They began, as connoisseurs, to discuss possible injuries and illnesses: appendectomy, pulmonary embolus, renal colic.

'Okay,' said Jo. 'So we're agreed on the chest pains. That would get you admitted overnight.'

'I think I need to be unconscious,' I said. 'Then Fine will not be able to challenge me.'

'Really unconscious or just faking?' asked Jo.

'They could tell if I was faking, couldn't they?'

Further discussions followed.

'Okay,' said Jo, 'how about a suicide attempt? That would also explain why we were bringing you in.'

It didn't take long to work out the details. Anne and Jo would take me in. Molly would stay close to the phone, in case anything went wrong.

'The dosage won't be dangerous,' said Jo. 'Just enough to knock you out and leave a credible trace in your bloods.'

We decided that 1.30 p.m. the following afternoon was the best time. I could either speak to Aragon soon after waking up, or at any time during the next day.

'They'll have to admit you, and keep you under observation,' said Anne. 'But once you're in, you should be able to move around pretty easily. Fine can't throw you out if you're in a nightie and on a drip. We can help you find where Simon is.'

I phoned Grzegorz first thing on Tuesday morning, to tell him what I had found out, what I had already done, and what I intended to do.

'Fucking police,' he said.

'It is not their fault,' I said. 'They are doing their jobs as well as they can.'

'The problem is, no-one really intelligent ever becomes a policeman.'

'But –' I said.

'Please repeat back to me the chain of evidence,' he said.

Grzegorz had a good memory.

'If anything happens to me when –'

'I thought you said it was completely safe.'

'The drugs are. I don't know about Simon Aragon. He may have punched Skelton so he may attack me. And security won't help.'

'Do you want me to be there? I could come down.'

'You can come during visiting hours if I am still there tomorrow. I expect it to be over by then.'

'Alright. If that's what you want. You can always call me, you know that.'

'You are a good friend.'

Then I felt myself weaken.

'Have you spoken to Skelton since last night?'

'No. It was a while ago. He was fine then. He still wants you back.'

'He does?'

'He's changed, though. At first, he was resigned. Now, he is resolved.'

'To do what?'

'To win you back.'

'You make me sound like a princess.'

'I think that is how he sees you.'

We talked a little longer. As I hung up, I felt myself glowing. I have always wanted to be a princess. I did not have time to examine my emotion, however. My phone rang a minute later.

'It's Anne. I just saw Skelton. He's working as a porter.'

I was too surprised to speak.

'Can you hear me? I've just seen him. He's working in the hospital as a porter. Isn't it incredible?'

'It is.'

Anne was breathless, and not only from excitement. I could hear the rustle of her walking.

'He says he got the idea from a conversation with me.'

'What did you say?'

'I think I said something like there are only insiders and outsiders, as far as hospital is concerned. And that if you are an outsider, you'd never really know what goes on inside a hospital.'

'Were those the words you used?'

Somehow it seemed important to know exactly what had caused Skelton to make this decision.

'Roughly. I can't remember exactly. I may have said it was a monster. That working there was like being in a nightmare. The belly of the beast. I wasn't exaggerating.'

'No,' I said.

'It's good, though, isn't it? He might be able to help us with our plan, if he's around.'

'I don't want him involved.'

'I just thought –'

'It was a good idea. Perhaps, in an emergency.'

'I'm going to be late for class,' said Anne.

'Watch Simon today,' I said. 'Call me afterwards to tell me how he seems.'

'Roger and out,' said Anne. Her laughter was cut off with a click.

I thought about Skelton.

30.

Twenty minutes later, I was pushing a still completely unconscious Kumiko up to a medical ward. Anne and Jo were alongside me.

'What exactly happened?'

'We just found her in her room,' Jo said. 'She'd taken a whole bottle of pills.'

'She didn't leave a note?'

'Nothing,' said Anne.

We took the nearest lifts.

Before we left A&E, Kumiko had been taken off to be treated for opioid poisoning. This involved an injection of something or other, to counteract the Diazepam.

As the doors opened on the seventeenth floor, I saw Mr Fine standing there, arms tightly folded. He seemed to be expecting us.

'This young woman is expressly forbidden to enter hospital property,' he said.

'This young woman is in a coma,' replied Jo. 'Now, get out of the way.'

'She's faking it,' said Fine.

'Oh, don't be so stupid,' said Anne.

Mr Fine stepped aside, but started to follow us down the corridor as soon as we were past him.

We pushed the trolley along into the ward, then lined it up beside the bed. Mr Fine watched us lift Kumiko across, without offering to help. He hung around for another five minutes before wordlessly departing.

'Why?' I asked.

'Until she wakes up,' said Anne, 'we're as much in the dark as you are.'

I sat down to wait by her bedside.

'Don't you have to be somewhere else?'

'I'm off shift now,' I said. 'So I'm going to stay here until she wakes up.'

This happened around half past ten.

Anne and Jo were still there, too, although they had come and gone individually several times.

Kumiko was very groggy. We gave her some water to drink. Her eyes had taken me in, but the first thing she said, almost as a question, was, 'Hello, Skelton.' I had been worried she would tell me to go away.

'Kumi,' I said.

'So it worked,' said Kumiko to Anne and Jo.

'What do you mean?' said I.

'He doesn't know?' Kumiko asked.

'No,' said Anne. 'He thinks you tried to commit suicide.'

Kumiko smiled at me.

'It was a trick.'

I was furious, with Kumiko especially, but I kept quiet.

'I needed to wake up in hospital. And here I am.'

She took another sip of water, then coughed for a while.

'Is he around?' she asked of Jo.

'No,' said Anne. 'He's gone home. You'll have to wait till tomorrow.'

'Who?' I asked.

'You know,' said Kumiko.

'Simon Aragon?'

'The Police won't do anything. I've told them what I know.'

'Will you tell me?'

Kumiko closed her eyes. 'Give me a few minutes. Could I have a cup of coffee? Black.'

I went to get her some – taking the opportunity to think things through. When I returned, she was far more alert. It took about ten minutes for her to describe how she had reduced her number of suspects to just one.

Then I told Kumiko what I knew of Aragon – from playing poker against him, and from last night when I'd found him reading her letter.

'What about you?' she asked. 'Did you find evidence against him, too?'

'I wasn't really looking. I got sidetracked.'

'Tell me,' Kumiko said.

I realized, just then, that I should feel embarrassed to be there with Kumiko and Anne together.

'I'll tell you,' I said, then turned to Anne and Jo. 'But I'm afraid you'll have to leave.'

'You can trust them,' said Kumiko. 'They are my good friends.'

I wanted to say, 'Who let you take a dangerous overdose of drugs.'

'It's serious,' I said. 'I can't risk it.'

Kumiko nodded at Anne and Jo, and they took her meaning. 'We'll come back,' said Jo.

I pulled my chair closer to the bedside. It felt wonderful just to be physically present in the same space as Kumiko, let alone talking so intimately with her. I didn't take her hand, although I wanted to more than anything.

'It's about King Death,' I said. 'I think you know who I mean.'

A Nurse came and pulled the curtain around the empty bed to our left. I thought this was a little strange, but didn't question it at the time. Now, of course, I realize that this was where Fine must have hidden when he spied on us. He could easily have asked the Nurse to create a hiding place – then snuck in there whilst we were absorbed in talk.

It took me longer than Kumiko to explain my investigations. I got confused, then had to double back and restate the things of which I was absolutely certain.

'But I don't see how I can prove anything,' I said. 'It's all circumstantial.'

'You have convinced me,' said Kumiko.

'I'm certainly not going to confront either of them. I can't even prove that they've ever met.'

I was at a dead end.

'What do they have in common?' Kumiko asked.

'They're very different.'

We sat in silence, not uncomfortable.

Kumiko finished the last of her coffee. 'I wish I could have a cigarette,' she said. 'I started again.'

This was a definite message. I wanted to say, 'It doesn't matter.' As if we were already talking about reconciliation. But then I had another thought –

'Smokers,' I said. 'They're both smokers. Nick said that Vic Goosen used to be one of the heaviest, but he gave up. *That's* where they could have met. And, by giving up, Goosen was trying to avoid accidentally meeting Fine. He smokes like anything, too. In fact, it's almost impossible that they didn't meet. And they both work nights. No-one else around. Fine gets talking about how much he hates his wife ...'

'It sounds good,' said Kumiko.

'I need proof.'

'Proof is hard to find.'

Anne and Jo returned – smelling of cigarettes.

'Finished?' asked Jo.

Kumiko nodded.

Anne and Jo brought another couple of chairs over, and we talked for a while about Simon Aragon. But then the same Nurse I had seen drawing the curtains approached us. I recognized her as the one who had prevented me from seeing Paul White.

'Visiting time over a *long* time ago, now. It only because you're staff I let you stay so long. Time fi you go.'

'Please,' I said. 'I'll sleep in the chair.'

'That not allowed,' said the Nurse, and went away.

It seemed that Kumiko was happy to be left alone that night.

'You can come again in the morning,' she said.

'No,' I said. 'Someone should be here with you. I'm sure I could persuade the Nurse to let me stay.'

'No chance,' said Jo.

Kumiko needed to be protected. I was sure of that.

'Wait here,' I said, then realized how ridiculous a thing it was to say.

'See you tomorrow,' said Jo.

Anne squeezed Kumiko's hand.

'Thanks for not dying,' she said.

I took the same lift as them downstairs, and said goodbye next to the entrance. Then I went into the Porterage, and had them beep Wally. He arrived ten minutes later.

'Come with me,' I said, already nervous something might have happened upstairs. 'There's someone I want you to meet.'

As we travelled up, I told Wally what I'd spoken about with Kumiko. 'She knows,' I said. 'That's why I'm worried.'

'It is wise,' he said.

Kumiko was very charming with Wally. It wasn't difficult to see that he thought she was beautiful. He almost became flustered.

'It is a very great pleasure,' he said.

'Can you keep an eye on her?' I asked. 'Make sure she's okay.'

'Of course,' he said to her. 'Though I will not wake you up.'

'And you have your mobile?' I asked.

'Yes,' said Kumiko.

'Is it on?'

'I will be fine.'

'Call if you want me. I'm going to be nearby.'

The Nurse came back. 'Okay. Now time fi to go.'

Wally accompanied me to the lift.

'You should go home,' he said. 'You are looking tired.'

'I'm staying here. I'll be in the locker room if she needs me.'

'You must also be careful,' said Wally.

I didn't expect to sleep, but I started to doze almost as soon as I lay down on the bench.

The next thing I knew, there was something covering my mouth – and then I didn't know anything at all.

31.

The girls told me what happened.

Anatomy class began, as usual, at 10 a.m.

Simon Aragon was looking terrible. He had shaved but badly. There were cuts on his neck covered with toilet paper. His hair was standing up. Black circles were around his eyes.

By contrast, Timothy Kendall seemed bright and happy.

At the end of class, which concentrated on the spleen, Simon Aragon asked Anne if she could stay to help clean up.

Suspicious, she tried to get out of it.

Molly and Jo came across to see what was going on.

Simon Aragon immediately went and spoke to Dr Speed, who said of course Anne must stay behind, if her help was needed.

Jo offered to help, too. But Simon Aragon said there was no need for that.

'We'll wait for you outside,' Molly said, so that Simon Aragon heard.

Once everyone was gone, Simon Aragon began shouting at Anne. Anne said later she remembered every word. This is what she told me.

'Why did you write that letter? Why are you accusing me of this?' She said that he snarled when he spoke. She even thought he would bite her.

'I didn't,' she said, trying to move towards the door.

Simon Aragon stood in her way.

'I know you did because your boyfriend told me you did.'

'What boyfriend?' Anne asked.

'He was almost gloating about you ruining my life.'

Anne knew he meant Skelton.

'You disguised your handwriting,' he said, 'but I know it's you. I've found out that you've been seeing him.'

'So you didn't do it?'

'No.'

'Well, if you didn't, who did?'

'One of you. A student. I don't know. It wasn't me.'

'But someone saw you putting the heart back in the Clown.'

'Yes,' said Simon Aragon. 'It was in the wrong body. Someone had moved it to Pandora. I heard what Paul White said. I heard him say the day before that someone had swapped the hearts. I was trying to see, discreetly, if what he said was true. Without involving Dr Speed, and getting all of you lot in the shit. Of course, I recognized straight away that it couldn't be a young woman's heart. I checked the other bodies, then replaced it where I found a gap. That's what Pavel Smid saw.'

'I believe you,' said Anne, although she was very confused. 'Why didn't you tell Dr Speed?'

'I did. He said it didn't matter. I tried to explain.'

'He knew?' asked Anne.

'Yes.'

Simon Aragon seemed exhausted.

'Can I leave now?' Anne asked. 'Or are you going to hurt me?'

'Of course I'm not going to hurt you. Did you write the letter?'

'No.'

'Do you know who did?'

'Yes.'

'Who is she? Molly?'

'How do you know it's a woman?'

'That man Skelton told me. Last night.'

'So he never said my name?'

'I called a couple of students. They'd heard you'd been out with him. I assumed –'

'Wrong. Can I go?'

'You can go.'

Anne waited. Simon Aragon stepped aside. Anne hurried past him.

Molly and Jo had stayed, just as they promised.

When they saw how upset Anne was, they brought her straight home, where I heard the whole story.

'Do you believe him?' asked Jo.

'No,' I said. 'And I still want to speak to him.'

'But from what he told Anne, someone else could have done it.'

'You mean Timothy Kendall?' I asked.

'He has an alibi,' said Molly. 'Jenny.'

'But I didn't check it. I was too eager for it to be Simon Aragon.'

'Do you want her number?' asked Jo.

'If you have it.'

Jo fetched her address book from her room. 'Perhaps it's better if I speak to her first,' said Jo. 'To explain.'

She dialled. Jenny answered.

'It's about yesterday morning,' said Jo.

I waited in silence as the conversation went forwards. Paul White's name was mentioned.

'So, will you speak to her?' Jo finally asked.

I heard the reply, then took the phone.

'Hello,' I said. 'This is Kumiko Ozu. Thank you for answering some questions. Could you tell me were you with Timothy Kendall on the night of April the thirtieth?'

'Yes.'

'All night?'

'No, he left around two o'clock.'

'On the morning of May first?'

'I checked my diary. Of course, I was all flustered in class. It was such a cruel thing for him to say. He has apologized since.'

'He did?'

'He said he couldn't have people thinking the letter was true.'

'You weren't with him at 5 a.m. on May first? You are absolutely sure?'

'He never stays the whole night. When he said he needed an alibi, I thought it was for stealing the thing. And he was with me after the class before. He didn't stay behind. We had lunch.'

'But he might have gone back in the afternoon.'

'I suppose so. But he's on rounds in the hospital then.'

'And the class before that. On the Friday. Did you leave with him?'

'Oh, I never did that. People would have seen.'

'Did you meet up with him?'

'Hang on. I'll check.'

She came back a couple of minutes later.

'No. We met that evening, though. We had an Italian meal.'

Timothy Kendall could have stolen the heart on either of these occasions.

'Have you forgiven him?'

'A little. I wanted people to know we were going out. I hated it being secret. And now it's not a secret any more.'

'You will see him again?'

'Oh, I'm so sad, aren't I?'

I told her I didn't know Timothy Kendall at all.

'Can I speak to Jo again?' she asked.

I passed the phone back.

Jo took it upstairs to her room, and didn't return for ten minutes. 'She thinks you think he did it,' she said.

'I am not sure.'

'It's so frustrating,' said Anne.

'I need to speak to him, too.'

'They'll both be on rounds tomorrow,' said Molly. 'You could kill two birds . . .'

'I could,' I said. But I wasn't sure I had even one stone.

I went upstairs to prepare for the overdose. Whilst doing this, I realized that I had another way of checking out Simon Aragon's story. He had told Anne that Dr Speed knew about the heart found outside a body on May first. If he was lying about this, he was probably lying about everything else.

I would delay taking the pills.

Jo supplied me with Dr Speed's work number.

I called, but got his voicemail.

Ten minutes later, I tried again, and again got voicemail.

303

So I left a message, introducing myself as the woman who had asked the first question at his lecture.

'I think I have proof now that Paul White is innocent. But I need your help.'

By 5 p.m. he had still not phoned back.

Another call to his work number only went straight to voicemail. I couldn't even tell, as with an answerphone, whether he'd picked up his messages.

I went and knocked on Jo's door. 'Do you have Dr Speed's home address?'

'No,' she said. 'He's not as accessible as Dr Norfolk was. Didn't you get to speak to him?'

I shook my head.

'What time is it?' Jo asked, then looked at the black alarm clock on her bedside table. 'Speed will still be in his office. He leaves around six. He always cycles home. You might catch him if you waited on St Thomas Street. I could come with you.'

'I can recognize him,' I said.

I caught a bus at 5.15 p.m. and was in place by 5.50.

There were many cyclists at that time.

In the end I spotted Dr Speed coming towards me on an old-fashioned bicycle with a basket on the front. He was wearing a helmet and a reflective jerkin.

I waved my hands and shouted his name. 'Please stop! Please stop!'

He gave me a terrified look and swerved past me, although I had not stepped into his path.

I turned to run after him.

Thinking this might happen, I had waited not too far from the lights. As Dr Speed approached them, they went amber. He stopped and looked round.

'What do you want?' he asked.

'To ask one question.'

'Oh. It's you. You left those messages.'

'I did. Please will you help me?'

He stepped off his bike and pulled it off the road.

'You have two minutes. What is your question?'

I asked him whether Simon Aragon had spoken to him about finding a heart in the wrong body on May first.

'Why is this important?'

'Because Paul White could be a good doctor.'

'He could have been. Is he a friend of yours? You're not a student. I know all the students.'

'No.' I quickly explained my involvement.

'Well, I'm afraid if Simon told me something in confidence, I can't share it with you.'

'But he didn't tell you anything, did he?'

'He told me something.'

'Was it that?'

'I really can't say.' He prepared to mount his bicycle again.

'If he told you anything else, then he is the person who stole the heart.'

'That's a very serious accusation. Do you have any evidence?'

'Yes.'

'Look, if you mean what you say, then you'll have to put it all in a letter or an email. You have my number. I suppose you know how to get in touch?'

I told him that I did.

'Then let me have it as soon as possible. Good night.'

The light was green. He cycled away.

Half an hour later, I arrived back home and told the girls everything. We decided to go ahead with the plan.

I swallowed all the pills at the kitchen table. As I did so, I realized that part of me must sincerely want to die.

32.

A surprise.

Skelton was there, with Anne and Jo, when I woke up.

I felt sick.

I asked for coffee and Skelton went to get me some.

While he was gone, I asked how he heard I was being admitted.

'He was in A&E when we brought you,' said Jo.

She asked me some medical questions, then told me to take it easy.

I lay with my eyes closed until Skelton returned.

The coffee tasted more strongly of coffee than any I'd drunk since I had my first cup at fourteen.

It was a relief to be alive. I was glad to see Skelton.

He wanted to know why I had overdosed. Together with the girls, I explained.

Skelton had something to tell me. But he wouldn't speak until Anne and Jo left the ward.

I was shocked to hear that it was about the murder of King Death, Monica's father. He said he believed that Vic Goosen had killed Dr Norfolk and disposed of his body as medical waste.

I told him what Monica's mother had told me: that Vic Goosen knew Dr Norfolk from medical school, that he had always been jealous of his success, that he had applied repeatedly for the lecturer position.

Skelton was pleased but said, 'It's not enough. I have no proof. I'm not very good at this.'

He looked so sad. I wanted to comfort him, like I used to. It would have been very easy to take his hand.

The girls returned. Soon, a Jamaican nurse told them to leave. I hated to be alone in the hospital ward, but I said I was fine. Skelton wanted to stay. When he saw that he couldn't, he went and brought a friend of his, a porter called Wally. Wally was shy. He told me he would watch over me as I slept.

A few minutes later, I was on my own.

I could say that nothing happened, before the big thing happened. It would be untrue. There were many small events. I knew sleep would not visit me.

At 11.17 p.m., my phone buzzed. A text had come, from Skelton.

> AM IN PATHOLOGY DEPT FLOOR MINUS TWO. CALL
> POLICE NOW! THEN GET WALLY. NOT SECURITY.
> THEY WILL KILL ME. GOOSEN AND FINE. THEY DID
> MURDER. DO NOT COME YOURSELF. I LOVE YOU. S

I knew it wasn't a joke. I got out of bed immediately. The floor under my feet felt like sponge. I would call the police while looking for Wally.

The go-away nurse came out of her office.

'Where you think you are going?'

'It is an emergency. Where is Wally the porter?'

I was dialling 999.

'You can't use that here. People here trying to sleep. Go back to bed.'

By mistake, I added another 9, so had to start again.

'I need the bathroom,' I said. 'Where is it?'

She pointed to a door further along the corridor.

'I watching you,' she said. 'You get this once, that's it.'

'Hello, you're through to the police.'

I went into the toilets.

'I'm at Guy's hospital,' I began to explain. Once I got to the words, 'He says they are going to kill him,' I knew the operator didn't believe me.

'What is your name?'

'Kumiko Ozu.' I spelled it for her.

'Right,' she said, 'I'm going to have to pass this on to the relevant force and then get them to ring you back.'

I knew what that meant. They wouldn't come. I was stupid. I should have given a different name.

The nurse was waiting for me outside the door.

'All finish?' she said. 'Now, back to bed.'

I started walking in the right direction, then broke into a sprint.

'Hey, you stop!'

The nurse was fat. She didn't have a chance of catching me.

I ran through another ward, then slowed to a walk. I was wearing a hospital gown, open at the back. It was obvious I was a patient, who shouldn't be wandering about.

There were some emergency stairs. Out the window, I could see London Bridge station, glowing yellow, with trains at two of the platforms.

I went down one floor and then headed towards the lifts.

Skelton hadn't told me how to contact Wally. All I could think of was to phone directory inquiries.

When they answered, I asked for Guy's switchboard.

The phone rang and rang, then connected just as I pressed the call-button for the lift. It came within seconds.

'I need to contact a porter,' I said, as the doors opened. 'His name is –'

'I'll put you through to the porterage.'

In the lift, I pressed for –2.

I began to descend.

'Porterage.'

'I need to speak to Wally.'

'Who is this?'

'It is an emergency.'

'You can't speak to him. He only has a beeper. I can't call him. What is it about?'

'Send him a message. Tell him to go to Pathology immediately. Tell him Skelton is there.'

'Skelton? What about Skelton?'

'He is in danger,' I said.

The lift stopped and a nurse got in.

I hung up.

33

I woke up in the dark with something soft over my face.

I could hear voices.

When I tried to move my hand, it touched fabric – the other hand did, too.

I lifted them up, and with them came a thin layer of cloth, like a bedsheet.

I pulled at it until it slid off my face.

It was still dark, where I was, although lighter down towards my feet. All I could see in front of me was deep grey.

Sliding my fingertips up on either side, they felt flat metal. Up further, and they came to a low roof, also metal.

Then I realized that the thin cloth covering me *was* a sheet, one of the sheets we used to cover corpses. And that I was in one of the drawers where the corpses were stored.

I stopped a scream.

The voices continued talking. I tried to listen to what they were saying, but they were just too muffled.

I was pretty sure who one of them was: Vic Goosen. And if he was planning to do to me what he did to Dr Norfolk, I was in extreme danger.

I needed to let someone know I was here.

When I checked my pocket, my phone was still there. But, holding it up to my face, I saw it had no reception.

If I made a phone call, they would probably hear me. So, it would have to be a text.

I activated the keypad and scrolled through the menus until I came to the one which turned off the clicking noises. Doing this, of course, made several clicking noises. But I spaced them out as much as possible, so as to make them ignorable. It worked; I hadn't been heard.

Then I composed a text to Kumiko. She was the only person I could think of. Wally just had a pager. Grzegorz was too far away. Anne, too. And I couldn't text 999.

I told Kumiko where I was, what to do. Most of all, I told her to stay away. Then, as it might be my last chance, I put in that I loved her.

Stretching as much as I could, I pushed the phone down towards my feet. Perhaps, closer to the door, a signal could get through.

A minute later, I retrieved the phone. The message hadn't been sent. It would have to be closer still – or outside the drawer altogether.

Quiet as I could, I tried to sit up. I lifted myself onto my elbows, then pushed with my hands.

Almost immediately, my head touched the metal roof. There was very little room to manoeuvre. I wasn't sure if I'd be able to turn round.

Trying a different approach, I shifted round onto my stomach. Then brought myself up into a crawling position.

The sliding drawer tray beneath me started to tremble. If I wasn't careful, it would start knocking against the door.

All this time, the voices kept talking. They were getting

louder, however. I wasn't sure if this was because those speaking were approaching.

The first speaker was Vic Goosen. The other one, I thought, was probably Mr Fine.

If I didn't get a message out soon, my body might never be found.

I twisted round and lay down, then tried to send the text again. But this time, I pulled my leg up until I could tuck the phone into my sock. Then, as it was attempting to find a signal, I stretched my leg out again until it was gently touching the door.

When I brought it back again, the text still hadn't been sent.

The voices were now audible.

'No,' I heard Goosen say. 'That wouldn't work. You heard what he said. He knows.'

'But if we just frightened him.'

Yes, it was definitely Fine.

'He's already told one person. Who else is he going to tell? This is the only certain way.'

'Look, I got into this for one thing.'

'And you *got* it. Now you have to make it safe.'

'I thought it was bloody safe.'

'It'll be just like last time.'

'No. Norfolk was only on the one tape. We'd arranged it. This time he's on three. And what about her? She knows just as much.'

'First him, then her. We've got all night. You've wasted enough time already. He might wake up.'

I had perhaps one more chance.

Lifting my knee until it was braced against my chest, I undid my left shoe and then pulled off the sock. Setting the phone up to send I jammed it in between my big and second toes. Then I held this out in the slight gap at the edge of the door.

Just then, I heard a loud electronic buzzing.

How could that be? I was sure I'd put the phone on silent.

'What's that?' asked Fine.

'His beeper, I expect. But why is it going off now? He's not on shift.'

'We should turn it off,' said Fine.

I tried to pull my foot back into the drawer. If I could get the sheet back over my head, and they didn't notice my shoe was off ...

But the phone slipped out from between my toes, and I heard it clatter to the floor.

'That wasn't his beeper,' said Fine. 'That was his fucking phone.'

I heard footsteps approaching.

Then Goosen opened the door and let the light in. I could see Fine, holding up my mobile.

'Hello,' Goosen said to me, in a way that no-one had ever said hello before.

'It's just sent a text,' Fine said. 'We're in shit.'

Not as much as I was in.

'Well, now we have to kill him,' said Goosen.

Reaching across, Goosen took the handle of the door and slammed it shut. It was completely dark, again. And this time, the drawer was airtight – if no-one came to my rescue, I would suffocate in very few minutes.

I tried to calm down, not to hyperventilate, as that would finish me off even faster. I lay back and listened. And I braced my hands above my head. If someone opened the door, I could gain a few seconds by pushing my way out. As long as Kumiko had been awake, or had been woken up by my text – as long as she called the Police immediately …

In my heart, though, I had already given myself up for dead.

34.

'Let him out!'

Those were the first words I heard, when I followed the signs and reached Pathology.

Approaching quietly, on bare feet, I could see Wally standing in the doorway.

Then he disappeared into the room.

I heard sounds of struggle, grunts and curses. I tiptoed closer to see who was fighting.

Wally lay on the floor. One man I didn't know was beneath him, another, in security guard uniform, was on top, trying to pull him off: Fine.

I had only seen pathology departments in movies. Everything in the room seemed to be made of shiny metal. Especially the wall of doors at the far end.

'You!' said Fine.

Wally looked up as well.

'Skelton is in the drawer on the left!' he shouted. 'The middle drawer on the left! He will suffocate.'

Wally's hands, as I could see, were around the unknown man's throat.

'Save him!' shouted Wally.

I started to move towards the drawers, keeping to the edge of the room.

Fine tried to stand up, but Wally grabbed him around the waist.

'Run!' said Wally. 'Run!'

I was almost there when Fine caught me by the wrist. Wally was still holding on to him, by the ankle. The other man was trying to claw his way up Wally.

I seized the door handle with my right hand and was about to turn it when Fine tugged me towards him.

He broke my grip.

Then I saw Wally elbow the other man in the face. His nose went bloody immediately, and his hands went to his nose.

Wally then climbed up Fine, pulling at his uniform.

I was being dragged further away from the door.

Then Wally got his hands to Fine's collar. He yanked him back, yanking me as well.

In order to defend himself, Fine had to let go of my hand.

I staggered back to the door handle and turned it.

The drawer opened a crack, then burst out. A tray slid into the room, and on the tray was Skelton, gasping for breath.

He rolled sideways. Fell to the floor. Curled up.

Fine now had his hands around Wally's neck. And, behind them, the other man was slowly standing up.

I watched, horrified, as the man went across to a tray of medical instruments and picked out two scalpels.

'Look out!' I shouted.

Wally struggled to turn around, to see what I meant.

'He's got knives,' I said.

Skelton went motionless, then started trying to stand up.

The man came towards Wally.

'Hold him still,' he said to Fine.

I had to do something.

Next to the corpse laid out in front of me was a metal bowl half-full of organs. I picked it up and threw it spinning at the man's face.

He tried to duck but it hit his forehead. He reeled back. When he came back into view, a gash had opened above his left eye. The scalpels were still in his hands.

Wally dipped to one knee, and threw Fine over his shoulder. It was a judo move.

As he went down, Fine's thigh hit the corner of one of the corpse-trolleys. It span away, and the body began to fall off, head first.

Skelton was now on his feet beside me.

Wally, backing away from the man, joined us.

'Don't be stupid, Goosen,' he said. 'It is over.'

The man, Goosen, sidled round until he was between us and the door.

Fine stood up and began to come towards us.

'Let us leave,' said Wally.

'I'll fucking kill you,' said Fine.

'We will kill all of them,' said Goosen.

35.

When the door of the drawer opened, I pushed with my hands and slid out into the room.

All I could do for a while was breathe and feel amazing joy at still being alive.

Then I began to take in what was going on. Kumiko was there. I felt angry with her for having put herself in danger. Wally was there too. But Goosen and Fine were facing us – Goosen armed with scalpels. And Goosen was threatening to kill us.

'Him first,' he said, nodding towards Wally. 'The other two will be easy.'

We needed to get to the door.

Fine backed away until he was up against a work surface. Then he began to feel around for a weapon. There were plenty to choose from.

Wally didn't hesitate. With a loud shout, he charged straight at Goosen, keeping his head down and ramming his shoulder into Goosen's gut.

Once he'd made contact, Wally kept driving Goosen back – until he banged into Fine.

Then he turned round to face us.

'What are you waiting for? Go!'

The door was close. We moved towards it, keeping our eyes on Wally, who was holding off Goosen and Fine.

'We can't leave you,' I said.

Just then, Goosen's hand, still grasping the scalpel, came

out in front of Wally's neck. With a terribly under-control gesture, it traced a bulging red line across Wally's throat. Blood spurted everywhere, and I knew he would die.

Kumiko grabbed my hand and pulled me out the door.

We ran for the lifts.

I looked back, and saw Goosen running after us, blood dripping down his arm.

'This way,' I said to Kumiko.

We stood a better chance on the stairs. The lifts sometimes took three or four minutes to come.

Kumiko was wearing a hospital gown that rode up as she ran. We'd be so obvious on the streets.

Up one flight, then another.

Goosen wasn't very fast. I could hear him, puffing away behind us.

We ran out into a corridor and then along into A&E. I looked back, and saw Goosen's face looking at us furiously through shatterproof glass. Then it disappeared.

'Did you call the Police?' I asked.

'Yes,' said Kumiko. 'They said they'd call back. They didn't believe me. They never believe me.'

We were walking towards the main entrance. I knew that we were attracting attention.

My phone was still down in Pathology.

'Let me call,' I said.

Ahead of us was a woman sitting on one of the waiting-room chairs. One of her shoes was off and her ankle was swollen up. A bright red fleece was on the chair beside her. As we went past, I grabbed it and passed it to Kumiko.

'Put this on.'

'Hey,' said the woman. 'Hey, come back.' She tried to stand up, then fell back in the chair.

I dialled 999 as we continued towards the door.

A Security Guard came in from the smoking bay. It was Kev. He was speaking on his radio, and looking around – for *us*, that was pretty clear.

We stopped.

Kumiko was now wearing the fleece. It came down quite low on her, but the papery hospital gown still stuck out around her legs.

'Hello. Emergency Services. Which service do you require?'

'Fire Brigade,' I said, looking towards the Security Guard who, for the moment, was just blocking our exit.

Kumiko looked at me.

'I'll put you through.'

'Fire service always come,' I said. 'They have to.'

'That man stole my fleece!' shouted the woman further back. 'Stop him.'

The Security Guard nodded, as if that's what he'd been intending all along. He continued to speak into the radio.

'He killed him,' said Kumiko.

'I know.'

I could hear the phone ringing.

'How are we going to get out?' asked Kumiko.

'Don't worry,' I said.

The phone continued to ring for what seemed like minutes, then, 'Fire Brigade.'

I walked with Kumiko over to where we kept the wheelchairs.

'I am at Guy's Hospital, near London Bridge,' I said. 'There is a chemical fire in the Pathology Department. Sub-basement level.'

'Could you just confirm –?'

'Guy's Hospital. Serious fire,' I said, then hung up.

I grabbed a wheelchair.

'You, too,' I said to Kumiko.

She got the idea immediately.

We lined them up side by side, and then charged towards the Security Guard. Metal footpads stuck out at the front, ready to hack at his ankles.

In the event, he stepped aside at the last minute – allowing us to crash past him.

I lost control of my wheelchair and it veered into Kumiko's. The two of them became entangled – began dragging on the floor.

'Leave them,' I said.

Kev was close behind.

I got the other side of the chairs and pushed them back into him.

Kumiko was already running away from the hospital. I went after her, as fast as I could.

When I looked back, I saw Kev was following us – keeping a distance, talking into his radio.

36.

Wally saved our lives by sacrificing his own.

We ran up the stairs to A&E.

Skelton called the fire brigade, as I should have done when the police were useless.

Then he improvised an escape past the security guard. We knocked him over with wheelchairs. I don't know what I would have done. Each decision had to be made so quickly. Skelton was more at home with this than me.

Outside the hospital, all I thought about was to get away.

I felt the pavement beneath my bare feet. It was quite soft.

We ran across the road, and down the small alley that led to Borough High Street.

'He's still behind us,' said Skelton.

I looked back. The security guard was not letting us go.

Far away, I heard the sound of sirens.

We went past the morgue, and out onto the main road.

There were not so many people around. I felt exposed, with bare legs and no shoes. Skelton had stolen a fleece from a woman in A&E. It made me sweat.

Skelton looked around. 'No buses,' he said. 'No taxis.'

The security guard came out of the alley. He was only ten metres away from us.

We waited at the bus-stop. Still nothing came.

Then we saw the security guard turn round and look back down the alley.

Skelton grabbed my hand and pulled me into the road. There was a gap between cars, but someone braked hard and honked their horn.

We crossed the southbound lane. The northbound one was much busier.

I looked behind us, and saw Fine run into view.

Skelton held up his hands, stopping the traffic.

Almost at the opposite kerb, a moped delivering pizza swerved round us.

We sprinted down Stoney Street. We were back at the market. Up there, on the roofs, was where I first saw the heart.

'Come on,' said Skelton.

I was slowing him down.

Fine was catching up. I could see he was carrying something in his hand. The other security guard wasn't with him.

'In here,' Skelton said.

We were at the door to Becky's house.

I stepped into the dark.

Skelton immediately shut the heavy door and braced his shoulder against it.

A few seconds later, Fine started to push on the out-side.

I joined Skelton. Together we were strong enough.

Then Fine gave up.

We could hear him on his radio.

He called for the other security guard to come and assist him again.

'Becky!' shouted Skelton, into the dark of the house. 'Anyone!'

'I think he has a gun,' I said. 'I think he went to get a gun.'

'Stay here,' whispered Skelton.

He searched blindly around the room. When he came back, he had a wooden chair without a seat. He jammed this against the door.

'Becky!' he shouted again.

Then he lifted me off the ground and carried me towards the stairs.

'Shh,' he said.

I could hear glass crunching beneath the soles of his shoes.

He took me up to the second floor, then into a room off the landing. He put me down.

We could hear thumps from downstairs, followed by scraping. Fine was into the house.

'There's a sofa,' he said. 'Get behind it. Keep quiet.'

He went and hid behind the door.

For a minute, there was only the sound of our breathing. Then Fine's tinkling footsteps began to approach. Sometimes they were louder, as when he came up the stairs, sometimes quieter, as when he searched a room. He also shouted. 'Come on out! Come on! Give yourselves up!'

I heard Skelton whispering. He was speaking into my phone, trying to persuade the police to come.

Then it got too dangerous to make noise, and he kept quiet.

Outside, there were more sirens.

Fine came onto the second-floor landing. He went into

the room opposite. 'Come out!' Then across into our hiding place.

It was very dark, but he had a torch.

The outline of the sofa was projected onto the wallpaper behind me. I could see graffitied names; Jonesy was one of them.

Fine stepped into the room.

He was standing next to Skelton, only the width of the door between them.

'What you doing in my house?' said a voice I recognized as Becky's. 'Get out.'

The light swept from the wall as Fine turned round.

'Are you hiding them?' Fine asked.

'Who? What are you on about?'

I thought it was safe to look out from behind the sofa. Fine had his back to the door. Skelton was moving round, ready to attack.

37.

Fine was still after us.

No buses or taxis came along, so we had to run to Becky's house and hide.

I called the Police and they said they would send someone along.

'He's armed,' I said.

'We will send someone along straight away,' they said.

We were on the top floor of the house: Kumiko behind the sofa, me behind the door.

Fine came upstairs, checking every room.

Just as he crossed the landing, closing in on us, Becky climbed through the window, down from the roof.

'What you think you're doing?' she said.

Fine turned around to see who it was.

I wanted to protect her, as well as Kumiko. With his back to me, I thought I could grab his gun.

I had to move before Becky saw me and said something.

With a lunge, I took his right hand in mine and tried to pull his fingers away from the handle.

The gun went off, firing I didn't know where.

Fine was at the top of the stairs.

He was too strong for me. His fingers couldn't be moved.

I pushed him, and he fell away, backwards.

Another bang from the gun – the bullet whistling past me.

Beneath that sound, though, had been the softer bang of Fine's head hitting the floor or the wall.

Kumiko was by my side.

'Is he —?' she asked.

There was a grunt of pain followed by a roar of anger.

Becky took my hand. 'Out the window,' she said. 'You can get on the roof.'

I made Kumiko go first. Becky showed her the way, then followed after. I watched their backs.

Fine was crawling up the stairs. His breathing was ragged.

I swung out onto the scaffolding.

A bullet grazed my leg.

And then I pulled myself up onto the roof.

Becky had already taken hold of a couple of empty wine bottles. When Fine stuck his head out the window, she hurled them down at him.

'The train tracks,' said Becky. 'You can get away over them. I'll keep the bastard stuck here for a while.'

'Thanks,' I said.

A train went past, heading from Blackfriars to London Bridge.

Again, I let Kumiko go first.

We could run along the tracks to the station. We should have gone there first of all.

I looked back, and saw Fine climbing out of the window. Becky threw another bottle at him, but it bounced off his back. She reached down to pick up another. Fine quickly mounted the scaffolding, and was on the roof beside her.

I stopped.

For a moment, I thought Fine might simply push

Becky down to the street. He wasn't interested in her, however.

With a jump, Fine was with us on the train tracks.

Kumiko was ahead, jumping from sleeper to sleeper.

A Police car turned onto Stoney Street, blue lights on but no siren.

I turned my eyes forwards, and saw that Kumiko, head down, was running straight towards a train. It was coming on the northbound tracks.

I shouted to her.

I don't know if she heard, but she looked up and saw it.

Then she turned to look at me, and her expression changed to horror.

At first I thought she had seen Fine, taking aim. But when I glanced round, I saw another train coming southbound.

We were across the bridge. The roofs of Borough Market were to our right – just where the heart had been.

I ran to catch Kumiko up.

Already, the front of the train dwarfed her. I couldn't see a driver. It had bright lights at the front.

I turned back again to see what Fine was doing. He was halfway across the bridge, and had no escape to either side.

When I looked forward, I saw Kumiko had started trying to climb across onto the roofs.

I heard a scream from behind me.

The train was fifteen feet away – and now it put its brakes on.

I thought the scream was from Fine. I had no time to check.

I grabbed Kumiko by the shoulders and forced her down onto the track. Becky had better be right about this.

The northbound train screeched closer to us, going too fast to stop.

I looked back towards Fine.

He, caught in the headlights, was climbing over the side of the bridge. The gun was still in his hands.

I ducked my head down, and pressed Kumiko's down, too.

And then we were under the train. The sense of its weight on top of us was enough to take the breath from my lungs. But it didn't come close to scraping us.

One carriage went past, then another.

The train on the southbound side came through much faster, honking its horn.

There was an absurd moment of calm. Whatever the circumstances, this was the first time I'd held Kumiko since she walked out.

Above us, the train continued to slow down.

I thought of the travellers, wondering what this was about.

Kumiko shouted, 'I thought we were dead.'

I hugged her tighter. It felt like I'd won her back.

The train was only five carriages long, and by the time it stopped, it was halfway over the bridge.

Whatever else, we were probably in serious trouble now. The police would be making their way up through Becky's house.

Kumiko and I stood up, brushed ourselves down.

I could see Becky on the roof, jumping and clapping and whooping as if at a rock concert.

Then she pointed towards the bridge.

Together, we ran towards the back of the train.

'You bastard,' shouted Becky, towards something under the bridge.

I saw a hand, clinging onto the edge of the metal beam. Fingers just holding on.

When I leaned over to have a better look, Fine shot at me. Luckily, he was waving around so much that it missed.

I looked back at Becky. She had started to throw bottles again. It was the Police, wanting to get on her roof.

The fingers were slipping.

'Drop the gun,' I shouted to Fine. 'I'll pull you up.'

I wasn't going to risk another peek.

The fingers disappeared.

38

I thought we would die in the house. But Becky arrived, and distracted Fine enough to let us escape.

Up onto the roof we went. Then across to the rail tracks.

Fine followed, armed.

We ran.

Two trains came at the same time.

Skelton knocked me to the ground and saved my life.

I was buried beneath a train, beneath him.

Fine jumped off the bridge, the gun still in his hand. He wanted to kill Skelton and me, perhaps more than he wanted to live.

It turned out that way.

He lost his grip.

I saw him falling – and as he fell, he put the gun to his head and pulled the trigger.

You wouldn't think there was time. There was.

The police climbed up onto the roof of Becky's house, although she tried to keep them off by throwing things at them.

The last things she threw were her shoes.

Skelton took my hand.

'Come on,' he said. 'We need to get back to the hospital.'

He didn't want to be arrested. Not yet.

We ran along the track.

No trains came in our direction. The controller must have stopped them all.

The sleepers made my feet black with dirt.

People looked at us as we climbed off the tracks and onto the platform.

Down the tunnel towards the exit.

We jumped the barriers.

The ticket collectors didn't chase us. I think they thought we looked too mad.

Past the taxi rank and across the pedestrian bridge, we kept running.

Then we were at the hospital.

Two fire engines were parked outside, blue lights but no sirens. Only one fireman.

Also, an empty police car.

In A&E, I returned the fleece to the woman Skelton stole it from. She was sitting in the same place.

Firemen walked past us, back towards their appliances. They were shaking their heads.

'I mean, honestly,' one said.

We took the stairs down to Pathology.

More firemen – and now they tried to stop us.

But Skelton, in his uniform, persuaded them he needed to take me somewhere.

I recognized the voice of the policeman. It was PC Wagner.

We turned the corner, and saw –

Wally lay on one of the trolleys, stripped naked. He was so pale from blood loss that he had to be dead. A hand was sticking out of his stomach. The fingers looked like the red crown of a cockatoo.

On the next trolley was Goosen. Blood was shining

on the floor beneath him. He had no right hand. His throat was also cut. An electric saw rested on his chest.

'What the hell are they doing in here?' said PC Wagner.

'We are witnesses,' I said. 'You must take our statements.'

The other police officer, a woman, was shaking her head.

'It's a confession,' said Skelton. 'That's how he did it.'

He was pointing to the fingers of the hand.

'That's what he did to Dr Norfolk.'

'This is a crime scene,' said PC Wagner.

'Really?' I said. 'You are very observant.'

'You must leave immediately, in case you contaminate it.'

'We are here already,' I said.

Skelton was looking at Wally. I put my arm around Skelton's back. He put his arm around my shoulder.

We were together.

39

Fine was dead even before he hit the ground. The bullet went in one ear and out the other.

Becky saw everything, and was able to give a statement to the Police.

Of course, once they began to take her seriously, they had to listen to everything she had to say. Particularly as Kumiko and I were both insistent upon the importance of her evidence.

We ran to the hospital, and saw what we saw, then said what we had to say.

The Doctors insisted on keeping Kumiko in that night. As far as they were concerned, she was still recovering from the overdose. However, she was able to talk briefly to a female Officer – and told her about who stole the heart and why. The Officer listened, took notes and nodded.

I, meanwhile, spent several hours at the Police Station speaking to PC Wagner, among other, more senior, Officers.

They were already trying to track down Simon Aragon. It turned out he had taken a flight to Pisa, then driven to Castelnuovo del Garfagnana, to La Camera Inglese. He wanted, as he later said, to see Monica Norfolk. He wanted to tell her what he'd done, before she heard from anyone else. He wanted her to understand *why*.

But, as it turned out, she and her mother must have

passed him in the air. They were on a plane back home. Monica had finally persuaded her mother that they needed to go and see Paul White. This they did as soon as they were back – around the same time that Kumiko was arriving, unconscious, at the hospital.

Paul White protested his innocence. Monica's mother believed him. He was exonerated by Dr Speed a few days later – Speed having acted as his name would suggest. There was no point waiting for the Police to finish investigating; not when Simon Aragon had made such a full confession to them. Paul White needed as much time as possible to catch up on all the work he'd missed.

Kumiko came out of hospital on the Thursday morning, and was taken immediately to Southwark Police Station. She made a special request to speak to PC Wagner, in the presence of his senior Officer. And as this was now a murder investigation, her request was granted – although the third Officer, the Detective Inspector, would have been present anyway.

Kumiko filled them all in on the details of her deductions. In return, they charged her with a second count of trespass – for returning to Becky's house. I was called in later that day, and also charged. However, I was told – in confidence – that both charges were merely for the sake of appearances, and they would be dropped before we got anywhere near a court. On this, the Police were true to their word.

Simon Aragon was arrested during the course of the morning. He had parked his hire car at the bottom of the track up to La Camera Inglese. The housekeeper there discovered him around 7 a.m., sleeping in what was normally Monica's bed. She managed to cover her mouth, and not wake him with a scream. A call to the local *cara-binieri* brought two Officers up the hill. Aragon was roused by the gentle prod of a gun barrel. He made no trouble.

When Monica's mother heard from them, an hour or so later, she already knew about events at Guy's. Paul White had called Monica, and told her everything. Acting on her suggestion, the *carabinieri* contacted Southwark Police, who began arrangements for Aragon's extradition. Because he still wanted to see Monica, he did not contest this – and was back within a couple of days.

Meanwhile, Kumiko had moved back to Camberwell. I had thought there was a small chance she would come home to King's Cross, but she was firm, as always.

'We will see,' she said.

I took comfort from the plural. At least we were together in that.

The Police investigation began with a search of Pathology. Here, they found several things of interest. Most of all, a list dating from the time of Dr Norfolk's disappearance, and comprising twenty names of the then recently deceased.

This matched, almost exactly, a list discovered in Wally's small and incredibly tidy top-floor flat on Trinity Church Square.

As it turned out, Wally's father and mother, eighty-seven and eighty-four years old respectively, were alive to hear news of their estranged third son's heroic death.

Wally, as copious notes in German made clear, had spent his two compassionate leaves on flying visits to Iceland and Senegal. In both cases, his mission had been the same: to try to persuade relatives of those on the list to agree to an exhumation. Wally had been reluctant to divulge the reasons this might be necessary, which might explain his lack of success. His list of names was also a list of an equal number of crosses. Those relatives of the deceased who were within easier reach, some within walking distance of Guy's, had already been visited. None of them, it seemed, had come remotely close to allowing their loved ones to be dug up.

The Police, though, now made it a matter of compulsion.

One week later, the body of Jacob Spendwell was exhumed from West Norwood Cemetery. It was not badly decayed, but a subsequent autopsy – conducted by a forensic scientist – discovered the left half of a male human skull inserted into the chest cavity. Dental records confirmed that the skull was that of Dr Norfolk. And his wife and daughter were, at last, able to grieve without restraint.

A second exhumation, on Siobhan Connolly, brought forth the bones of the hand and forearm.

At this point, Mrs Norfolk intervened to call a halt. She had no intention of putting eighteen other families through distress merely to assemble the broken body of her husband. The Police, though, were intent on finding out the way in which Dr Norfolk had been killed.

Examination of the storage drawers in Pathology, however, revealed that the door of one of them was seriously dented – the suffocating Dr Norfolk had done his best to kick his way out. This was taken as evidence enough.

A search of Mr Fine's home disclosed a collection of video-cassettes, each annotated with a member of staff's name. Included among these was one that showed me stealing codeine from a pharmacy. Others, also, including Nick and Kev, were visible engaged in compromising activities. More importantly, one tape labelled 'King Death' contained footage of Dr Norfolk re-entering the hospital building by a side entrance, in company with Goosen, a couple of minutes after the previous last-sighting.

As he strides across the screen, Dr Norfolk is seen to check his wristwatch. Goosen walks along behind him.

There was considerable press interest, right from the moment news of Fine's death hit the morning papers. And once the Japanese media heard about Kumiko's involvement, things became even more intense. She was portrayed as a heroine, who had managed to create an entirely new aesthetic discipline by combining performance art with successful criminal investigation.

During this time, I saw Kumiko almost every day – although she insisted that I come and visit her at 'the house of girls', which is what she called it.

I also continued to work as a Porter at the hospital. With Wally's death, they were yet another hand short – and I decided that I would fulfil my obligation by working out a month's notice. Minus one day's holiday.

This did little to endear me to my agent, who had already begun to receive inquiries from 'major players, including one American hip-hop star' as to my availability for session work.

In the end, I was able to pick and choose what I wanted to do, fitting the recording in around day- and nightshifts at Guy's. I missed Wally's impassive guidance. I missed Wally. And Nick seemed to keep out of my way as much as possible. Perhaps he was guilty about telling

Kev that I'd been asking questions about his boss. It wasn't malicious. At least, I don't believe so.

For staying on, I earned the eternal devotion of Barbara. And, along with everything else, I felt very proud to have been able to hold down what is, by a long chalk, the most difficult job I've ever attempted. Warning vulnerable people of upcoming bumps is a very necessary thing. I wish someone had been able to do it for me.

Kumiko and I attended two funerals within a week. First, Wally's cremation – for which his parents made the trip over from Austria. They took his ashes back with them, to be scattered in the corner of his favourite field, high up in the mountains. And second, the interral of a small box containing Dr Norfolk's skull. The grave plot was for Dr and Mrs Norfolk. There was room on the stone for her epitaph. Paul White stood by Monica's side throughout the brief ceremony. Over two hundred people were present in the small country churchyard, many of them Dr Norfolk's former students.

'The Heart' went to number one and stayed there for three weeks.

Simon Aragon was charged with various offences, including theft of hospital property. He lost his job. Monica took out a restraining order on him. He fled the country. Was captured. Held on remand.

Paul White quickly caught up on his studies. Soon, he was challenging Pavel Smid for the position of Dr Speed's favourite.

As soon as she was done with the Police, Becky disappeared. She pushed a final note through the door of the house in Clerkenwell. All it said was *See you*, but it was addressed to both of us.

The day I finished work at the hospital, I found a Get Well Soon card wedged into my locker – one of the sort they sold in the hospital shop. The front showed a bunch of violets. On the inside, drawn in black marker pen, was a skull wearing a crown at an angle exactly halfway between jaunty and rakish. The message read, 'Bye-bye, Skeleton.'

That evening, I went round to the house of girls and asked Kumiko, quite formally, if she would move back in with me.

'No,' she said.

40.

I knew I loved Skelton.

I realized when he was there at my bedside, after the overdose.

I had loved him all along. I had just been furious with him, for not being a different person.

But I was very proud. And I did not want to admit my mistake.

When I make my mind up, it is definite, and when I am wrong, I am definitely wrong.

Perhaps it wasn't a mistake. By moving out, I forced Skelton to become stronger, to become different.

What I didn't know, although I should have done, is that Skelton is very good at improvising. Not just in music.

I think he has written about what happened after the climax. We agreed he could, although we haven't read each other's stories yet. That is for the future.

I do know, because he has told me, that he learnt about King Death because Grzegorz mentioned I was reading about Keats. That was an important crossover. He needed to know I was interested in King Death to understand my thinking.

Things have taken a while to settle down.

Jo's relationship with the sixth-former continues to develop. Molly and Pavel split up. He said he couldn't spare any time from his studies. Anne and Grzegorz, who met when he came to visit me in hospital, have been out a few times, though they both insist it isn't serious.

Whenever Skelton came round to see me, I wanted to tell him things would be alright. He looked so anxious.

Then, when he asked me to move back in with him, I said no. That would be a return. We had made a new start. I wanted to continue with that start.

So, after no, I said, 'But we can go on a first date.'

Anne will advise me what to wear.